A
SHATTERED
CIRCLE

KEVIN EGAN

A TOM DOHERTY ASSOCIATES BOOK
NEW YORK

A SHATTERED CIRCLE

Copyright © 2017 by Kevin Egan

A Forge Book
Published by Tom Doherty Associates
175 Fifth Avenue
New York, NY 10010

www.tor-forge.com

Forge® is a registered trademark of Macmillan Publishing Group, LLC.

Library of Congress Cataloging-in-Publication Data

Names: Egan, Kevin (Lawyer), author.
Title: A shattered circle / Kevin Egan.
Description: First edition. | New York : Forge, 2017.
Identifiers: LCCN 2016043747 (print) | LCCN 2016051791 (ebook) |
    ISBN 9780765383693 (hardcover) | ISBN 9781466892842 (e-book)
Subjects: LCSH: Judges—New York (State)—New York—Fiction. |
    Murder—Investigation—Fiction. | BISAC: FICTION / Legal. |
    GSAFD: Suspense fiction. | Mystery fiction. | Legal stories.
Classification: LCC PS3605.G355 S53 2017 (print) | LCC PS3605.G355 (ebook) |
    DDC 813/.6—dc23
LC record available at https://lccn.loc.gov/2016043747

Our books may be purchased in bulk for promotional, educational, or business use.
Please contact your local bookseller or the Macmillan Corporate and Premium
Sales Department at 1-800-221-7945, extension 5442, or by e-mail at
MacmillanSpecialMarkets@macmillan.com.

First Edition: March 2017

Printed in the United States of America

0 9 8 7 6 5 4 3 2 1

To Jon,
an absent friend whose wisdom, intellect,
and decency are sorely missed

ACKNOWLEDGMENTS

Many thanks to Kristin Sevick, Bess Cozby, Eliani Torres, and Elizabeth Catalano for helping to shape this novel.

A
SHATTERED
CIRCLE

A
SHATTERED
CIRCLE

CHAPTER 1

Ken Palmer felt the big old Buick pull to the right when he was halfway across the field. He was off road, in a car not designed for off-road driving, and instead of stopping to confirm what he already suspected, he kept his foot on the gas. The double dirt track crossed an alfalfa field owned by a client. The alfalfa was just starting to push up among last year's stalks, the field blending into a dull greenish brown as it stretched into the distance.

The car pulled harder, and Palmer gripped the steering wheel tighter, twisting himself to keep the wheels on the double track that now curved sharply left as the Beaverkill showed itself beyond the tree trunks. His suspicion blossomed into conviction; his right front tire was going flat. But he had no reason to stop, no reason to change plans. He had rescheduled his appointments and adjourned his court appearances for his annual day of hooky. A flat tire was not about to stop him.

It was mid-April, which meant that fishermen from all over creation had descended on the Trout Fishing Capital of the World. Most of the outsiders gravitated to the public fishing areas about twenty miles south, where the Willowemoc joined the Beaverkill at a place called Junction Pool. This land was owned by one of Palmer's clients who hadn't sold out to the state, which meant this three-mile section of the Upper Beaverkill was private property. Palmer could fly-fish the day away without any company. And he definitely did not want any company, because company and the river didn't mix well for him. He'd invited the prospective client now and then, once entertained a lawyer up from the big city. None appreciated the river; none mustered the quiet patience necessary to make the day worthwhile. And so, a wiser man now, it was just him. One day a year, for many years.

The track ended at a thin line of trees, then turned into hard-pan as solid as asphalt. Palmer got out to check the tire. It was flat, all right, but not shredded. Cell phone service was spotty, but he raised enough of a signal to connect with Simcoe's Garage.

"Ken Palmer here. Need someone to change a tire."

"You in a rush?" said Darwin.

Palmer explained where he was.

"I'll see who I can rustle up. Just as long as you ain't in a hurry."

"I ain't," said Palmer. He knew Darwin would rustle somebody up. The garage was a hangout for every idler between Lew Beach and Roscoe. Somebody would be willing to pocket a few bucks for changing a flat tire.

Palmer opened the trunk of the car, where he neatly laid out all his gear. He stepped into his waders, then pulled on his vest, which had pockets for flies, tippets, leaders, even his cell phone if he were of a mind. He wasn't. He peeled back the rubberized liner to expose the spare tire, then tossed the phone onto the front seat of the car. He couldn't truly disconnect from the office with that thing in his pocket.

The hardpan sloped down to the river, meeting the water at a tiny patch of sand. Upstream was a stretch of riffles, but they smoothed out as the water dived into a deep, wide pool where Palmer knew the trout liked to gather. He waded out till the water was knee-deep and he could see the dark edge of the pool. He flicked his wrist and launched a blue-winged olive mayfly toward the pool.

In that moment, everything fell away. The flat tire, the office, the clients clamoring about their problems. It was the perfect day. Bright overcast, mild temperature, the birds chirping, the soothing rush of the river against his waders. He didn't give a damn when Darwin Simcoe sent someone to change his tire. He was here for the day.

He caught four browns the first hour, then switched out the blue-winged olive for a little black caddis fly and caught three more. He heard a car pull up, a door slam, and then he saw a man looking appraisingly at the flat tire. The man waved, and Palmer waved back.

Palmer flicked his wrist and whipped the fly over the pool. A trout struck, and he hooked it. This is some lucky day, he thought as he reeled in the trout. He grabbed it, lifted it out of the water, turned toward the bank to display his latest prize. But the man did not look his way. He had the spare tire leaning against the back bumper and was elbow deep in the trunk, rooting around for the jack.

Oh well, thought Palmer, not every local gave a damn about trout. He pinned the rod under his arm, squeezed the fish's mouth, and worked out the hook. Eight caught, eight released. Still early.

He stayed in the water, flicking flies over the pool until he heard the trunk slam and saw the man dusting his hands. The man did not look familiar; at least he wasn't a Swayze or a Berkeley or Reid, the usual collection who hung out at the garage, eating pork rinds and generally getting in the way until Darwin pressed them into service. But he had done his job and done it quickly, and so Palmer slogged toward the sand patch, running numbers in his head. Twenty seemed too much, but ten not enough. Fifteen, he decided. He'd give the man fifteen bucks.

The man crossed the hardpan slope. Maybe he wasn't a Swayze or a Berkeley or a Reid, but as he got closer, there was something about the slope of his shoulders, the swing of his arms, and the tilt of his head that formed a vaguely familiar pattern in the cortex of Palmer's brain.

Palmer set his fly rod down on a large flat rock where the water was ankle deep. He patted his waders, trying to remember if he had his wallet in his pants pocket or if he'd left it on the seat of the car along with his cell phone.

The man came down off the slope, onto the sand, and then into the water.

"Mr. Palmer?" he said.

"Yes," said Palmer.

"Mr. Kenneth Palmer?"

Palmer nodded.

"I changed your tire."

"Thank you." Palmer located his wallet in his back left pocket and worked his hand inside his waders. "Just want to pay you for your trouble."

"No trouble, Mr. Palmer. Besides, I'm here to pay you."

"Pay me?" Palmer's hand reached his wallet. "For what?"

The man mumbled a name.

"Who?" said Palmer.

The man cleared his throat and repeated the name.

"But you're not one of them," said Palmer.

"That was the whole point, wasn't it?" said the man. A smile slowly spread across his face; then he lunged.

Palmer backed away, but the man grabbed him in a bear hug. Palmer bucked and thrashed, but with one arm in his waders and the other pinned to his side, he couldn't break the man's hold. The man waded out to his waist, tightening his arms around Palmer's chest as if to squeeze every molecule of air out of Palmer's lungs. At the edge of the pool, he loosened his hold. Palmer managed one long breath before the man spun him around and shoved him facedown.

Palmer tried to get his feet under him, but the man pressed him deeper into the cold, smooth water. Palmer flailed his arms and kicked his legs, but the water dampened the force of his blows. Three feet away, he could see the edge of the pool where the eight trout he had caught and released on his day of hooky now hid in the dark depths. His lungs hurt; his neck hurt. He kicked one more time. The air exploded from his lungs, and as he drew in a chest full of cold water, he saw the darkness of the pool swirling up to envelop him.

CHAPTER 2

The taxi swung east off Broadway, the sky suddenly opening on the August sun hanging hot and brilliant over Brooklyn. Barbara squinted until the taxi completed its turn and the roofline plunged the backseat into shade. She and Bill were subway people, she because of her humble beginnings and Bill because he saw himself as a regular guy who happened to become what he had become. She remembered how he looked on the subway— refusing to sit even with empty seats, standing with his back to the double doors, *The New York Times* opened and then folded precisely in the lost art of broadsheet reading. She remembered his wide stance, his flexed arms, his reading glasses low on his nose, his eyes focused. It was an image of confidence and strength, two qualities she found extremely sexy.

Now they rode in cabs. Bill slumped beside her, head turned to watch the Federal Building slide past the window. The *Daily News* lay on his lap, still folded in its plastic bag. She pinched a shred of lint off his sleeve and flicked it away with her thumb. It took Bill a moment to react to the tiny tug, another moment to break away from the window, still another to search out her eyes. It was then he smiled.

"Hello, dear," she said, and patted the top of his hand. He still looked so damn good, so damn distinguished. The judge from central casting.

"Hello, dear," he replied.

The cab pulled to the curb between two orange cones that reserved the space where cabs or car service dropped off judges at the side entrance to the New York County Courthouse. Barbara opened the door just enough for her thin frame to squeeze through as traffic zipped past. She went around the back of the cab, opened the rear door, and paid the cabbie as Bill unfolded himself, tall and lanky, onto the sidewalk.

"Here we are again," said Barbara. She tugged the cuffs of his white shirt, smoothed the lapels of his gray chalk-striped suit, and straightened his blue tie. "Back for another day."

A flagstone path crossed a triangular park formed by the northwest face of the hexagonal courthouse and the right-angle corner of Centre and Worth Streets. In an hour or so, couples newly wed in the City Clerk's Office would pose for pictures in this park. But right now it was quiet, with lawyers making last-minute changes to court papers, office workers meeting for coffee, and bums stretching out on benches.

Barbara locked her elbow on Bill's arm as they headed down the path toward a court officer standing beside a brass door.

"Morning, Judge," the officer said. "Morning, Mrs. Lonergan."

Barbara felt Bill's arm tighten as if jolted with energy.

"You're doing a great job," he said, his voice hearty.

The officer grinned.

"Don't listen to what they're saying about you in Chinatown," Bill continued. "You're doing a great job. A helluva job."

"Thanks, Judge." The officer pulled open the brass door.

Barbara released Bill's arm and let him walk in ahead of her.

"Sixteen years he's been telling me I'm doing a great job," the officer whispered to Barbara. "Does anyone ever do a bad job?"

"Not often," Barbara whispered back.

Inside the door was a small foyer. A stairway led up to the main lobby, and beside the stairway was a key-operated elevator reserved for judges, chambers staff, and senior administrators. Barbara and Bill took the elevator to the fifth floor, then walked two faces of the hexagonal corridor before reaching a door bearing a gold name-plate that read: MR. JUSTICE LONERGAN.

Like most chambers at 60 Centre Street, Judge Lonergan's was a three-room suite. In geometric terms, one room was a square, another a narrow rectangle, and the last, because it butted up against the angle of the hexagon, a trapezoid. A Supreme Court Justice—the official title of those who presided at 60 Centre, though they answered to "judge"—was entitled to a law clerk and a confidential secretary. Technology—first in the form of desktop computers, then later in a second generation of laptops, tablets, and smartphones—reduced the secretary's workload while increasing the size and complexity of each judge's caseload. Consequently, many judges opted to replace their secretaries with a second law clerk. In this respect, Judge Lonergan was in a distinct minority.

Barbara unlocked the door into the trapezoid-shaped room. She led Bill through the law clerk's office, down the short avenue of doors that connected the three rooms, and sat him in the big leather chair behind his desk.

"Don't move," she said. "I'll be right back."

She went to her desk in the middle room, dumped her purse into the big bottom drawer, and stripped off her linen jacket. Her cotton blouse already felt heavy with perspiration. But it would dry quickly in the frigid chambers air, and she was not going anywhere or seeing anyone today, so the dark half-moons below her armpits made no difference. Today would be a normal day or, more precisely, a new-normal day.

Back in the square, inner office, she found the judge facing the window.

"No birds," he said.

"Not yet." She grabbed his hands. "Up with you."

The judge allowed her to pull him up to his feet. She peeled off his suit jacket, gave it a shake, and hooked it onto the coat-tree, where his robe hung from a hanger. She unbuttoned his shirt cuffs and folded them back, exposing the wrists she loved so much.

"There," she said. "Comfortable?"

The windows on the chambers floors had steel frames and thick leaded-glass panes, a combination so heavy that Barbara's two-handed exertion succeeded in raising the sash one squeaky foot. She spread a thin layer of birdseed on the granite sill, then used her entire weight to push the window closed.

"Here," she said, laying a field guide to northeastern birds on the desk in front of Bill. "See what comes to visit."

She set Bill's door ajar to shield him from any unexpected visitors, then went into the outer office. Larry Seagle, the law clerk, had come in while Barbara fed the birds. He was a small but athletically pre-served man with wiry hair dusted gray and brown eyes magnified by wire-rimmed glasses.

Larry stood at the printer, waiting as the last of several pages settled into the tray. He plucked out the pages and sat behind his desk. Barbara sat opposite, watching him attach a page to each of ten file folders with rubber bands.

"Ready when you are," he said.

"Let's wait awhile," said Barbara. "He needs to settle down."

"No problem," said Larry. He was only a few years younger than the judge, but moved with the vigor and spoke with the voice of a much younger man.

Barbara stretched out her legs, slumped down in the chair, and let her head drop back over the backrest. She needed to settle down herself after the two-hour ordeal of getting Bill out of bed, into his suit, downtown in a cab, and into chambers. It wasn't so much the physical effort as the need for constant vigilance that drained her. But now they were in chambers, in the courthouse that Bill deeply loved. That love may have been temporarily scrambled now, but she could still sense it pulsing off him.

After a few minutes, she locked the chambers door and led Larry into the judge's office. Bill stared at two house finches pecking at the few seeds that remained on the sill. Barbara gently removed the field guide from his hand and pulled up a chair beside him.

"We have a case here, Bill," she said. She lifted the first case summary Larry had written.

Bill patted his pockets, then ran his hand under the desk blotter. He was looking for the field guide, which Barbara had slipped behind her back.

"Over here, Bill." She snapped her fingers. "Look at me."

Bill dropped the blotter and turned his chair to face her.

"Do you want to hear about the case?"

"Yes," he said.

"There's this woman," said Barbara. "She goes to a department store. That morning, a carpet-cleaning company shampooed all the carpets in the store. The woman walks across a carpet. It's still wet, and she's wearing rubber-soled shoes."

"I remember now," said Bill. His eyes narrowed in concentration. "She walks off the carpet and onto a tile floor, where she slips and falls. She says the carpet wasn't properly dried, so the water on her rubber soles caused her to fall when she stepped onto the tiles. She's suing the store and the carpet company. So who's asking for what?"

Barbara turned to Larry, who sat on the sofa. She arched her eyebrows; he nodded.

"The store and the carpet company are both asking you to dismiss the case against them," said Barbara. "The store says it didn't clean the carpets. The carpet company says it owed the woman no duty."

"They can't both be right," said Bill. "I would deny both their motions."

Barbara wrote *Deny* across the top of the summary and handed it to Larry.

They worked that way for over an hour, Barbara reading the case summaries until Bill's mind engaged—suddenly, it always seemed—and he opined on how the decision should come out. Two months ago, shortly after the incident, Bill barely could concentrate. One month ago, he could discuss three, maybe four cases before his attention wavered. In the last week, though, he seemed to improve each day. Six cases, then seven. Yesterday, eight. Today, Barbara was reading the ninth case summary when Bill suddenly lifted out of his chair and shuffled past her to the window.

"No more," he said, tapping a finger on the glass.

"Bill, honey, come sit."

"No more," he said.

"Bill—"

Larry cleared his throat. Barbara turned toward him, and he made a slashing motion across his neck.

"Best day yet," he mouthed.

Barbara joined Bill at the window and snaked her arm around his waist.

"Where did they go?" he said.

"Wherever birds go," said Barbara. "They'll come back. You want them to come back?"

"Yes."

"Come sit down, honey," Barbara told Bill. He backed away from her as she yanked open the window and spread more seed. He was sitting when she turned back around, the field guide open on his lap.

Barbara slipped out of Bill's office and closed the door behind her. She sat down at her desk, pinched the bridge of her nose, and swallowed back the lump in her throat.

"Best day yet," she muttered.

CHAPTER 3

Robert Cannon heard the unmistakable sound of many voices blending into a dull drone the moment the elevator door opened. Straight ahead, through a large window, was the brass dome of the rotunda roof. The corridor circled the dome, breaking off into radiating hallways that led to paired courtrooms. There would be six of them, he thought, since the building was shaped like a hexagon. He passed three, seeing only a custodian pushing a dry mop in one and a lawyer seated on a bench with his briefcase open on his lap in another.

The fourth hallway was crowded, and Cannon sidestepped through knots of lawyers as well as his belly and the carry case tucked under his arm would allow. He expected this activity to be connected with the courtroom of Justice Lonergan, but when he pushed through the leather-bound courtroom door, he found nothing but silence and saw no one but a court officer seated at a desk in the far corner. His sneakers made no noise on the mottled cork floor as he walked through the gallery of wooden benches to the velvet cord that hung across the opening in the courtroom rail. He knew enough not to unhook the cord—one didn't enter a courtroom well even with no judge on the bench— and he stood for several long moments before he cleared his throat to announce his presence.

The officer looked up.

"I'm here to see Judge Lonergan," said Cannon.

"About?" said the officer.

"A personal matter."

"And?"

"That's everything, unless you want details."

"Save it for the judge," said the officer. "He's up in chambers."

"I don't want to disturb him in his chambers," said Cannon.

"That's your only choice. He has nothing on his calendar for today, so I don't expect him here. Go to the security desk on five. The officer will see if the judge is available."

Working the fifth-floor security desk was a standard assignment for a court officer at 60 Centre Street. The desk guarded the public entrance to more than a dozen judges' chambers, which made it a popular destination for lawyers, messengers, lunch deliveries, and members of the general public under the mistaken impression that they could visit a judge the way a student could drop in on a college professor. Foxx rarely worked the desk. But it was early August, almost the exact midpoint of the summer, and with many officers on vacation, Captain Kearney had little choice but to assign Foxx to this sedentary post. It was an easy gig, with long stretches of time passing soporifically between minor interruptions. Foxx, in fact, was dozing when a muffled cough returned him to consciousness. The cough sounded vaguely like Ellen, the reason for his current fatigue, but he opened his eyes to find a portly man with a walrus mustache looming over him.

"Quiet day, huh?" said the man. Plastic-framed glasses tilted so that the earpieces reached behind his ears. Wispy hairs receded from a forehead etched with lines like a music staff.

"Not anymore," said Foxx. He purposely did not stifle a yawn.

"I'm here to see Judge Lonergan."

"Is he expecting you?" said Foxx.

"No."

"Can you tell me why you're here to see him?"

"It's a personal matter."

Foxx leaned back in his chair, summoning a stare that was a few notches down from his most baleful. *One of the main duties of the desk officer is threat assessment,* preached Captain Kearney, and right now Foxx tried to assess the man in front of him. He seemed harmless with his gut and his glasses, and he wasn't emitting the desperate energy of a whack job. He looked like just another faceless member of the public that washed up on the courthouse each day.

"Your name?" said Foxx. He picked up the desk phone.

"Robert Cannon. But he might not remember me by name. It's been several years."

"Have a seat," said Foxx.

There were four benches in the small lobby, two on each wall. Foxx waited for the man to settle on one before punching in the number to Judge Lonergan's chambers.

Barbara Lonergan sounded surprisingly cheery on the phone, especially since Foxx knew her default demeanor to be deadpan. He turned his head and muffled his mouth with his hand.

"Fella here is asking to see the judge. His name is Robert Cannon. Says it's a personal matter."

"Is he a lawyer?" said Barbara.

"I'd say no."

"And his name again?"

"Cannon. Robert Cannon."

"I don't know anyone by that name," said Barbara. "Do you have any suggestions?"

"You come out here and screen him yourself."

"I'll be out in a minute," said Barbara.

Foxx relayed that the judge's secretary would be out soon and then opened his newspaper.

"I had a job a lot like yours," Cannon offered.

Foxx looked up.

"Delaware County court."

"Okay," said Foxx.

"Thirty years. Been retired five now. Very different up there."

"Smaller, I suppose." Foxx turned a page of his newspaper and leaned in close to signal he was reading.

"How many judges do you have in this building?"

"About forty."

"We had two," said Cannon. "So you see what I mean?"

"About what?"

"About it being different up there."

Foxx heard the fire door open down the corridor to his right and the smart click of heels on the terrazzo floor. Barbara Lonergan was unique among the confidential secretaries in that she also was the judge's wife. She was a nifty-looking fiftysomething with intelligent eyes, youthful hair, nice figure, and great legs, and on this visual assessment alone, Foxx would take her for a tumble. But after two weeks of working this security desk and several attempts at small talk as she rooted through the black box where messengers deposited hand-deliveries, he hadn't detected any spark of personality or hint of innuendo. Pretty as she was, Barbara Lonergan struck him as about as sexy as a nun.

Barbara nodded curtly at Foxx and crossed directly to Cannon, who rose quickly from the bench. "I understand you want to see Judge Lonergan about a personal matter," she said.

"I do."

"Can you tell me anything about it?"

"I'd rather talk to the judge directly."

"Well, Mr. Cannon, here's the problem: I've been Judge Lonergan's secretary for many years, and I never once heard mention of your name."

"I doubt you would. But I have this." Cannon plucked a business card from his shirt pocket and handed it to Barbara. "I went to his old law firm this morning. They told me that the Mr. Lonergan I wanted to see was now Judge Lonergan."

"This card is at least twenty years old," said Barbara.

"Flip it over," said Cannon.

On the other side, written in Bill's painfully neat script, was: *Call if you ever have a legal problem—Billy L.*

"I was a court officer in Delaware County court," said Cannon. "He was on trial. He stayed over a weekend and asked me to drive him around the countryside because he was looking to buy a summer home. He wanted to pay me. I wouldn't take a dime. And so—"

"And so he offered free legal advice in the future," said Barbara. "You know that as a judge, he's not allowed to give advice."

"This wouldn't be that kind of legal advice."

"What kind of legal advice would it be?"

"I'd rather discuss that directly with him," said Cannon.

Barbara tapped a finger against the edge of the card. "I'll show him the card and let him decide." Barbara headed back the way she had come.

Cannon sat down on the bench closest to Foxx.

"Nice lady," he said.

Foxx said nothing.

———

Rather than return to chambers, Barbara headed to the library to photocopy the business card. When she started working as Bill's secretary, before they were married, he kept a box of these cards in his desk. *In case I ever return to private practice,* he would say, though the twinkle in his eye indicated that was not likely to happen. She remembered that he often had lunch with former clients, though he scrupulously insisted on paying his own way. Eventually these lunches trailed off. And after they married, she dumped the box of cards into the trash. Bill never asked about them.

Barbara lingered in the library for a spell before returning to the security desk.

"I'm sorry," she told Cannon. "The judge is involved in a conference call with no end in sight."

"I can wait," said Cannon.

"I'm afraid that's not possible today." She handed back the

business card. "I made a photocopy to show him. Is there a number where he can reach you?"

"Sure," said Cannon. "Will he call today?"

"Most likely, but no promises," said Barbara. She borrowed a pen from Foxx, and Cannon leaned on a corner of the desk to write his phone number.

"I know this all sounds very mysterious," said Cannon. "You can tell him it involves Ken Palmer. That should ring a bell."

———————

Back in her office, Barbara cracked the door to peek in on Bill. His chair faced the window and the field guide was open on his lap, but he was asleep.

She closed the door and shoved the photocopy of the business card deep into the top drawer of her desk. A judge often was a target, not only of angry litigants but also of random people under the misapprehension that the judge could be the answer to their problems if not their prayers. Bill, especially the open, friendly, backslapping Bill, was particularly vulnerable to the latter group, who confused open with accessible, friendly with familiar, backslapping with deep human interest.

The old Bill would have seen his business card and, whether he remembered this Robert Cannon or not, would have invited him back to chambers and talked to him forever. But that Bill didn't exist anymore, and there was no reason to tell the new Bill.

CHAPTER 4

He visited the plot for the first time later that April. The plot was surrounded by an iron fence and screened from the main house by a stand of arborvitae that had grown together to form a solid wall. Long ago, he had been able to peer through the conical bushes to the playground with its state-of-the-art redwood climbing structures and thick foam rubber padding, its railroad ties and wood chips. The swing set did not have strap seats or bucket seats or even the heads and tails of fanciful animals. Instead, it had flying machines: a dirigible, a biplane, a fighter jet, and a helicopter. He liked to think that the boy asked for it, insisted on it, kicked his tiny sneakered feet at the wood chips until they bought it for him. He hated how they spoiled the boy, but the swing set that he never could have afforded and never would have dreamed existed was an exception. It proved he and the boy had a connection.

He did not bother peeking around the arborvitae now. Seeing that the swing set might have been taken down or seeing that it still stood with those faded flying machines quivering in the raw breeze, each would have saddened him in its own way. He plodded toward the iron gate, his big work shoes sucking in the mud. Three stones stood in the plot, all there ever would be. Two singles and one double. The singles were fully engraved with names and dates. The double had only the names of the eventual occupants. Eventual, he snorted.

He stood before the only one that mattered to him. The stone was well cut, the front finely polished except for the roughened panel where the name and dates appeared. The characters were engraved in a clean, sharp, sans serif font.

The wind had blown a pile of last fall's leaves against the back of the stone. He scraped them into a cold, slimy handful and dumped them over the iron fence. He shivered. This had been a cold place when he knew it, and it felt even colder now. Spring came late here, fall came early, winter stayed too long, and summer not long enough. It was the story of his life, he knew now. Summer never was long enough.

He went back to the grave and said a prayer. He wasn't one to pray, but he was here and so he said a prayer. When the last words faded from his mind, he slipped the pebble and the vial from his pocket. The stone was set on a granite plinth with an inch all around. He knelt behind the stone, opened the vial, and tapped a dollop of white slurry onto the plinth. The slurry was a chemical concoction designed to bind stone to stone. Not forever, of course, but then nothing was.

He let the slurry set for a minute, then pressed in the pebble. He stood up, dusted his hands, and walked around to the front of the grave. As he wasn't one to pray, he also wasn't one to speak aloud to the dead. But he had prayed today and now he spoke.

"Got one, kiddo," he said.

And then he walked away.

CHAPTER 5

Andrew Norwood tossed the magazine back onto the coffee table. The glossy cover hit the polished wood with a satisfying crack, but the receptionist did not lift her head. Norwood knew she heard it because her eyes, which he could plainly see from the lobby sofa, drifted momentarily away from the fashion magazine she was reading. Norwood had been stewing on the sofa for twenty minutes. The phone had not rung once, and the only two people who arrived obviously worked here. They breezed in casually, unhurriedly, with their ties loosened, their suit jackets draped over their arms, and oversized coffee cups in their hands.

Another minute passed. Norwood stood up and cracked his spine, less to stretch than to make a point. And when he sat back down, his point not taken, the first tremor of anger rumbled in his gut.

"Are you part of the charade?" he said aloud. "Or do you just amuse yourself all day on the taxpayers' dime?"

The receptionist looked up. "Excuse me?"

"Don't play dumb." Norwood smirked. "Judicial Conduct Commission. It should be the Judicial Charade Commission. You don't really investigate these clowns. You certainly don't discipline them, either."

"Sir, someone will be with you shortly," said the receptionist.

"That's what you said twenty minutes ago." Norwood looked at his watch. "Make that twenty-two minutes ago."

"Sir, as I said—"

"I know what you said. And I know your game, too. Hold out a false promise, then frustrate people until they give up. What's driving this place? Money? Politics?"

The receptionist opened her mouth as if to answer, but Norwood cut her off.

"Don't say a word. It was an unfair question. Money and politics, they're really the same thing."

Norwood lifted a pile of magazines and slammed them down on the table. The receptionist jumped at the sound. She picked up the phone and curled away from Norwood's steady, angry gaze. She whispered sharply, listened to a reply, then lay the phone back on its cradle.

"Someone will be with you shortly," she said.

"Yeah, yeah. Shortly. I know the drill. 'Shortly' means just a few seconds longer than I'm prepared to wait."

He pushed a button to activate the stopwatch setting on his watch to time exactly how long "shortly" would be. But as the numbers raced past two minutes, a shadow darkened the doorway behind the reception desk, and one of the men he had seen arriving earlier emerged.

"Mr. Norwood?" he said. His tie was now properly knotted, but his sleeves were rolled up to expose thickly muscled forearms. "I'm Bob Brundage."

He held out his hand, and Norwood, suddenly cowed by the sheer bulk of the man, accepted the handshake.

"I believe I can help you," said Brundage. "Right this way."

Norwood followed Brundage past the reception desk, through the doorway, and down a corridor to a small, windowless office. They sat across from each other at a desk that was clear except for a telephone and a thick file folder.

"I'm sorry this has taken so long," said Brundage.

Norwood wondered exactly what he meant. The wait in the lobby? The four months since he'd filed his complaint? So many timelines ran in his head. He said nothing, and Brundage continued.

"By way of explanation, I am a staff attorney. I usually work with an investigator. Neither I nor the investigator can investigate a complaint without the commission's approval."

"The commission takes its damn sweet time," said Norwood.

"I'm afraid that's the nature of the beast," said Brundage. "The commission meets once a month and reviews all complaints received since the last meeting in the order they are received. Your complaint just missed the April meeting. The May meeting was canceled because not enough commission members were available. There was no scheduled meeting in June. But—" He patted the file folder. "—it was the first complaint reviewed at the July meeting. It's been approved."

"What does that mean?" said Norwood.

"It means that a majority of the commission believes your complaint has merit."

"So that wing nut'll be thrown off the bench?" said Norwood.

"You're getting way ahead of yourself," said Brundage. "It means that my investigator and I will investigate your complaint."

He slipped a few pages out from the folder and laid them on the desk. Norwood recognized the complaint form he had printed from the commission Web site and filled out in neat block printing with a black pen.

"A judicial grievance is technically an administrative proceeding," said Brundage, "but it mirrors a lawsuit in several respects. Your complaint is like a complaint in a lawsuit. Nothing is proved yet, but for now, the commission accepts your allegations as true. My first task is to hear the judge's side of the story. After that, the commission takes a second look, weighs your complaint against the judge's answer, and decides how to proceed."

"More months of waiting?" said Norwood.

"I don't expect so," said Brundage. "Judges usually leap to their own defense very quickly."

"I don't know about this guy," said Norwood. "It took him three weeks to hear three days of testimony, with all his schmoozing and taking recesses for who the hell knew why. Then he took about two minutes to write his decision, from the looks of it."

Brundage drew breath as if to respond, then began to page through the complaint. His eyes narrowed in concentration, which made his brow look especially thick.

"Your case was about restoring a car," he said.

"Not just a car," said Norwood. "It was a Maxwell. One of the last ones made before Chrysler took them over. My father had it as a young man. I remember riding in it as a boy. He maintained it for many years, but eventually it began to deteriorate. He left it to me in his will and instructed me to restore it. I didn't need the instruction. I wanted to restore it in his honor."

Brundage closed the complaint back into the file.

"There is something about your first car, isn't there?" he said. "My first car was a '67 Camaro. It was in terrible condition, but it was mine. I still dream about it occasionally."

"Really?" said Norwood. "I'm glad you do."

They spent time talking about favorite cars from their respective eras, and then Brundage steered the conversation back to the grievance procedure. The complaint would be served on the judge within the next day or two, and then the process would formally begin. Brundage handed Norwood a business card and reconfirmed Norwood's contact information. Then he walked him back to the reception area.

"Is there anything else I can do to help?" said Norwood. "Anything else I can send you?"

"Not right now. If I need anything else from you, it will be after my investigator and I have interviewed the judge."

"You mean if he lies through his teeth?"

Brundage grinned tightly.

"The best thing you can do right now, Mr. Norwood, is be patient. The commission accepted your grievance. It rejects many others. Trust the process."

He reached out his hand, and again Norwood accepted his handshake.

———

Chambers shifted gears as one o'clock approached. Barbara stopped typing Larry's hastily scrawled decisions and moved into Bill's office. Larry stopped hastily scrawling decisions and changed into oversized gray shorts and a sleeveless T-shirt. By the time Larry opened the door to the judge's office and announced that he would be back by two, Barbara and Bill were seated across from each other at one end of Bill's wide desk. Bill responded that Larry "was doing a great job." Barbara simply waved.

Lunch arrived at precisely one o'clock, delivered by a short man wearing white pants and a white smock: tuna salad on whole wheat and a lemonade for Bill, turkey and lettuce on rye toast and unsweetened iced tea for Barbara. It was a standing order, automatically delivered unless Barbara phoned the deli to cancel by noon. She tipped the deliveryman five dollars.

They spoke little as they ate because the point of lunch was not to converse or to relax or to plan the rest of the workday. The point was to eat as quickly and efficiently as possible, then head out for their midday walk.

They descended a little-used stairway to the rear door. A security post was set up there, consisting of a single magnetometer and a table. Two court officers sat on stools.

"You're doing a great job," Bill told them as he and Barbara skirted the magnetometer.

Both officers laughed, and then echoed, "You're doing a great job yourself, Judge."

Outside, a short set of steps led up to a narrow courtyard that curved between 60 Centre Street and the federal courthouse. The buildings blocked the sunlight, but the air was hot and thick. Barbara climbed two steps ahead of Bill, then turned to face him. They were at eye level now, and she fixed him with a pair of sunglasses, then set a straw hat on his head. He lifted a hand to brush it off, but she caught his wrist.

"That's your hat," she said. "You need your hat because the sun is strong."

Bill obediently lowered his hand.

With her elbow firmly locked on his arm, Barbara guided Bill through the courtyard and out into the sun. By slightly altering the pressure of her elbow, Barbara could sway Bill left or right, speed up his pace, or bring him to a stop. They crossed Worth Street to Columbus Park, which separated the huge Criminal Courts complex from Chinatown. The park had basketball and volleyball courts, a soccer field of artificial turf, handball courts, swings and climbing gyms, benches, and patches of pavement that could be adapted to city games like boxball.

As they reached the basketball courts, Bill gripped the staves of the iron fence and stared intently at the game. The players ran up and down the court, dribbling, passing, fighting for rebounds when the ball rattled off the rim.

"You were a good player," said Barbara.

"I know," said Bill. He spoke these two words without a hint of question or wonder.

"The Knicks drafted you, but your knee—"

"Blew it out," said Bill.

They watched the game until the players, tired and hot, took a time-out. Bill's fingers slipped from the fence, Barbara locked her elbow around his arm, and they resumed walking.

———

She had come to understand that the important events do not always announce themselves. Rome did not fall all at once; the Great Depression did not begin the day after Black Tuesday. Her Black

Tuesday—rather, their Black Tuesday, she sometimes needed to remind herself—was not a Tuesday at all. It was Memorial Day.

They spent the long weekend at the Berkshire house and, as was their custom, rose early on Monday morning to go to brunch at the Red Lion Inn in Stockbridge. Car service was not due until five o'clock, and they spent the afternoon on the porch, drinking iced tea and trading sections of the Sunday New York Times. At about four o'clock, as Barbara fixed sandwiches in the kitchen, Bill noticed that a lightbulb had burned out in the wagon-wheel chandelier that hung from the center beam of the cathedral ceiling in the main room. Barbara told him to leave the bulb for the caretaker, but Bill, who could be as stubborn as he was affable, opened a stepladder in front of the fireplace.

Later, as she remembered it, he must have miscounted as he backed down the stepladder. His foot missed the last step, and he tumbled backwards. Had he landed a few inches to the left, his head would have found the opening of the firebox. Instead, it found the fieldstone face.

She drove him to an urgent care clinic in Great Barrington. Neither of them could say whether he had lost consciousness. The doctor found nothing of concern in a basic neurological exam. He gave the standard warnings: be mindful of abnormal headaches, don't let him fall asleep for the next several hours, follow up with your own physicians in New York. He wrote an order for a CT scan.

Car service took them back to the city four hours later than planned. It was a three-hour drive, and she kept an eye on Bill the entire trip. He nodded off once or twice, but he often nodded off during long car rides. Reading in a car made him dizzy, and the world outside the window was dark. When the car pulled up in front of their apartment, he thanked the driver for doing a great job. Vintage Bill Lonergan. One day passed, and then a second. He seemed fine, and so she held off scheduling the follow-up exam. And then . . .

It was a normal midweek morning. Bill had a hearing scheduled for eleven and decided to sleep in for an extra hour and a half. Barbara went to the courthouse at the regular time. The law clerk had the morning off, so she was alone in chambers. At nine forty-five, she called home to make sure Bill was getting ready to leave. No answer. She waited five minutes and called again. Still no answer.

At eleven fifteen, she called the courtroom. No, the judge didn't go directly to the courtroom, the court officer told her, and the lawyers on the hearing were getting impatient. She made up an excuse for the officer to convey and hung up the phone. Her hands shook.

At eleven thirty, she started making phone calls: to the dry cleaner where Bill took his shirts, to the gourmet deli where they ordered in food, to the coffee shop where Bill read the *Times* on Sunday mornings, to the wine store that stocked Bill's favorite upstate pinot noir. No one had seen him. At noon, she called her super and asked him to check the apartment. The judge wasn't there, and his hat and raincoat were gone from the coat-tree in the foyer.

At twelve thirty, she began calling hospital ERs.

Shortly after one, the private line rang. The caller was the administrative assistant for the chief operations officer at Madison Square Garden. Barbara needed to get there immediately.

She jumped into a taxi. A security guard met her at the Garden's employee entrance and took her to the executive suite. The operations officer told her that one of his men found the judge sitting courtside. No one was sure how he got into the building or how he made it all the way down there. But he seemed like a nice enough guy, so they started asking him questions, and he told them he was playing in a game that night. *For who?* they asked. *Seton Hall,* the judge said. On a whim, someone looked up some old programs— and sure enough, the judge was right about having a game, only he was about forty-five years too late.

The men seemed amused, but Barbara wasn't. She demanded to see the judge immediately, and they led her into an adjoining office with a large TV screen and a varnished pine bench that was a relic from many years ago. The judge sat on the bench, with his sleeves rolled up to his elbows. He held a basketball in his hands.

———

The incident, as she called Bill's wandering, galvanized Barbara. Using her own persistence, as well as the prestige of Bill's judicial office, she arranged for an immediate battery of neurological tests at one of the finest hospitals in the city. The conclusion, as Barbara understood it, was that Bill was suffering from traumatic dementia. His prognosis, which the doctor called "guarded," depended on whether the blow exposed a latent neurological condition.

"Such as?" Barbara asked.

"Well, to put it bluntly," said the doctor, "Alzheimer's. Does it run in his family?"

Bill couldn't answer the question, and Barbara, who married Bill late in life, knew nothing of his family's medical history. And so it was determined that nothing could be determined right now.

That night, Barbara lay awake while Bill snored beside her. She had invested everything in her husband, and now their lives could come crashing down because Bill missed a step on a stepladder. It wasn't going to happen; she couldn't let it happen. But how?

Her answer came in the form of three words that sounded suspiciously like a police department motto she must have heard somewhere. *Preserve, protect, defend.*

She would draw a very small and very tight circle around her husband. She would reveal little and admit nothing until she knew which path Bill's recovery would follow.

———

It had taken the entire summer, but she was beginning to understand the new geography of Bill's mind. The law still interested him and the meaningless banter with courthouse staff still amused him. But nothing engaged him like watching the basketball players run up and down the court in Columbus Park. Though his basket-ball career was much further removed in time than legal issues or courthouse faces, there seemed to be a special immediacy to these memories. Bill, she theorized, remembered the game with his muscles as well as his mind.

They continued their walk around the park, up past the pagoda at the north end, then back down behind the Criminal Courts complex. They walked slowly, drifting right and left as necessary on the crowded sidewalk. At one point, they passed Larry playing boxball on a patch of pavement marked by electrician's tape. He looked ridiculous with a sweatband squeezing his wiry hair and large plastic goggles magnifying his eyes.

They strolled a second circuit around the park, then crossed Worth Street and returned to the courthouse through the rear entrance. Bill complimented the court officers on doing a great job. They all laughed.

CHAPTER 6

After the Lonergans settled themselves in chambers and after Larry returned flushed and sweaty from his boxball game, Barbara excused herself for the ladies' room. Judge Lonergan's chambers was one of the few with its own private lavatory, a feature that started as a luxury but now had become a necessity. Back when the chambers population was two-thirds female, the lavatory was a distinctly feminine environment with bud vases, scented water, and plush pastel hand towels. Bill rarely used it then, preferring to head out to the men's room and chat with whomever he met along the way. Now, after Bill fell into himself, he had the exclusive use of the chambers lavatory, and it was Barbara who saw her ladies' room excursions as an excuse for getting away.

Barbara lingered in the ladies' room, happy to be alone despite the heat from the bright sunshine streaming in through the window that overlooked the interior light courts. A day with Bill, even a good day like today, was physically and mentally exhausting. She constantly worried about what he might do, what he might say, whom they might encounter at an inconvenient moment. She constantly needed to think ahead, war-game the most routine activities to foresee any potential problem. She could control what happened in chambers, but little else.

Barbara left the ladies' room and climbed to the sixth floor. Judge Neville Patterson, the administrative judge, literally maintained an open-door policy in his chambers. All court employees, from the newest data-entry clerk to the most senior administrator, were encouraged to wander in, state their business to Bertha, the judge's longtime confidential secretary, and wait for Judge Patterson to see them.

Barbara was exempt from these formalities. As soon as she crossed the chambers threshold, she saw Bertha press the intercom button on her phone. From behind a closed door, she heard three faint buzzes. A moment later, Judge Patterson opened the door and waved her inside. He was a trim man with a thin beard gone mostly white and shaggy hair the color of pewter. He closed the door behind him, then walked quickly to the big swivel chair behind his desk.

"I saw the motion reports for the last term." The judge lifted a stack of papers and fanned it in front of his face. "Bill's productivity is one of the best in the courthouse. His condition is improving, I take it?"

"It is," said Barbara.

"And Bill's former law clerk?"

"Still quiet as a mouse. She found a job fairly quickly, which eased the pain."

"Clerking for your husband looks good on anyone's résumé."

"I know. I hated firing her like that. But with Bill's condition that first month or so, it was easier having another man in chambers."

Judge Patterson cocked his head, boring into Barbara with one eye. The truth, which Barbara refused to admit, was that Bill's former law clerk was too ethical to stay within the small circle she had drawn.

"Plus Larry's a smart man," she added.

"He is," said Patterson. "He's just problematic in other ways. I thank you for taking him on. He deserved another chance."

"we all," said Barbara.

"ave a concern," said the judge. "I know I agreed to wait recovered. But as good as the motion production has been, I'm seeing a drop in our trial numbers. I can't afford to have a good trial judge like Bill on the sidelines much longer."

Barbara slumped in the chair, and Judge Patterson came around the desk to stand behind her.

"I'm sorry to dump my administrative problems on you," he said, gently kneading her shoulders with his thumbs. "It's just that I get pressure from on high. I've been running interference, but the fact is that if anyone sees that Bill Lonergan hasn't held a trial since May, I'd have a lot of explaining to do."

"I understand," said Barbara.

"I'm not talking immediately," said Patterson. "This term is shot. You're taking the August term for vacation. There's no need for any change until you come back after Labor Day."

Labor Day. It sounded so far into the future. She hoped Bill would be fully recovered by then.

"Are you going anywhere exciting?"

"The Berkshires," said Barbara. "As usual."

They were silent for a while. Judge Patterson kept kneading her shoulders, and Barbara closed her eyes to allow herself just a few precious moments of relaxation. Outside, the phone rang, and a moment later, Judge Patterson's phone buzzed.

Barbara heard from the tenor of Patterson's voice that it was an important call, perhaps from one of his superiors up the administrative chain. She slowly stood up and quietly backed around the chair. As she left chambers, Bertha pretended not to notice.

CHAPTER 7

Foxx was much less attuned to summer nightfall than he had been as a boy. Back then, he noticed the slow, incremental progress of the night as the combined effects of the earth's tilted axis and its yearly revolution around the sun shaved off a minute of light each day. Now, summer nightfall was static. He didn't, as he once read Daisy Buchanan to say, wait for the longest day of the year only to miss it. He didn't think of it at all. But there always was one night, usually in early August, when he realized that the days had gotten much shorter. Last evening, he reached the corner of City Island Avenue in what he remembered as full light. Tonight, at precisely the same time, the streetlights blazed.

Foxx paused at the corner to consider what his observation meant and decided it meant nothing except that he didn't notice now what he had noticed as a kid. He stubbed out his sixth and last cigarette of the day against a telephone pole, then slowly unfolded the wrapper of a stick of cinnamon gum. A few blocks later, he spat out the gum and went into Artie's.

The tables were crowded, the bar not. Foxx claimed a stool in the middle, which left an empty one on each side. At the far end, Ellen backed away from the service bar with a tray of drinks balanced on her shoulder and the palm of one hand. She wore white sneakers, a black pleated skirt, and a white tank top. Her black hair was pulled back, then gathered into a loose ponytail. Foxx looked her up and down and back up again, catching her wink at the end and responding in kind.

The bartender set a pint of Guinness in front of Foxx.

"Duff was here," he said. "Has something he needs to tell you. Said he'd be back. Not to let you leave."

Foxx looked at the clock above the mirror. Ellen's shift ended in an hour. He ordered a steak sandwich and a salad. As he waited for his food, he alternated sips of Guinness with glances at Ellen. He liked watching her work. He liked the way she moved, especially when she spun away from a table and her skirt twirled with her.

Foxx was on his second pint and halfway through his sandwich when a hand clamped on the back of his neck and a gravelly voice said, "Foxx-y."

"Hey, Duff," Foxx said to the image in the mirror.

Duff looked like he had been designed with a collection of pipe cleaners. Tall and thin, bony and loose-jointed, elongated face with a high forehead and sweeping chin. He had worked for eons at 60 Centre Street as a court officer, then as a clerk, then as a senior administrator. He took the stool beside Foxx, caught the bartender's eye, and held his thumb and forefinger an inch apart. The bartender poured a shot of Bushmills and set it on the bar. Duff knocked it back.

"Grandkids are a great invention," he said. "You have any?"

"I have a date tonight," said Foxx. "It's a start."

A puzzled look crossed Duff's face; then he coughed out a laugh. "Old Foxx-y." He clapped Foxx's shoulder. "Still the same."

"What do you need to tell me?" said Foxx.

Duff stopped laughing. "I saw Ralphie Rago," he said.

Foxx tore off a hunk of sandwich and stared into the mirror, chewing.

"That's what you do, you know, when you're retired and you're not watching your grandkids. You visit people. Hospitals, nursing homes, shut-ins."

"Ralphie isn't any of those," said Foxx.

"I remember you two as kids," Duff said, seeming not to hear, "riding up and down the avenue on your little bikes with big handlebars. I never saw one of you without the other. And if I did, the other wasn't very far away." He signaled for another shot.

"What's your point?" said Foxx.

"My point is that you need to see him."

"He's way upstate," said Foxx.

"Not for now. He has a medical issue, so he's transferred down to Valhalla for a while."

"Are you asking or is he asking?" said Foxx.

"Does it matter?" said Duff. "Both."

"Is he bad off?"

"That's what you'll need to see for yourself." Duff knocked back his shot, then clapped his hand again on Foxx's shoulder. This time the hand pressed down with the effort of getting off the stool.

Foxx had another pint while waiting for Ellen's shift to end, then another when Ellen joined him at the bar.

"What was Duff talking to you about?" she said.

"Something he thinks I need to do."

"Which is?"

Foxx shook his head, then ran his fingertips down the length of Ellen's arm. She had nice arms, toned arms, arms that looked like the products of gym workouts when all she did was heft trays of food and drinks. They finished their pints and decamped from the bar, walking along the avenue, then up the slight hill to the dead-end street that Foxx called home. They went halfway up the front steps, then sat down.

It was a beautifully calm night, and beyond the boatyard, the quarter moon lit a dark Long Island Sound that was as smooth as glass. Salt laced the air, and the quiet—without the whoosh of traffic, the calls of seagulls, the slap of ropes against rigging—was total.

"Hey," said Foxx. They had spoken hardly a word since he shook his head back at Artie's. He was thinking about what Duff told him, and he knew that she was thinking about whatever he was thinking about. And he didn't want either of them to be thinking about this at the moment.

He put his arm around her shoulder, and she tumbled across his lap. He rubbed a hand up the back of her thigh, burrowed it under her skirt, worked his fingers into her panties.

Her face slid against his.

"Let's go inside," she whispered.

"Let's not," he said. He stood her up and planted her one step below him, his knees pinning hers together until he slipped her panties down past them.

Afterwards, they did go inside. Foxx lay in the bedroom, his head dangling over the foot of the bed so he could see into the kitchen. Ellen stood at the stove, scrambling half a dozen eggs. She wore one of his old uniform shirts and nothing else.

"Duff told me I need to visit an old friend who lived in the house next door," said Foxx.

"There is no house next door," said Ellen.

"There was."

Ellen divided the eggs between two plates and pulled four pieces of toast out of the toaster. She brought the plates to the kitchen table, and Foxx rolled off the bed to join her.

"Where is he now?" said Ellen.

Foxx speared a piece of egg into his mouth, then put down his fork. Ralphie Rago, he told Ellen, was his first friend, his best friend, the friend he wrapped his childhood around. The Rago cottage was an exact duplicate of the Foxx cottage. Ralphie's father worked for the court system. His mother was a homemaker because in those days a mother could be a homemaker and the family still could stay afloat on a single breadwinner's salary. A fence ran between the two houses. The fence was made of wooden staves bound together by wire the same thickness as coat hangers. He met Ralphie one summer morning looking over that fence. Ralphie had a big head, pudgy features, a round belly beneath a yellow T-shirt, wide hips made wider by baggy khakis.

Hi, I'm Ralphie, he said with a smile because Ralphie's face was set in a perpetual smile that melted away only when he became very angry.

They were the only two kids on the poorly paved street that ran past a boatyard and ended at a boneyard, and they were inseparable for four whole summers and three full school years. Ralphie was pleasant company, his calm demeanor and hulking physique the direct opposite of Foxx's rat-a-tat talk and whippet-thin frame. But then things changed. Their fifth-grade teacher, a nun named Sister Edith, took an instant dislike to Ralphie. *Slow as molasses in the middle of winter,* she would say. Out loud. To the entire class. With Ralphie sitting in the front row.

Ralphie needed to repeat fifth grade, then took another two years to get through sixth. Meanwhile, Foxx moved on—to high school, to girls, to Ripple and Schaefer. If he saw Ralphie at all, it was over the fence. They would talk, but not for very long because Ralphie had atrophied both mentally and socially. He had become the Baby Huey cartoon character, a child packaged in a huge body.

More years passed. Foxx went to college, took the civil service exam, came off the list and into the court officers' academy. He was assigned to Bronx Supreme, moved into an apartment near Arthur Avenue, and tended bar for extra cash. He thought about his old friend only during his infrequent visits home. Ralphie was now a recluse.

And then, offstage and at a distance, Ralphie's life turned. Foxx could not remember the year, or even the chronology, but Mr. Rago somehow pulled enough strings to arrange Ralphie a custodian's job at 60 Centre Street. It was the perfect situation for Ralphie. He could go out into the world, trade an honest day's work for an honest day's pay, and then return home. Foxx recalled visiting one Christmas and crossing over to the Ragos' cottage. He and Ralphie sat on the porch, drinking beer in the bitter cold and reminiscing about their favorite games and their favorite toys. It was the last time they actually spoke.

A few months later, Ralphie was arrested for murder. He had been found in a basement office at 60 Centre Street, along with the body of a law clerk. Ralphie told the police that he had been cleaning the office for about twenty minutes before finding the body behind the desk. He stuck with that story right to the end of the trial, when he took the stand as his first, last, and only defense witness.

The jury convicted in three hours; then the judge maxed Ralphie at twenty-five to life.

———

"I visited the Ragos with my father the next Christmas," said Foxx. "Ralphie already had been away for five months by then. Five out of three hundred. The Ragos looked like they'd aged a hundred years. Their cottage was a shambles. We sat with them, tried not to rush out, though that's what we both wanted to do. Mrs. Rago insisted we have tea. So we had tea. As I drank it, I saw a mouse peek out from behind the refrigerator. We never went back again. At least I didn't."

"Where are they now?" said Ellen.

"Dead, I think," said Foxx. "They sold the cottage. The buyer knocked it down, then never built anything. Funny thing is, when I was a young scared kid, I used to feel safe because Ralphie's house was between mine and the cemetery. Now there's nothing in between.

"Anyway, Duff told me I needed to visit Ralphie. He wouldn't have said that without good reason."

CHAPTER 8

Getting to see Ralphie Rago was even easier than Kieran Duff had told him. The inmate medical facility was jointly operated by the county jail and a medical college. Inmates from prisons as far away as the Catskills who needed more than routine medical attention were transferred there for treatment.

"You can tin your way in," Kieran Duff had said.

Foxx listened doubtfully. "Tinning" meant flashing your shield. It usually worked on the subway and sometimes worked at Citi Field if the Mets were particularly horrendous and their opponent even worse. But to visit a convicted killer in a secure medical facility?

"Ralphie's been a model inmate for twenty-three years. Just don't show up with a hacksaw baked in a cake."

Amazingly, the tin worked. The guard asked Foxx a few extra questions, then played the do-you-know game with some 60 Centre Street names before letting Foxx pass.

The block was basically a straight-line corridor with private cubicles on either side. The air was hot and smelled of rubbing alcohol. Ralphie Rago lay uncovered on a bed and wore only a pull-up diaper. The resemblance to Baby Huey was completely gone. Ralphie looked like a stick figure. His arms, legs, and torso were wasted practically to nothing. But his head, owing to his skull, was still large and round. His eyes and mouth looked like horizontal dashes, his nose like two dots. A tube connected an IV bag to a port on the top of Ralphie's left hand. A monitor beeped, registering his vital signs.

Foxx moved closer, and the two dashes that were Ralphie's eyes fluttered and then opened. The dash that was his mouth twitched into a grin.

"Hey, Foxx," he rasped. "Duff said you'd visit."

"Of course," said Foxx. He gently took Ralphie's right hand into his, feeling the finger bones beneath the paper-thin skin.

"How's the old street?"

"Different," said Foxx. "Not as nice as we knew it."

"They ever move in, those people who bought?"

"Nah, never did. Still a vacant lot." A thought made Foxx smile inside. "Now there's nothing between me and the ghosts."

"Never actually saw one. Just told you so you'd think . . ." Ralphie drifted.

"Think what?"

"That I was brave."

"You were brave," said Foxx. "Still are."

Ralphie's hand wriggled free and groped along the side of the bed.

"What are you looking for?" said Foxx.

"I want to sit up. Sit me up."

Foxx found the bed control dangling by its wire below the mattress. He pressed the button, and the mattress contracted, raising Ralphie's head and bending up his knees.

"Need a couple of favors," said Ralphie. "One big, one small."

"Okay," said Foxx.

"I ain't ever going back to prison," said Ralphie, "so the doctors here need someone to make decisions for me when I can't do it anymore."

"You want to make me your health-care proxy?"

"That's what it's called?"

"Yeah."

"Then that's what I'm asking."

"You talked this over with Duff?"

Ralphie nodded. "He said you'd do it."

"He did, huh?" said Foxx. Duff sure had snookered him.

"All the papers are out at the nurses' station. You just need to tell them. They'll fill in your name. Then I'll sign."

"I can't be running up here."

"You don't need to run up here. You can do it by phone. Okay?"

"Okay," said Foxx.

"But if you want to visit, I wouldn't mind."

"Sure," said Foxx. "What's the small one?"

"That is the small one. The big one, you need to listen."

Foxx nodded, then realized Ralphie maybe didn't see. His eyes seemed unfocused.

"Yeah," said Foxx. "I'll listen."

"You probably already know what it's about."

"The murder?"

"I didn't do it, Foxx. I found the body, just like I always said I did. But that was all. I didn't do it."

"The way I remember the trial, your lawyer didn't put up much of a defense, except you taking the stand."

"Yeah, well, the evidence made it look bad for me," said Ralphie. "And I didn't have the best lawyer. Another one mighta stopped me from taking the stand. But I had no defense except what I knew was true and I wanted to tell it."

"You might have gotten a shorter sentence and been out long before."

"Long before this sentence?" said Ralphie. "You're right about that, but you need to understand. The world was a hard place for me. I had that job, but I had no real friends anymore. Anyone who meant anything to me had moved on."

He paused long enough for Foxx to field the implication that he was one of those who had moved on.

"I understand, Foxx. You couldn't hang back and not live your life on my account. Turned out, being inside wasn't so bad. God protects fools, and I had guys in there who protected me. Out of pity, maybe, or some weird sense of justice. I don't know. But I had them watching over me, a bed and three squares a day, no job I needed to get to in the morning and no nights at home without any friends or anything interesting to do. So being inside wasn't half bad, except for one thing. My mom and dad were devastated. They wasted their life savings defending me, mortgaged the house, too, and here they would probably die before I got out, which is what happened."

"I'm sorry," said Foxx.

"Yeah, well, I went to each of their funerals. Those were the only two times I been out except for when I got sick."

"What is it, exactly?"

"Colon," said Ralphie. "Had some bleeding on and off for a few years. Not exactly a red flag inside, you know? Then one day I bent down to pick up something off the floor and felt like my guts were being torn out. It was already Stage Four."

"I'm sorry."

"You already said that," said Ralphie, "but now here's what I want. Maybe you believe I didn't do it, maybe you don't. I don't care, because I know I didn't do it, and that's been good enough for me. But soon I'll be gone, and when I'm gone, it won't be enough for me to know I didn't do it. I want other people to know it, too. I want to be remembered well. Find out who did it, Foxx."

"You want me to investigate that murder?" said Foxx. "Now? All these years later?"

"I know it's long ago. I know lots of things changed, but lots of things didn't change."

"Like what?"

"You'll see, Foxx. Just start looking and you'll see."

"But what can I see that the cops didn't see?"

"Things," said Ralphie.

"Like what? Can you give me a hint?"

"I can't. But I know things were going on that I couldn't see or didn't understand."

"And I'm supposed to find them?" said Foxx. "Now?"

"You're good at asking questions, Foxx. You don't buy bullshit. And you're a pain in the ass."

"You're not pulling the friend card?"

"I already did," said Ralphie.

———

After lunch, after the usual midday stroll around Columbus Park, after settling Bill back behind his desk and spreading birdseed on the sill outside the window, after visiting the ladies' room and successfully resisting the temptation to drop in on Judge Patterson if only to feel his hands on her shoulders, Barbara returned to her desk. The morning had been a step backwards in Bill's recovery. Bill listened to Larry's first case summary, rendered his opinion on how the case should be decided, then balked at listening to anything else. He was tired, she could tell, and so was she. Larry cajoled three more rulings out of the judge before he totally shut down.

Now the four case folders were on Barbara's desk, and she had neither the ambition nor the energy even to loosen Larry's handwritten decisions from beneath the rubber bands, let alone spread her fingers on the keyboard and start to type. Vacation was still well more than a week off, and she knew better than to wish away an element as precious as time.

The phone rang, and Barbara, suddenly feeling inert as well as tired, let it ring. Twice, three times. Voice mail usually picked up after four, but the fourth ring cut off short and the blinking dark triangle beside line one went steady.

Larry poked his head in.

"Hand-delivery out at the desk for the judge," he said.

"Can you go out and get it, please?" said Barbara.

"The officer says it's a bit more complicated than that," said Larry.

"How complicated can a hand-delivery be?" said Barbara. She picked up her phone. "Officer, this is Barbara Lonergan. What seems to be the problem?"

"I have someone out here who insists that his hand-delivery means in-hand." The officer muffled his voice. "I told him the judge won't come out and I won't let him back to chambers. Seems kinda sketchy to me."

"I see. Ask him exactly what he is to deliver in-hand."

After a muffled exchange, the officer said, "He says it's confidential."

"I'll be right out," said Barbara.

The messenger looked like the typical summer intern—young, pale, nerdy.

"I was expecting the judge himself," he said as Barbara drew up to the desk.

"I am the judge's secretary," she said.

"I have my instructions," he said. He held a blank manila envelope in his hand. "I am to give this only to Judge Lonergan. No one else."

"Well, I have my instructions from Judge Lonergan," said Barbara. "He is in the middle of a very important conference call and he instructed me to accept whatever you are delivering."

"This is a confidential communication," the young man said as if uttering a magical incantation. "I can't hand it over to a secretary."

"And I'm not only the judge's secretary. I am also his wife."

The young man looked sideways as if thinking, then backed away to make a cell phone call. Barbara and the court officer looked at each other.

"Sorry you needed to come out here," the officer said. "You can see how persistent he is."

"Not a problem," said Barbara. "But if he somehow gets past me, you have my permission to shoot."

The officer laughed; Barbara didn't.

The young man ended his call and returned to the desk. "I am to verify that you will accept this on behalf of Justice William Lonergan," he said.

The formality struck Barbara as weirdly stilted, as if this boy wanted to inflate his own importance.

"Sure," said Barbara. She reached for the envelope, but he pulled it away.

"I need to hear you say it," he said.

"Say what?"

"What I just told you to say."

Barbara sighed. "I accept this on behalf of Justice William Lonergan."

"You heard it, right?" the boy asked the officer.

The officer grunted. The boy handed the envelope to Barbara, turned on his heel, and walked off toward the elevators.

"You ever see anything like that?" said Barbara.

"No, ma'am," said the officer.

"Well, thank you for your caution. I wouldn't have wanted him back in chambers."

"Not a problem, ma'am."

Barbara drifted down the corridor and pushed through the fire door. She could tell that the manila held a smaller envelope inside and that the smaller envelope was thick. She waited until she reached the first angle of the corridor, then ducked into an alcove. The smaller envelope was ivory in color with the return address printed in chocolate-brown raised lettering. Barbara groped blindly for the wall as the courthouse suddenly tilted.

CHAPTER 9

The Lonergans ate dinner, as they did every night, side by side on separate snack tables in their den with its big-screen TV tuned to a cable channel devoted to pro basketball. Every show looked the same to Barbara—interviews intercut with game footage. But Bill seemed to enjoy the shows; at least he watched them without complaint, much as he watched the birds feeding outside the chambers window.

After dinner, she helped him into his pajamas and tucked him into bed. Routine, she had learned courtesy of several hard lessons, was a virtue. Bill's mind demanded routine because it could not tolerate any surprises, and Barbara found that she liked routine, too. The time between bedding Bill down for the night and eventually crawling in beside him—whether it be twenty minutes or two hours—was the only time she had to herself anymore.

Tonight was different.

After satisfying herself that Bill was asleep and would stay asleep, she quietly left the apartment. Outside, she flagged down a cab.

Arnold Delinsky was a partner in a mega-firm that occupied three floors in the office tower over Grand Central Terminal. In his latter years, owing to his calm demeanor and political connections, he had developed a niche practice within the firm's wide range of specialties: his clients were exclusively judges.

"It happens more than you think," he told Barbara. Despite the hour, the corridors outside Delinsky's office buzzed with activity.

"The reason it happens more than you think is that most judicial complaints lack merit. In my experience, fifty percent are based on sour grapes and forty-nine percent are based on ignorance of the law."

"That leaves one percent," said Barbara.

"Even a blind squirrel finds the occasional acorn," said Delinsky. He had a completely bald head, small eyes, a big nose, and lips that squiggled above an underbite. "May I see the complaint?"

Barbara took the envelope out of her purse, then leaned forward on the edge of her chair as Delinsky began to read. The complaint consisted of four pages—two pages of a printed form filled out by the complainant and a two-page letter on Judicial Conduct Commission stationery that recast the complaint in legal terms. Barbara had tried to read the letter several times since it arrived that afternoon. She never made it past the first dense paragraph of legalese.

Delinsky read slowly, hunching lower over his desk as he turned each page. Finally finished, he pushed himself up and steepled his hands in front of his face.

"Bill never received anything like this," said Barbara.

"How old is the judge now?" said Delinsky.

"Sixty-six."

"I've seen this often. A judge has a sterling reputation, an impeccable career. He's seen more than most lawyers ever see and forgotten more than most lawyers ever knew. But he gets old. He starts to say inappropriate things. People might think he's lost his filter, but that's not what's going on. His time on the bench is growing short, so he gets impatient. He doesn't suffer fools gladly. He has no time for lawyer tricks and lawyer talk, so he cuts through it."

Barbara glanced over her shoulder. The office door was open, and beyond the empty secretary's desk in the outer office, a conversation drifted along the corridor. She got up, closed the door, and sat back down.

"How confidential is this meeting?" she said.

"It's a bit odd that the judge isn't here," said Delinsky. "But if we were involved in a court proceeding, I could speak to the judge with you present and not surrender the attorney–client privilege. So whatever you tell me will not leave this room."

Barbara took a deep breath. "Bill has lost it," she said. "Mentally."

"Alzheimer's?"

"That's the big question," said Barbara. "Bill fell off a ladder and hit his head. The doctors diagnosed it as traumatic dementia, but they are not sure if it accelerated a latent condition like Alzheimer's."

"When did he fall?"

"Memorial Day."

"After the trial that gave rise to this complaint," said Delinsky.

"Almost two months after."

"How bad is he?"

"On a scale, mild to moderate," said Barbara.

"And he continues to work?"

"He does. Judge Patterson temporarily assigned him to work on motions only. He doesn't hear oral argument, but he discusses every case with his law clerk. Quite amazing, really, the way the right comment or the right question literally can unlock all his knowledge."

"So Patterson is on board?"

"Well," said Barbara. "I didn't tell him about the fall. He thinks Bill is suffering from depression."

"What about his law clerk?"

"That's complicated, but under control."

Delinsky paged through the complaint again.

"Let me explain how this will likely play out," he said. "Whether the complaint has merit or not, the commission has decided to investigate. That investigation will consist of a one-on-one interview between the investigating attorney and the judge.

"The interview is formal. I can be present, but you, for instance, cannot, and neither can the complainant. A court reporter will take down every word. The commission then reviews the transcript. If, when they weigh the complaint against the judge's side of the story, the commission believes that the complaint does not have merit, the complaint is dismissed. But if the complaint survives the interview stage, it goes to a hearing."

"Is the hearing public?"

"Absolutely not," said Delinsky. "And if the judge prevails, the entire proceeding, even the fact that there was a complaint, is kept confidential."

"So if you win this for Bill, it's like it never happened."

"In layperson's terms."

"And the court system wouldn't know, either?"

Delinsky leaned forward. "Who or what are you afraid of, Mrs. Lonergan?"

"Bill had a longtime law clerk. Wonderful young lady. Very sharp. Very loyal. Unfortunately, very ethical. When Bill took sick, I knew he couldn't keep her as a law clerk and remain on the bench."

"She would reveal his condition," said Delinsky.

Barbara nodded. "She left while Bill was still undergoing tests. And Bill, that is, I, started looking for a replacement. I was put in contact with someone who had gotten into trouble and was barred from working in the courts."

"But not barred from working as a judge's personal appointment," said Delinsky.

"Exactly," said Barbara. "But before we even hired him, Bill received a letter from the inspector general that explained the clerk had agreed not to seek court employment as part of a plea bargain and suggested that Bill follow the spirit of that bargain. I took the letter to Judge Patterson, and he told me Bill was under no obligation even to respond."

Delinsky pressed his hands to the side of his nose for several seconds, then dropped them to the desk.

"This is all very interesting," he said, "but ultimately meaningless. I've never heard of the IG's office and the Judicial Conduct Commission working together or even sharing information. I suppose that if the judge was told about the new law clerk's record, the IG could open a fraud investigation. But that's not likely to happen because of this complaint."

Barbara let out a deep breath.

"So what happens if the judge loses the hearing?" she said.

"There are three usual outcomes," said Delinsky. "Admonishment, which is a warning. Censure, which is a stronger warning that may come with conditions. And removal for cause, which is what it sounds like."

Barbara sat back in her chair.

"When would the interview be held?" she said.

"We can move as quickly or as slowly as we want," said Delinsky. "Within limits, of course."

"We plan to be away for the entire August term."

Delinsky looked at his calendar.

"I could squeeze it in before you leave. But I would need to meet with the judge no later than tomorrow to go over the complaint and prep him."

"What about after we get back?" said Barbara.

"I expect the commission would honor a judge's vacation plans," said Delinsky.

"I'll need to think about it and let you know."

Delinsky summoned a clerk to photocopy the complaint and the commission's letter. He kept the copies and handed the originals back to Barbara.

"Before you go, I need to know whether you really want to pursue this," he said.

"Why would you even ask that?" said Barbara.

"Your husband has had a long, successful career. I'm sure he could retire tomorrow, and the two of you would live comfortably. More than comfortably. Why do you need to fight a battle you may not win?"

"What about the ninety-nine percent failure rate of judicial complaints?" said Barbara.

"Because there's a fourth possible outcome that applies in very few cases but could apply in yours. Even if the commission dismisses the complaint, it may find that the judge can no longer handle his duties. If so, it can direct a disability retirement."

"Why would it do that if it dismisses the complaint?" said Barbara.

"It could form its own conclusion during the interview, or the hearing if it gets that far."

Barbara folded the pages back into the envelope, stuffed the envelope back into her purse, and snapped the purse shut.

"Mr. Delinsky, I know what you are saying. I also know my husband. He did nothing wrong in that trial, and I will not have him punished for it. And even in his compromised state, he can still do good for people. I see that every day. But beyond that, my husband needs the bench. Being a judge is not a job to him. It is his lifeblood. If he is forced to retire, he will be dead in six months. I cannot let that happen."

———

Foxx stood on his porch, smoking a cigarette and watching the lights on the water. Ellen was asleep in his bed. They had just had sex, but what lingered in Foxx's mind was his visit with Ralphie Rago.

He opened the screen door to flick away his cigarette, then quickly lit another. He was thinking about how easy it had been to jettison Ralphie Rago as a friend and simply move on. But he was beginning to suspect that there are things you can't really get past, especially things that were important to you when you were young. Like the lights on the water, like meeting Ralphie over the fence, like the house that no longer stood as a buffer between your bedroom and the ghosts flickering in the old cemetery. He could see that now, not clearly just yet, but as a harbinger of what it will feel like to be old.

He heard a faint creak of wood behind him, the sound of a footstep on the soft spot in the kitchen floor. A moment later, Ellen pressed up behind him. She nuzzled his shoulder with her chin, worked her fingers into the waistband of his boxers.

"Whatcha thinkin', Foxx?" she whispered.

He told her about visiting Ralphie Rago but not about the harbinger.

"Why did he ask you now?"

"I was his best friend."

"But why now?"

"He's dying. He needs to know who really killed the guy."

"I'll ask it a different way," said Ellen. "Why did he ask you and why did he ask you now?"

"I can't answer any other way."

"Maybe he asked you because you were his best friend. But maybe he asked you because he thinks the answer is still at 60 Centre."

"But it was twenty-five years ago," said Foxx.

"It's an old building, Foxx. What's twenty-five years to an old building?"

CHAPTER 10

Maxine Rosen slept late on the Saturday of Memorial Day weekend. She had worked on a report until midnight, then drove directly from her office in Binghamton to her summer house in the Hudson Valley. The house had a musty smell—she hadn't been there since New Year's—but the morning dawned clear and breezy, and she opened all the windows before burrowing back into bed for another hour of sleep.

At noon, she went into the village and bought herself food for the weekend. She loved the village, which had the rustic, upscale ambience one might expect of an enclave populated mostly by weekenders from Manhattan. She planned to close her practice in three years, and the hardscrabble hill country of the Southern Tier was not where she intended to spend her retirement.

Back home, she fixed a BLT and mixed a gin and tonic. She ate on the back deck, her laptop open so she could read that report one last time. She found a few typos, changed a few other words, then e-mailed the report to the judge and to counsel on the case. The husband was paying 100 percent of her fee, so his attorney received her invoice as well.

The gardeners arrived for their first visit of the new season. Their big mower thundered, their leaf blowers hummed, their trimmers whined. Maxine remembered one particular visit, years ago now. The gardeners descended and then all but one departed, the straggler bagging the piles of winter detritus scooped out of the shrubbery and blown away from the foundation. It was a hot day. She offered him a drink, he accepted, and what ensued she remembered as a French art film, with she playing the part of an aging Gallic starlet and he the earthy handyman. Or maybe what she remembered was a parody of a French art film. She wasn't sure anymore.

She closed her laptop, brought her empty plate and tumbler inside, and fixed herself a second drink. Outside, the gardeners still swarmed. She never had seen the earthy handyman again, or maybe she had. Again, she wasn't sure. She lay on the chaise. The sun felt warm on her arms and legs. She took a healthy slug of the gin and tonic, then closed her eyes and lifted her chin so the sun hit her face directly.

She drifted to the buzz of the lawn equipment. Then the buzz stopped and she thought she heard the truck drive away. But maybe she hadn't because a thin whine persisted. She opened her eyes and turned onto her elbow. A single gardener was down below, trimming the edges of the rock garden.

Maxine drained off her drink and closed her eyes. The sound of the trimmer sent a pleasant chill down her spine, and she remembered being young and lolling in bed while her mother vacuumed their apartment. She drifted again, then woke up to silence. And a presence.

She opened her eyes. The gardener sat on the edge of the chaise.

"Hi," he said gently.

Maxine pushed herself up. The gardener was leaning on his hand, and his hand was between her knees, and when she pushed herself up, one knee rubbed against his wrist. It felt scratchy.

"You startled me," she said.

"I am sorry," he said. He smiled sweetly. "Remember me?"

She thought back to the afternoon of her French art film. His face, she realized now, had faded from her memory, and if this were the same gardener, he was taller and much more handsome than she remembered.

He caressed the side of her face with his knuckles. They felt scratchy, too, and the reaction they evoked in her was not a chill and was not in her spine. She rolled toward him, pinning his other wrist with her knees.

"Do you?" he whispered. His thumb traced the line of her jaw, then trailed lightly across her lips.

"Here," she whispered, her eyes hooded. The word caught in her throat, so she repeated, "Here. A day like this."

His thumbnail etched a straight line down her chin to the center of her throat. He worked his other hand out from between her knees, and then both hands were at her neck, both thumbs boring into her throat.

Maxine's eyes shot open. She grabbed at his wrists, but could not pry them away. She kicked her legs, but he swung over her and sat on her thighs. His thumbs pressed harder.

He spoke a name, and his voice, shedding its earlier sweetness, sounded harsh and accusatory.

He spoke the name again.

"Now do you remember?" he said.

And just as the last spark faded in Maxine's frenzied brain, she did remember.

CHAPTER 11

Barbara watched the painfully slow progress of the digital clock on her nightstand. She had separated the strands of her many problems and come up with tentative solutions meant only to mollify her worried mind and usher her to sleep. But sleep would not come. Beside her, Bill began to grunt and twitch, entering his second dream cycle since she had joined him in bed. She wondered what dreams his addled mind conjured to get him through the night. Did they revisit scenes from the eras of his life? His basketball years, his career as a lawyer, his first marriage, his time on the bench? What role did she play in his nightly cinema?

She pushed up on an elbow to listen and watch, but his grunts never resolved into intelligible words, his twitches never found the rhythm of recognizable gestures. After twenty minutes, he slowly sank toward the deeper reaches of the sleep cycle, and she slipped out of bed.

She glided down the hallway, one hand skimming along the wall because her vision was spotty in the darkness. She found her way into the kitchen and poured herself a small glass of milk. In the den, she lowered the panel in the section of bookcase that served as a bar and added a hefty shot of Scotch. It was a putrid combination—two things she disliked intensely—but one her mother induced her to try when a horrible toothache kept her up all night. Now, as an adult, it worked as a sleep remedy.

She forced the drink down and toddled back to the bedroom.

But sleep would not come, and she needed to think of something, anything, to get her mind off her fears.

———————

There were places Barbara would not go, not even in her memories.

The move came without warning. It was a stormy day in the dirty part of November, with a turbulent gray sky, glistening bare trees, mounds of mushy roadside leaves. Instead of going to school, Barbara piled into the backseat of the family's green Ford station wagon with her twin brother and several cardboard suitcases. Her parents were in the front seat, her father driving. They said little to each other, and when they did, it was only in whispers. Up ahead, the taillights of the moving van blurred between the strokes of the wipers.

Eight hours later, they arrived in a nasty dusk. A clapboard house on the side of a hill, a barn below. When the engine cut, she heard only the whistling wind and the spattering rain.

In the morning, her new life looked no better.

That first winter was long and dark, perpetually cold. She and her brother took nightly turns hiding a small transistor radio under their pillows. If the sky conditions were right, the radio pulled in stations from home. The signal would waver and then sink back into static, but even a few notes of a song from last summer or the mention of a familiar place name made her feel warm again.

Their birthday was in late April, and that first birthday on the farm, their parents surprised them with special gifts—a bicycle for her, a BB gun for him. Strict rules came with each. She could not ride the bicycle without announcing exactly where she was going and when she would return. He could not shoot anything that lived.

There was a pond on the farm that the former owner used for watering cows. The water rose and fell with the rainfall, sometimes brimming up near the top of the grassy berm, other times sinking completely beneath a thick sheath of mud. Frogs lived in the pond, which was not far from the big rusted oil drum where her father burned garbage.

One day, her father dumped a pile of old newspapers into the oil drum and tossed in a match. As the flames rose, he noticed a strange silence. He strolled to the pond. On the top of the berm, a frog lay on its back. He flipped it with his toe and saw a hole the exact size of a BB at the base of its skull.

She was in her room, tying her sneakers, when she heard her father whip into the house and shout her brother's name. She ran down the stairs, passing her father on the way as he unlooped his belt from his pants. She went into the kitchen and quickly told her mother exactly where she was going and exactly when she would return.

The old farmhouse had grates in the ceilings to allow heat to rise to the second floor. Her brother's room was directly above the kitchen. She heard him cry *I didn't!* then the crack of leather on flesh.

Outside, she jumped on her bicycle and pedaled down the driveway. The big balloon tires hissed like radio static as they crunched over the broken shale of the dirt road. But the sound of the belt slaps didn't fade from her ear until she was a mile away.

She lived on the farm for twelve years, graduated from high school, earned an associate's degree from the community college, then fled to New York City. She arrived with no big-city dreams, just an intense desire to escape the silent hills and the broken-down farms and the slowly dying towns. Outside the Greyhound's windows, tall buildings loomed and people teemed on the sidewalks. She felt safer already.

A high school friend let Barbara sleep on her sofa. A job with a temp agency kept her afloat. Two years later, an opening in the courthouse steno pool brought her to Lower Manhattan. She arrived early for the first day of her new job. There was a park across the street, and she sat on a bench and gazed up at the imposing building. The temp agency had sent her to more places than she cared to remember, but she never had seen anything quite like the wide stone steps and the massive stone columns that seemed to bulge beneath the weight of the pediment.

She pinned her purse under her elbow, gripped her brown-bag lunch with her other hand, and breathed deeply to quell her quivering heart. Because she knew. She knew the moment that she laid her eyes on this sooty old building in this backwater of Manhattan that here was where she belonged. And she knew that something special was going to happen.

The interior of the courthouse reflected New York City's difficult financial times. The mural gracing the rotunda dome had faded. The marble columns had a fuzzy layer of smoke, grit, and oil. Light fixtures were broken. Water trickled uselessly in the drinking fountains. Windows were either sealed shut with layers of paint or stuck open in broken tracks.

The steno pool "girls," as they were called, worked in a bland interior office with dusty windows that looked out over litter-strewn spaces called light courts, which she later learned was an ancient architectural method of illuminating the interior of a large building. The girls pounded typewriters on tiny desks set up in two parallel rows. From nine to one and then from two to five, they did nothing but type decisions handwritten on legal-sized sheets of yellow paper sent down from the rarefied heights of the judges' chambers.

The girl who occupied the desk beside hers was named Bertha. They were about the same age and started their jobs on the same day, but Bertha seemed to flout every rule. She arrived late in the morning, departed early in the evening, took extra-long lunches, and, when she actually sat down to work, would procrastinate by fixing her makeup or brushing her hair.

"Aren't you worried about getting fired?" she whispered to Bertha after one particularly late arrival.

"I can't get fired," said Bertha.

"Why not?"

Bertha hooked the fingers of her two hands together and tried to pull her hands apart.

"Connections," she said.

Bertha was plump, brassy, and man-crazy, everything the thin, polite, and shy Barbara was not. Still, the two became friends, though Barbara needed to contribute little effort to the friendship. Bertha provided all the energy, all the plans, all the talk. Barbara needed only to show up, smile, and go along for the ride. Bertha dragged her to clubs, invited her to mixers, roped her into double dates. She also expounded on the courthouse as a husband-hunting ground.

"Forget about the judges," she would say. "They're successful, but they're old. The court officers are exciting, but what kind of future do they have? Becoming a courtroom clerk? And the clerks, what are they but court officers who have become boring? So where does that leave us? The law clerks. You want a husband, you find a law clerk. Not just any one. You got to know what you're looking for. You want one with an upside, one who wants to work here two or three years, learn the ropes, then cash in by going to work for a private firm. Or better yet, one who wants to become a judge."

———

Barbara did not sleep long. In fact, she had no sense of having slept at all. No memory of a dream or of the disconnected thoughts that often preceded sleep. But there was evidence of having slept: the pale light filtering in through the curtains and the new numbers on the clock. She knew now that the solution she had reached before her phantom sleep would not work. Her priority, first and foremost, was to keep Bill on the bench for as long as possible. To do that, she needed to defeat the judicial conduct complaint without it ever going to a hearing. And to do that, Bill needed to be in the best possible health, both mental and physical.

She made herself a pot of coffee, then went into the den. She drank down the first cup quickly because it was the second cup she needed. The second cup always hit her with a surge of strength, energy, and optimism. After the second cup, she switched on her laptop and began her hunt.

CHAPTER 12

Foxx untangled himself from Ellen and carefully slid out of the bed so he would not shake the mattress. In the kitchen, he put up a pot of coffee, scrambled three eggs, and toasted a bagel. He took his breakfast to the daybed on the porch. The weather promised to be thick and humid. The sky was white, the Long Island Sound gray, the air windless.

By eight o'clock, he had showered, shaved, and dressed. At eight thirty, he phoned Captain Kearney to bang in sick. At nine, he peeked in on Ellen, who still slept. He left a note, then left the cottage. He stopped to light a cigarette at what passed for the corner of his street—a broken curbstone, a patch of dried mud inlaid with bits of gravel and shards of glass, and some kind of exotic weed with little white flowers. Then he loped down the hill to the avenue.

Vincent J. Scannell, Esq., had a street-level office not far from the seawall where the avenue ended. He was a big-gutted, red-faced man with a shock of gray-blond hair and sad-looking eyes. He had cornered the transactional law market on City Island, mostly real estate closings, lease negotiations, and probate work. But he had to have started somewhere, and thirty years ago, his start had been assigned counsel work for indigent criminal defendants.

"Kieran Duff's good people," Scannell said, settling in behind his desk. "He vouches for you, that's good enough for me. Though I'm a little unclear about your interest in Ralphie Rago's case."

"Ralphie and I were childhood friends," said Foxx. "I visited him yesterday. He isn't doing well."

"I'm sorry to hear that," said Scannell. "He was my first true private pay criminal defense client. But a client like him, a case like his, they stay with you for a long time."

"He asked me to look into his case. He needs to know who did it before he dies."

"Duff didn't tell me you're a detective."

"I'm not," said Foxx.

"And you seriously think you can find the killer?"

"I don't think anything. I told Ralphie I'd try, so I'm going to try."

Scannell sighed enormously.

"I suppose you can start by reading the transcript," he said. "I'll need time to dig it out of storage. Duff only called me last night."

"I don't want the transcript," said Foxx. "I want to know what didn't get into the transcript."

Scannell unhinged his glasses and tossed them onto the desk.

"What do you remember about the case?" he said.

"Not much," said Foxx.

"Even though you and Ralphie were friends?"

"It was a time in my life when I didn't pay much attention to anything."

"Well, then you'll need the whole rundown," said Scannell. He took a deep breath. "The victim was a law clerk named Calvin Lozier. Ralphie discovered the body in a remote office at the bottom of a back stairway. He said he was sent to clean the office and was in there for about twenty minutes before he found Lozier's body behind the desk. He didn't think Lozier was dead, so he tried to lift him, then he tried to revive him. Then he realized he was dead and started yelling. A court officer heard the yelling and found Ralphie still hugging the body.

"The police questioned Ralphie, and he told them exactly what I told you plus one other detail. When Ralphie first went into the office, there was a brass lamp on the floor. He didn't think anything of it, just set it on the desk and then went about his business. Unfortunately, the lamp turned out to be the murder weapon—blunt force trauma to the skull was the official cause of death—and the only prints on the lamp belonged to Ralphie.

"Ralphie never lawyered up and he never changed his story, except at one point, he made a curious comment. He said that even though he thought Lozier was 'a bad man,' he didn't want anything to happen to him."

"What did he mean by that?" said Foxx.

Scannell raised a finger. "I was doing assigned counsel work in the Bronx when Ralphie's parents hired me to defend him. Put me in the big leagues right away. Not only my first privately paid client, but my first murder trial and my first felony case in Manhattan, too.

"But what I had was a completely circumstantial case, a client with a story I couldn't shake, and a curious comment that pointed to motive. What did I do with that? I started looking at the victim, and what did I find? I found two promising avenues of inquiry.

"The first one, let's call it political. As I said, Lozier was a law clerk, and like lots of law clerks, he was trying to become a judge."

"At the time of the murder?" said Foxx.

"Oh yeah," said Scannell. "He had a regular campaign organization. A manager, a few campaign workers, a war chest that wasn't huge but big enough to print a few posters and keep those campaign workers in pizza. But the problem was that he didn't have a chance. The nominating convention was about two weeks away when he was killed. I talked to the campaign manager, Sidney Dweck. There was only one slot open on the ballot in Manhattan, and Lozier wasn't going to get it. Nobody needed Lozier out of the way, because he wasn't in the way. He was tilting at windmills.

"So that ended the political avenue of inquiry. The other avenue, let's call it personal. Lozier had an underside. He was married, but he had been involved in several courthouse affairs, sometimes more than one at the same time."

"He was some kind of a stud?" said Foxx.

"Not to look at him," said Scannell. "But, you know, some guys just have a good line of shit."

"Is that why Ralphie called him a bad man?" said Foxx.

"I thought so then, and if you pressed me, I still think so now," said Scannell. "One thing I learned about Ralphie was that he had a primitive sense of morality. There was no nuance with him. Things were black or white."

"He was like that as a kid," said Foxx.

"Now, here is where it got interesting," said Scannell. "The room where Lozier was killed was outfitted like an office but wasn't an actual office. It was a place where people went to have sex. You needed the key, and the key was held by one of the custodians."

"Ralphie?" said Foxx.

Scannell held up his finger again. "You can see why this was important. If I could show that other people—lots of other people—had access to that room, it could substantiate Ralphie's story that he found the body and create reasonable doubt. And maybe one of these other people would be one of Lozier's jilted former lovers come back to take a chunk out of his head. But the problem was that I couldn't find anyone at 60 who could nail any of this down as a fact. Lots of people claimed to know about the room. They even called it the 'boom-boom room.' But no one ever admitted to using it or even could locate it on a diagram. From an element-of-proof standpoint, it was more like a local legend than a fact."

"What about the custodian?" said Foxx.

"Him, too. No one could identify him. But I hired an investigator, and he dug and dug and finally got a name. Orlando Cortez. He had the only key to the room and would arrange who got to use it and when. For a price.

"First, I tried to squeeze Cortez to give me names, but Cortez absolutely refused. He said some of them I wouldn't want to know. And if he gave me one that led to others, he didn't want that on his head."

"What did he mean you wouldn't want to know?" said Foxx.

Scannell shrugged.

"Judges?" said Foxx.

Scannell shrugged again.

"I didn't give up," he said. "I hit him with a trial subpoena and brought him in to testify. The DA immediately objected because Cortez wasn't on my witness list. The judge leaned the DA's way, then reversed himself and allowed me to make an offer of proof outside the presence of the jury. I did, or at least I tried. But Cortez talked circles around all my questions until finally the judge cut him loose. So without Cortez, I had no way to show other people had access to the room.

"I tried another offer of proof, this time the testimony of one of Lozier's ex-girlfriends. The judge shot that one down, too, saying the testimony would tarnish Lozier's reputation without furnishing the jury with evidence of any probative value."

"What about taking a plea?" said Foxx. "He'd have been out years ago."

"You think I'm an idiot?" said Scannell. "The DA offered eight to twelve. I tried to sell Ralphie on the deal. His parents tried to sell him on the deal. But he adamantly refused. That old black-and-white morality of his. He didn't do it, he knew he didn't do it, and he couldn't understand why no one else believed he didn't do it. I didn't want to put on any defense. The case was circumstantial, and the way the evidence went in, I thought there was a chance that at least one juror would hold out. But Ralphie not only didn't want to take a plea. He also wanted to testify. I tried to talk him out of it, but he insisted. The judge didn't want Ralphie to take the stand, either. He yelled and screamed and banged the table, trying to force Ralphie to plead guilty and take the deal. He even warned Ralphie that if he testified and the jury convicted, he would treat his testimony as perjury. Ralphie took the stand anyway. I asked him a question here and there, but mostly I just let him talk so the jury would see the gentle, harmless, trusting Ralphie Rago. Then the DA tied him in knots on cross.

"The jury convicted, and the judge, true to his word, gave him the maximum sentence of twenty-five to life."

Scannell grabbed a pen from a cup and leaned over a legal pad. "What's your address?" he said.

"I told you I don't need the transcript," said Foxx.

"I know. But I want to dig out my witness interview notes. They might help you."

Foxx gave Scannell his address.

"Across from the old boatyard, eh?" said Scannell. He dropped the pen, tore off the sheet of legal pad. "You'll have it by tonight."

Foxx got up, shook Scannell's hand, and turned toward the door.

"Hey, Foxx. I never was a crusader, never was much of a trial lawyer, either. Good thing this island became popular as it did. But there's one thing that's always stuck in my craw about Ralphie. I think someone set him up. Not sure who, not sure why. But that's what I believe. Maybe you'll see something in all this that I never saw myself."

CHAPTER 13

B arbara did not relax until the Town Car cleared the Bronx and sped up the Thruway. The driver reported that their ETA was 11 A.M., give or take, which meant that she had time to do what she needed to do and make it back home by late afternoon. Luckily, Larry had come to the apartment on short notice, arriving with the day's ten case summaries and sandwiches for lunch. He asked no questions, and Barbara gave no hint of her plans.

Barbara settled herself into the corner of the backseat and adjusted the reading lamp that curved over her shoulder. The brochure she had downloaded onto her laptop showed a large estate on gorgeously landscaped grounds. There were groves of fruit trees, weeping willows along the banks of a wide stream, rolling lawns divided by hedges, and stone paths curving through gardens of flowers and shrubs. The main building was a Georgian mansion with a redbrick facade and tall white columns. A large trapezoidal keystone anchored the two halves of the lintel above the imposing front door. Smaller keystones sat above all the windows of the facade.

Barbara read the entire brochure, then closed the laptop. The soothing vibration of the car and her fatigue from her fitful night of sleep quickly conspired against her. She dozed off and stayed asleep until the very last leg of the trip. The slow roads, as she called them, curved through areas quaintly labeled THICKLY SETTLED on yellow road signs. Soon the "thickly" became "thinly," the terrain less manicured. She remembered how proudly expansive Bill had been during their first excursion to the vacation home, how he recounted bits of local history, including the fact that the forest had slowly reclaimed the colonial farmland.

The car turned off the road, then climbed a short stretch through some trees. At the top of the climb was a clearing where a house with a fieldstone front and a big red barn stood on opposite sides of a circular driveway. The car slowly passed the barn and stopped in front of the house.

The driver opened the back door, and Barbara got out. She had not been here since Memorial Day weekend, and she was glad to see that Jack, the caretaker, had repaired the broken trellises and freshened the window frames with a new coat of green paint.

"I won't be going inside," she said. She started to walk toward the barn, and the driver hastily apologized for not stopping there.

"Nonsense," said Barbara. "I can use the exercise."

A flagpole stood in the center of the circle, surrounded by a flower bed where a late-summer mix of asters and zinnias bloomed. The barn, according to Bill, predated the house by a century. The Lonergans, like their predecessors in title, used the barn as a garage and for storage until Barbara came up with the idea of transforming the hayloft into guest rooms.

She lifted the wooden latch, and the two barn doors swung smoothly outward. She loved that first smell of the barn, a mix of gasoline and cut grass and old wood. Their car, a sensible sedan, was parked in the center. The rest of the barn was dedicated to Jack's equipment. Along one wall was a workbench with garden tools; along the other was a large red tractor mower caked with dried grass clippings. Behind the mower was a golf cart, which Jack used to travel the property.

Barbara started the sedan and pulled out into the sun.

"I expect to be at least three hours," she told the driver. "Follow the road back out and you'll hit town in less than a mile. Good restaurants. An old-style music shop, if that's your thing. I'll phone you when I'm done."

The Keystone was ten miles away, its only sign a pair of brick pillars on the side of the road with a concrete keystone embedded in each. A narrow lane started at those pillars and ran for a straight half mile between white pines of identical shape and height. The mansion slowly revealed itself in the distance, and when she reached the end of the white pines, the grounds spread open before her. The photos had been as accurate as the driving directions. There were the rolling lawns, the groves of fruit trees, the willows dipping toward the glassy water of the stream. She parked in a lot behind a hedgerow, then walked on a brick path to the front door of the mansion.

The lobby was large, the woodwork dark and ornate, the walls a pale blue. Overhead, three ceiling fans turned slowly. Barbara gave her name to the woman behind the reception desk. The woman checked her computer and asked her to take a seat in the waiting area. Dr. Feldman would be with her momentarily.

That prediction proved accurate as well. Barbara barely had time to sit on a sofa and grab a magazine from the end table when a young woman wearing a lab coat stuck out her hand and introduced herself as Dr. Stephanie Feldman.

"Thank you for seeing me on such short notice," said Barbara.

"Short notice is what we get quite often," said Dr. Feldman. "Families tend to deal with this until they suddenly can't anymore. Do you live in the area?"

She had thick hair and a thin face and a sprightly girlish aspect that made her seem impossibly young to be a doctor. But her voice sounded cultured and mature.

"New York, actually," said Barbara. "But we own a summer home here."

"And this is about your husband. Does he have a diagnosis?"

Barbara recounted Bill's fall on Memorial Day, his wandering incident, and the doctor's diagnosis of traumatic dementia.

"We can help," said Dr. Feldman. She led Barbara out the door and across a wide lawn. There were several people in sight. Residents, Barbara assumed. One walked a small black dog on a long, retractable leash. Another, a man about Bill's age, tossed a Frisbee with a young boy, possibly his grandson.

At the end of the lawn was a hedgerow with an iron gate hung between two brick pillars. Dr. Feldman opened the gate and ushered Barbara through. The world, it seemed, immediately hushed.

"We call this our contemplation garden," said the doctor as she latched the gate behind them. "It's less for the residents than for the families."

A path made of finely crushed red brick curved through flower beds and shrubs cut into precise geometric solids.

"Most people call the path a figure eight. I think of it as the symbol for infinity."

As they walked slowly on the path, the tiny bits of brick crunching noiselessly beneath their feet, Dr. Feldman explained that the Keystone was the brainchild of two financially successful brothers determined to find a different way to cope with their mother's mental decline. They read all the current literature on dementia, and since neither was a scientist nor a doctor, they had no preconceived notions, no reputations to cultivate, no grant money to protect.

"They decided to take a totally different tack," she said. "And so they came up with the theory."

"The brochure vaguely mentions a theory, but gives no detailed explanation."

"A marketing ploy, but truthfully, it is better shown rather than told."

"And the testimonials?" said Barbara. "Another marketing ploy?"

They had done a full circuit of the infinity path and went back out through the gate.

"We have two levels of care here," said Dr. Feldman. "Behind the main building are the condos. Those residents are the ones you see on the lawn. They may come and go as they please, though they must stay on the property, of course. We are headed to the secure unit, for residents who can't be left on their own. Both sets of residents benefit from therapy based on the theory."

Inside the main building, they rode a slow elevator to the second floor. The elevator opened into a lobby, and Dr. Feldman pressed four numbers on a keypad beside a set of double doors. A red light above the keypad turned green, and the locks within the doors turned back with a loud click. Inside, a corridor ran past several rooms. On each door, the room number and the name of the resident were set out in polished brass. Beside each door was a glass curio box where photographs and trinkets were displayed. The corridor carpet was padded but not plush. A shallow wooden shelf ran between each door. Light from clamshell sconces brightened the pastel yellow walls.

"Each resident has his or her own room." Dr. Feldman scraped her foot on the carpet and rubbed the shelf with her palm. "Accent on safety. No thick pile to catch the sole of a shoe, a handrail to help with balance."

"The doors are all closed," said Barbara.

"We don't let them stay in their rooms. It goes against the theory."

Dr. Feldman led Barbara to the end of the corridor and into a large room with many round tables. At each table sat two aides and two residents. The aides wore powder blue smocks and white pants, the residents wore stylish warm-up suits. Barbara silently followed the doctor on a serpentine path through the tables to the other side of the room. Each of the residents, Barbara noticed, was engaged in needlepoint, knitting, beading, or watercolor painting on postcard-size canvases.

"Arts and crafts hour?" she whispered.

Dr. Feldman held up a finger and looked at her watch. A two-tone gong sounded. The aides all rose and shifted from table to table. In a moment, the room was as quiet and settled as before.

"What you just saw," Dr. Feldman said, "is the theory in action.

The theory is that the combination of fine motor movements and many brief interactions with many different people slows the process of mental deterioration."

"Is it proven?" said Barbara.

"Empirically, but not scientifically," said the doctor, "which is why I wanted you to see this before I addressed the testimonials. Yes, family members claim that this therapy reverses mental deterioration. Their mother or their father seemingly gets better. But it's an illusion. The truth is that no spouse, no child, no family could provide the constant, multifaceted interactions that a trained staff can provide at a facility like the Keystone. It's just not humanly possible. What they see is not a reversal but a bounce back, a response to the proper stimuli."

"Isn't that the same as a reversal?" said Barbara.

"If your perceptions are your reality," said Dr. Feldman. "In fact, all the different flavors of dementia are one-way streets. The car may slow down, maybe even stop for a while. But it never shifts into reverse."

———

Back inside the Town Car, Barbara pulled down the window shades and asked the driver to raise the partition. She waited until they were on the highway, the engine thrumming and the tires rippling, before she called Delinsky.

"I want the hearing later rather than sooner," she said.

"Perfectly acceptable," said Delinsky. "I will contact Mr. Brundage, note my representation, and arrange a date. May I ask why you have decided to wait?"

"I want Bill to be in the best possible mental state for the hearing. I've enrolled him in a thirty-day program that looks promising."

"You think of everything, Mrs. Lonergan," said Delinsky.

Barbara silently agreed. It was her overarching job to think of everything.

"I'm looking at my calendar now," said Delinsky. "I may be able to move some things around the latter part of Labor Day week. If I can, you have a deal. If I can't, I'll set the hearing for the Tuesday and prep him on Monday."

The call ended, and Barbara lifted the shade long enough to spot the highway milepost passing outside the window. It was always this way: a problem arises, and through determination and effort she overcomes it. Yesterday at this time, she was standing at the doorway to a nightmare. Bill's world, as well as hers, would come crashing down around them. But now, like a field general, she had moved her assets into alignment.

She lifted her legs onto the seat and took a deep, settling breath. The backseat of the Town Car felt as comfortable as the four-poster at home, and her sleep, when it came, was divine.

CHAPTER 14

Though no longer related by a marriage that had ended many years ago, Cannon still had an open invitation to stay with his brother's ex-brother-in-law whenever he visited New York. Dave DiLallo was thicker than Cannon in every way. He was thicker through the middle, wore thicker glasses, and had a thicker shock of hair that had gone gray only around the temples. He also had a "thicker" career, having been twenty-five years in the NYPD rather than a sheriff's deputy and court officer.

Dave lived in the Howard Beach section of Queens. It didn't feel like New York City to Cannon, that is, if he assumed that Midtown Manhattan was the template for the entire city. The house had a garage and a driveway and a backyard. It also had a redwood deck, where Cannon sat while Dave futzed in the kitchen. Below the deck, a garden hose leaked water into a mound of dark brown mulch surrounding a cherry tree Dave had planted in the spring and needed to nurse through the heat of the summer. Above the deck, a jumbo jet moved slowly across the white sky, flaps spread and landing gear down as it descended toward JFK.

Dave came out with two BLTs and a pitcher of iced tea.

"Remember when you could go to an airport, and all you saw were Pan Am, TWA, United, Delta, maybe Eastern?" said Cannon.

"Times have changed," said Dave.

"Yeah. Tell me about it. I just watched ten planes land, and not one an American carrier."

Dave chomped on his BLT, splintering woody bits of bacon that landed on his plate. Since retiring, he focused his leisure time on "things big and metal that ran on a schedule." Railroad and aviation magazines covered his coffee table.

"I know you want to help your brother's kid," he said. "But I don't see how talking to this Judge Lonergan in New York City moves that ball down the field."

"I told you," said Cannon.

"Right. You told me all about what a great guy he was twenty-something years ago. But what's he going to do now?"

"Something," said Cannon.

"Something," said Dave.

"Okay, it's a crazy long shot. But I made a promise, and I can't go back empty-handed."

"I hope you didn't give this kid any false hope," said Dave.

"I didn't," said Cannon. "I wouldn't."

"Then who? Your brother. I can't see Buck—"

"Sarah," said Cannon.

Dave leaned back, grinning. "Now we're getting somewhere," he said.

"It was just after I retired," said Cannon, "and was trying to get my PI business going. She had a problem she wanted me to look into. Something between her and your ex. And then, well . . . It was brief. No more than a few times. I don't know how Buck found out."

"From what I've seen, Buck isn't stupid," said Dave.

"All I can say is that you haven't seen much and you haven't seen lately," said Cannon. "Buck's turned into a charlatan. Or maybe he always was, and I only came to see it later. These foster kids, he only got interested in taking care of them when his B and B business died."

"You mean he does it for the money?" said Dave.

"You'd think so because the simplest answer is usually the right answer, but things aren't ever simple with Buck. No, it's not the money. He does it for the glory, the prestige, for the awards he gets.

Delaware County Man of the Year. Should have been Woman of the Year because Sarah does all the work while Buck sits on the porch and rocks in his rocker."

"Those kids don't care," said Dave. "They get a fine place to live. Does the division of labor matter if the results are good works?"

"Don't get theological on me," said Cannon. "Buck's a phony, their marriage is a sham, and if it wasn't for those kids, Sarah would have left him."

"I get it," said Dave. "So what's Buck doing so god-awful wrong that brings you down here on this mission? Besides wanting to impress Sarah."

"It's not to impress Sarah," said Cannon, but he felt his eyes drop as he spoke and he knew Dave caught it. He bit off some of the BLT and went on as he chewed it down. "Buck hired this lawyer to defend Luke. Local guy. I've seen him in action, and he's competent enough, just no great shakes. And for something like this, you need great shakes.

"I tried to talk to Buck, but with what happened before, well, it's like a steel curtain slammed down between us. He's not fiery mad at me. Never was. With Buck, it's always a long, slow smolder. So I decided I can only do what I can do, and I can't do what I can't do. I poked around the edges of this case. Didn't find much of anything."

"Except for that guy you told me about," said Dave.

"Yeah, that guy," said Cannon. "The sheriff and the state boys looked into him. If they found anything, they never told me."

"You would've known," said Dave.

"Suppose so."

"You pitch that guy to the kid's attorney?"

"Yeah," said Cannon. "Hard to sound convincing when all you got are some vague feelings. So I was done until last week when Sarah came crying to me about Buck and the lawyer and how she thought they should be doing more."

"And so you decided this was a way to get Sarah back," said Dave.

"I know that's what it looks like to you," said Cannon. "But I feel like shit for what I did, for what we did back then. I really do. And there's nothing to get back, anyway. It was a fling, not a full-blown relationship with lots of sneaking around and making plans that never got done."

"But," said Dave.

"But I still felt I needed to do something, and that's when I came across a business card from this lawyer I met when I was a court officer. I told Sarah about him. Maybe I exaggerated some, made it sound I was more involved in that case than I was. But I said what I said, and Judge Lonergan's all I got right now."

––––––

Foxx toyed with the idea of returning to see Ralphie Rago, then decided a second visit would be more effective when he knew more. He went back to his cottage to await the delivery of Scannell's interview notes. Ellen was gone, but the scent of her body wash still hung in the bathroom atmosphere. His bed was made, hospital corners and all. His breakfast plate, coffee mug, and silverware were cleaned and drying in the drainboard beside the sink. He could get accustomed to Ellen's particular form of domesticity, though he worried that growing accustomed to anyone's anything usually preceded the death knell of his illusions.

He slathered peanut butter and jelly on a bagel, and when the sun moved far enough past the meridian, sat in the shade on the front steps. He smoked his third cigarette of the day. A car drove up from the avenue, then turned in his direction. He thought for a moment that the car bore Scannell's interview notes. But it made a broken U-turn and headed back to the avenue.

Foxx lit up his fourth, took a long drag, then leaned back on his elbows. It was ridiculous, he knew, to be investigating a murder that occurred a quarter century ago. But here he was, doing just that. He had no training or experience. Even the undercover work he occasionally did for the inspector general, whom he knew well enough to call Bev, wasn't exactly investigatory. Bev usually had him look into something that entailed observing and reporting rather than questioning and deducing. Still, he had a knack for making people uncomfortable, which counted for something.

The notes arrived in a Redweld, brought by a kid on a bike. Foxx gave him five bucks.

The Redweld was heavy. Several strips of masking tape covered the flap, and written on them in black marker were Ralphie's name and case number, swelled and blurred now from years of absorbing the salty air. Foxx arranged the notes on the kitchen table, then began to read. It took time to get comfortable with Scannell's messy mix of print and script, more time to decipher his system of symbols and abbreviations. Meanwhile, the world darkened outside the cottage.

Ellen came after her shift, laden with a shopping bag that held two take-out dinners. Rather than clean up the piles of notes, they ate on the porch, seated side by side on the daybed, plates on their laps. Foxx told her generally about his meeting with Scannell and specifically about the papers that covered the table. He hoped to find something he could pursue and thought that, together, they could dig out a thing or two that Scannell had missed.

"I don't know anything about this," said Ellen.

"Neither do I," said Foxx. "But if we don't try, I'm out of options before I begin."

They dumped their plates in the kitchen sink and took up positions on opposite sides of the table. Ellen tightened her ponytail and slipped on a pair of reading glasses. She was too vain to wear the glasses at Artie's, where she compensated by writing large on her order pads. But here, in the privacy of Foxx's cottage, her vanity vanished. Plus, Foxx liked the look for a particular reason that dated back to high school.

But there was no time for librarian fantasies now. Foxx read the interview notes for Sidney Dweck, Lozier's campaign manager;

Ellen read the notes for Wendy Lozier, the bereaved spouse. When they finished, they switched.

"Did you notice this?" said Ellen. She turned the notes toward Foxx and pointed to a snippet of underlined script.

Foxx read the words, then looked up.

"He sounds like a lawyer," said Ellen.

"He is a lawyer," said Foxx.

"I'm talking about Sidney Dweck, not Scannell," said Ellen.

CHAPTER 15

During Barbara's years in the courthouse steno pool, she knew the judges only as names that she typed on decisions. But she imagined them as kindly men with white hair and bushy eyebrows. At lunch hour on nice days, she would sit on the same park bench where she sat that first day, her knees pressed together to balance her lunch on her lap. She would watch the men going up and down the courthouse steps and wonder which were the judges.

One day, a young man settled on the bench, far enough not to intrude, but close enough to invite conversation. She finished her lunch, refolded her brown bag, smoothed it so she could use it again tomorrow. A breeze passed, and the bag sailed out of her hand and cartwheeled past the young man's feet. He caught it and handed it back. Conversation ensued. He said he was a law clerk for one of the judges. She told him, meekly, that she worked in the steno pool.

"Then you must know me," he said. He took a well-thumbed address book from his pocket and opened it on his lap. "See?"

She recognized the handwriting immediately.

"You are very busy," she said. "We get lots of your decisions to type."

"The judge's secretary can't keep up anymore," he said. "She'd probably be fired anyplace else, but our judge is a kindly man."

"Does he have white hair and bushy eyebrows?" she said.

"No," said the young man. "Why do you ask?"

He dropped by the bench several times over the next few weeks, and though he was friendly and talkative, he seemed always to have a wind at his back. They would chat amiably for five minutes, ten minutes, once for half an hour, but always until he took out his address book, checked his watch, and brusquely excused himself. Then, after a few weeks, the unseen wind at his back stopped blowing. It was mid-September, and the change in the weather dovetailed with a change in his demeanor. He would buy a falafel from the cart in the corner of the park, sit on the bench, and eat lunch with her. He didn't rush, didn't open his address book, didn't lift his head to see who might be passing on the sidewalk or climbing the courthouse steps. He would stay the entire hour, then guide her across Centre Street. Once, he held her by the elbow.

September turned into October. The leaves on the sycamores in the park began to curl, but the weather stayed mild. Their conversations were pleasant but vague. Still, she felt there was something going on, that somehow, almost without volition, they were tumbling toward each other.

It happened on a blustery day in late October. They were on the bench. Leaves scraped across the sidewalk. People hurried past. For all these days during all these weeks, they sat as they always sat—she to his right, he to her left, approximately a foot of bench between them. That day, he slid right up against her.

"Chilly," he said, as if that needed to be stated. He lifted his arm onto the back of the bench and let his fingers brush her shoulder.

She settled into him.

"It would be nice to go somewhere warm," he said.

"It would," she said.

"What if there was?" he said. "Would you?"

"I would."

They crossed Centre Street, his hand on her elbow. Inside the courthouse, they crossed the rotunda and took a back stairway she never had seen. At the bottom of the stairway was an alcove, and in that alcove was a door that looked like a closet. He plucked a single key from his shirt pocket, and the door turned out not to be a door to a closet but to a room with a desk, three chairs, a book-case, and two brass table lamps. But the main piece of furniture was a red velvet sofa.

"Fancy," she said.

He stood behind her, breathing her hair. She lifted her shoulders, and her coat slipped into his hands. She heard the buttons click when he tossed the coat onto the desk. And then she felt his hands cupping her breasts.

CHAPTER 16

Back in those happier days, he would take the plane up out of Stewart and then follow the Hudson before banking west. The flight plan always included a slow climb over the Catskills. At the appropriate time, he would announce "starboard" or "port," and then listen to the sound of them moving around in the cabin to look. They were like children, the way they loved gazing down at the estate, which from five thousand feet looked like an artistically constructed toy.

He was grounded now, in more ways than one. The brush had greened since his last visit, hiding the cuts he had made in the wire. He poked blindly with his hands, pricking his fingers several times before he located the first cut and carefully separated the barbed strands wide enough to shoulder through. The ground felt firm beneath his boots, its perpetual moisture not dried, just sucked up by the ferns and skunk cabbage that grew knee-high and thick.

He plodded slowly, lifting his knees and planting his feet carefully to leave less of a track behind him. In April, the black staves of the wrought iron fence had stood out against the brown mud and the gray tree trunks. Now there were bands of pink, white, and purple azaleas that held their blooms long after Mother's Day in the cool shade.

He reached the fence and opened the gate. The grass had been mowed and raked. There was no sign of anything dead, not the soggy mats of last year's oak leaves, not the stalks of daffodils he knew had come and gone since his last visit.

The first pebble was right where he had placed it, on the back edge of the granite plinth where the single gravestone stood. He bent down and flicked his fingernail against it. The pebble did not move.

He plucked the second pebble from his pocket. Gauging with his eye, he set it on the other end of the plinth, then nudged it slightly until it was the exact distance from one corner as the first pebble was from the opposite corner. Symmetry was important.

Satisfied with his measurement, he squeezed a droplet of slurry onto the plinth and set the pebble in place. The slurry dried quickly.

He stood up and walked around to the front of the stone. He tried to pray, but this time no prayer would come.

"Two down," he finally said. "I'm getting there, kiddo."

The rumble of a gas engine cut the silence. It could have been a lawn mower suddenly come to life or a tractor revved to climb the hill behind the big house or the scooter throttled by the security guard. He opened the gate, closed it behind him, let the latch fall. The engine kicked into a higher pitch. Not a mower. Certainly not a tractor. Had to be the scooter.

He headed back toward the cut in the wire, the ferns and skunk cabbage slapping at his boots because he didn't care about leaving tracks at the moment. He needed to get the hell out.

The scooter—because it was the scooter—burst through the arborvitae. He could tell from the sound that the guard had pulled up at the gate to the plot and stood straddling the sputtering engine.

"Hey, you!" the guard yelled. "You there!"

He didn't turn around. He knew that if he turned around and met the guard's eye, he would be compelled to go back. Instead, he kept walking.

"What do you think this is?"

He didn't rush now. He resumed the plodding gait that had brought him here, lifting each knee high and setting each foot down with care so as not to disturb the undergrowth. The scooter revved once, kicked down, and then faded back into silence.

CHAPTER 17

Foxx usually arrived at the courthouse with just enough time to change into his uniform and get to the fifth-floor desk before Captain Kearney red-lined the sign-in sheet. Three red lines in a month equaled one lost vacation day, a mathematical formula Foxx knew very well. Arriving an hour and a half early was like landing on another planet. He used his swipe card to open the brass door on the Pearl Street side of the building, then climbed up to the lobby. The coffee shop was locked, the security desk empty.

Foxx skirted the metal stanchions that demarcated the magnetometer lines and headed into the rotunda. The building felt less like a courthouse than like a church before the first Mass of the day. He saw no one, but could hear distant sounds—a door latch clicking shut, cartwheels bumping over a threshold, an elevator dinging on an upper floor.

Foxx changed into his uniform, but left his equipment belt and weapon in his locker. The custodial crew usually arrived by seven, and when Foxx didn't see any of them hanging around the head custodian's office, he knew that Orlando Cortez already had started his morning rounds. He cleared his mind and allowed his feet, or maybe his subconscious, or maybe just dumb luck to steer him into Orlando's path. He couldn't have picked a better interception point, a catwalk corridor on the third floor.

The catwalks followed the inside faces of the hexagon and

crossed the six radiating corridors. On one side of the catwalk was
a solid wall. On the other, windows opened into the interior light
courts. The catwalks were not air-conditioned, and the windows
remained open for the entire summer. By August, only a rare breeze
moved the air.

Foxx pushed into the catwalk from one end while Orlando
Cortez pushed in from the other. Cortez had a rolling trash can and
seemed to be amusing himself by spinning it so that it caromed off
one wall and into the other. He caught up with the can and spun
it again. The can rotated toward Foxx, who grabbed it and flung it
down the catwalk behind him.

"Hey!" said Cortez.

Foxx spread his feet to block the width of the catwalk and summoned his baleful stare. "We need to talk," he said.

"About what?"

"About Ralphie Rago."

"Who's that?"

"A guy who worked with you here about twenty-five years ago."

Cortez made a big show of looking up as if thinking. "Nah,
doesn't ring a bell."

"How about this?" said Foxx. "He was arrested for murder. Does
that ring a bell?"

"Oh, Ralphie Rago." Cortez slackened his jaw and swung his
arms. Then he snapped back into himself. "Is that who you mean?"

Anger bubbled in Foxx's chest. It wasn't just Cortez's dead-on,
mean-spirited impression of Ralphie. It was also knowing that
Cortez was playing him from the very beginning.

"Anyway, that's old business now," said Cortez. With his sinewy
neck, scraggly chin beard, and bulging eyes, he looked like a billy
goat. "Now, if you will excuse me, I need to work."

He stepped forward to shoulder past Foxx, but Foxx didn't
budge.

"I said I need to work," said Cortez.

"And I need to talk about Ralphie Rago."

"I told you, that's old business. Nobody gives a flying shit about him."

"I give a flying shit about him," said Foxx.

He braced an arm against the wall. Cortez stared at him, chewing the inside of his cheek. He cocked his head and narrowed his eyes, then chopped down on Foxx's arm. Foxx caught his wrist, then used Cortez's own momentum to spin him around and yank his arm up behind his back to a place it wasn't designed to reach.

"I need to talk about Ralphie Rago," he said.

Cortez sneered. "Fat chance, fuckhead."

Foxx yanked Cortez's arm until his wrist touched the back of his head. Cortez was one tough bastard. He should have been screaming, crying, howling in pain. But all he did was gasp and snort and close his eyes.

"Ralphie's lawyer called you to testify, but the judge cut you loose."

"I had nothing to tell them," Cortez said through his teeth.

"You had a lot to say, you just didn't say it."

Cortez said nothing, and Foxx pushed his arm higher.

Foxx kicked Cortez's legs out from under him and shoved him facedown on the floor.

"I want to know everyone who used that room."

"I didn't tell that dumb-ass lawyer, and I ain't telling you now."

Foxx pushed Cortez up against the wall. He didn't know what the hell to do. Anyone would've talked by now; anyone should've talked by now. But Cortez seemed willing to hunker down and take the pain until it blew over.

Well, if that was the plan . . .

Foxx yanked the arm one more time. He felt something change in Cortez, as if he'd reached a breaking point. With his free hand, Foxx pressed Cortez's face into the wall and rubbed it against the rough plaster.

"Okay, okay," said Cortez. "I'll talk. I'll tell you."

Foxx eased off. He let go of Cortez's head, dropped Cortez's arm, spun Cortez around but pinned him to the wall with a hand to his chest. A drop of blood oozed from Cortez's nose. He lifted a hand to wipe it, but Foxx slapped it down. Cortez sniffed the blood up his nostril.

"Rago was a weird dude," he said. "Like 'hang out near the ladies' room' weird, like 'stroke his broom handle' weird. He knew about that room. He asked me if he could hide in the closet and watch when someone was using it."

"You didn't say that to Scannell. You didn't say that when you were questioned in front of the judge."

"I didn't want to say it," said Cortez. "It would've made Rago look bad."

"So you really wanted to protect him," said Foxx.

"Yeah. That's right. Protect him."

Anger erupted in Foxx again. It wasn't just that Cortez was a liar. He was smug about it, too.

Foxx pulled Cortez off the wall, chopped him in the gut to double him over, then shoved him halfway out an open window.

"I need names," he said.

"You're not getting them," said Cortez.

Foxx kicked at his feet, and Cortez slid out the window until the only things holding him were two of Foxx's fingers hooked in his belt.

"Pretend you wanted to protect Ralphie," said Foxx. "Bullshit. You wanted to set him up."

"No way. Not me."

"Who then?"

"No one."

"I need names," said Foxx.

"No fuckin' way, man. You don't know who you're dealing with."

"Tell me who you're dealing with," said Foxx, "or they'll find you puddled down below."

Still, Cortez said nothing.

Foxx let him hang. Luckily, his anger gave way before his fingers. Cooling down, he realized that no one benefited from face-planting Cortez at the bottom of the light court. He lifted him back inside. Cortez dived for the floor, curled himself into a ball, and panted.

Foxx crossed the catwalk and headed down the back stairs. On the second floor, he found a trash can and retched hot bile.

CHAPTER 18

The Lonergans arrived at the courthouse at their usual early hour. The officer greeted them at the brass door, and the judge heartily complimented him on doing a great job. Barbara said nothing, just grinned tightly in a way that was intended to mean anything.

Chambers was quiet, even for a summer Thursday. No inquiring lawyers, no visitors at the security desk. Amazingly, the phone did not ring until well after ten.

Larry picked up. The caller spoke gruffly and quickly. Larry asked him to repeat himself, was able to grasp the important points on the second go-through, then put the man on hold to buzz Barbara.

"Someone's calling to talk to the judge. Says he was here a few days ago," said Larry. "A personal matter."

"I'll talk to him."

Barbara watched her phone console until the steady black triangle started blinking. She picked up the call and said a cautious hello.

"This must be Judge Lonergan's secretary."

"Yes."

"This is Robert Cannon."

"And?"

"We met a few days ago. I showed you one of the judge's old business cards. I haven't heard from him."

Now she remembered the older, heavyset man with the walrus mustache and thick plastic glasses. After being served with the judicial complaint, she hadn't given him a second thought.

"Mr. Cannon, the judge has been very busy, and without knowing exactly why you want to speak to him—"

"That's why I'm calling, ma'am," said Cannon. "I know I was vague because I thought that card and my name and mentioning Ken Palmer's name would arouse his interest. I realize that was a mistake, so I wanted to give him the whole story."

"Mr. Cannon . . . ," said Barbara. She did not have time for a story, or even part of a story, not with everything that transpired since her brief meeting with this Cannon character three days ago. But maybe it was better that she let him vent and then firmly disabuse him of any hope the judge would contact him.

"I'm sorry, Mr. Cannon. Continue."

"Thank you, ma'am. I'm a retired court officer from Delaware County. I met the judge when he came up to handle a case. We're a very small legal community in Delaware County, and we never did appreciate big-city lawyers coming up and throwing their weight around. So we weren't favorably disposed when this Bill Lonergan showed up. Except everyone who met him immediately took to him. He was friendly, personable, a regular guy, and a damn good lawyer to boot.

"The case lasted more than a week, and Mr. Lonergan, I mean, the judge stuck around for the weekend. He wanted to see the countryside because he was looking to buy a country home somewhere and hired me to drive him around for two days. That was when he gave me the card and told me if I ever needed a favor in the legal variety, I should call him.

"Well, all these years passed, and I never had a problem of a legal variety until a few months ago. I have a brother, and even though we don't get along now, I still consider him a good man. He raised his own children and now spends his time fostering kids with Down syndrome.

"Back in April, Ken Palmer was murdered while fly-fishing in one of our trout streams. He was a well-known lawyer, but more than that, he was one of the county elders. He also was involved in that same case as the judge, which I why his name should ring a bell. Anyway, the deputies found Luke, one of my brother's foster kids, fishing with Ken Palmer's rod about thirty yards upstream of the body.

"Now, you can imagine that this is a complicated defense with Luke's mental capacity and the kind of evidence the prosecution has. I work as a private investigator. I started to look into the evidence, but my brother didn't want my help. So I bit my tongue and stayed in the background, but then my brother hired this local hack to defend Luke, and I decided I couldn't keep my mouth shut anymore, so I pulled out that old business card and drove down to New York City to cash in on Bill Lonergan's offer. That's when I learned he was a judge."

"You understand how his being a judge prevents him from getting involved," said Barbara. "There are ethical rules he must follow."

"I know," said Cannon. "But since I'm here, I thought, or maybe hoped, that he might have some advice, or that he's seen something like this before, or maybe he knows a lawyer in the city who's handled something like this."

"Judge Lonergan never has been assigned to criminal court," said Barbara. "Was that case from long ago a criminal case?"

"No," said Cannon.

"I didn't think so. As far as I know, he never practiced criminal law as a lawyer."

"I understand," said Cannon. "But I still would like to speak with him, if only for my future peace of mind."

"I'm afraid that's impossible," said Barbara. "He's behind closed doors, in conference with several lawyers on a multimillion-dollar commercial dispute. I can't interrupt him and I don't know how long he will be. But I promise you that I will mention you, your brother, your brother's foster son, and Ken Palmer to him. If he has any advice to offer, we will get back to you."

After hanging up, Barbara looked in on the judge. He sat facing the window, his eyes open but unseeing. There was nothing to see anyway. Not a bird pecked on the windowsill; the seeds Barbara had spread were gone.

"Bill," she said gently. When he did not react, she repeated his name more sharply.

He shook himself out of his torpor and turned her way.

"Bill, do you remember someone named Ken Palmer?"

"Huh?" he said.

"Ken Palmer. Do you remember that name?"

Bill's eyes drifted back into their faraway gaze, and then a faint smile crossed his face. He lifted the field guide off his lap.

"I saw one," he said.

"Saw what?" said Barbara. "A bird?"

Bill pawed through the pages, then pointed at a photo.

"An eagle?" said Barbara. "You saw one?"

Bill nodded eagerly.

"When?" said Barbara.

"I don't know," said Bill.

Barbara could get through many days of the new Bill by putting one foot in front of the other. But at some moments, she felt the ground falling out from under her. This was one of those moments. She leaned heavily on the desk, forced herself to take a deep breath. Bill stared at her, not comprehending. Finally, she pushed herself off.

"Ken Palmer," she said. "Do you know him, Bill?"

He looked straight at her, his eyes completely focused.

"Who?" he said.

———

Andrew Norwood scooped his wallet, change, and keys out of the plastic tray and distributed them among his pants pockets as he headed toward the rotunda. The rotunda floor was two-toned marble, designed to look like a compass with bronze symbols of the zodiac inlaid along the outermost circle. In the center of the compass, a dozen tourists gathered around a woman wearing a ribbon on her lapel.

"The rotunda, as you can see, employs a variety of materials and colors, which is a hallmark of neoclassical public architecture. The main attraction is the enormous dome mural you see above, which was designed by Attilio Pusterla and was completed during the Great Depression by artists working under the auspices of the WPA. It is called *Law Through the Ages* and depicts the development of the law from ancient to modern times."

Norwood walked toward the elevator bank, smirking to himself about the irony of the mural. *Law Through the Ages.* The ages may have begun with the ancient Assyrians, but they certainly ended before his trial last April.

It was near lunch hour, and when the elevator door opened, several people got off and only Norwood got on. He rode up to the third floor, following a path he knew well. A central corridor circled the roof of the rotunda dome, and one of six radiating corridors led to Judge Lonergan's courtroom. Norwood passed the pair of permanent, built-in phone booths that no longer had phones, the spare wooden bench where he waited interminably while Judge Lonergan was "attending to other business in chambers."

Brundage had called to report that the complaint had been served on the judge and that the first stage of the proceedings— the private interview with the judge—would be held within a matter of days. Norwood liked the sound of that. Truth was, he always believed big lunks like Brundage to be as slow-witted as oxen. But Brundage came across as sharp, intelligent, and efficient. He would get this job done.

Now Norwood needed to get his part of the job done. He needed Judge Lonergan to see him. He needed to look Judge Lonergan in the eye. He didn't need to say anything, because the look would say it all. It would say, *I'm coming to get you.*

Norwood reached the courtroom doors. Cardboard covered the two tiny glass windows. He pushed on the doors, but the dead bolt held them.

"Dammit," he muttered.

He checked his watch. It was shortly after one, which meant he needed to wait almost an hour before court resumed. If he was lucky, that is. Lonergan seemed to keep to his own leisurely schedule, like being a judge was a hobby rather than a job. But Norwood had nothing else to do, and the symbolism of looking Lonergan in the eye was important.

He sat on the bench to wait.

———

The Lonergans had their usual one-o'clock lunch in chambers. Barbara watched carefully as Bill mashed and swallowed his tuna salad.

"Tiny bites, hon," she reminded him.

"That's good," she complimented him.

A flake of tuna tumbled from the corner of his mouth and stuck to his chin. She reached across the desk and wiped it with her napkin.

"Bill, do you remember anyone by the name of Ken Palmer?"

Bill stopped chewing. He lowered his eyes and stared through the desk, then snapped back to attention and started chewing again.

"What about Robert Cannon? Do you know anyone by that name?"

"Who's he?"

"A court officer who drove you around Upstate New York over a weekend when you were on trial. He said you were looking to buy a summer home. Must have been before you bought the Berkshire house."

Bill's eyes drifted again, but only for a moment. He reached into the folds of Barbara's wax paper sandwich wrapper and plucked a baby carrot from a plastic container. Barbara gently removed it from his hand and bit off half with a loud crunch.

After they finished lunch, they took their usual backstairs route to the basement and then headed out the back door. Bill, as usual, told the officers at the security post they were doing a great job, and the officers answered that he was doing a great job as well. The first stop on their walk was the basketball court at the bottom of Columbus Park. Barbara allowed Bill to watch quietly. When he had seen enough, they headed up Mulberry Street.

"You know, Bill," she said, gently holding his elbow, "vacation starts at the end of next week."

"Okay."

"We are going up to the country house."

"That's good. I like the country house. Didn't something happen there once?"

"Lots has happened there," said Barbara. "We go there often. What do you mean?"

Bill went silent.

"I made another plan, too." She waited for Bill to respond, then continued. "There's a place near the country house. It's very big and very beautiful. I thought we might try that for a while."

"Does it have a basketball court?"

"I think it does," said Barbara.

Bill said nothing. He leaned away from her, and she lost her grip on his elbow. She recovered quickly and wrapped her arm around him in time to steer through a group of oncoming teenagers.

Talking about the law was one thing. Once the gears of Bill's mind engaged, they churned up years of legal knowledge. But feeding him the kind of basic, contextual information that made up the fabric of daily life was like watching him eat. A tiny bite at a time was all he could handle. And she needed to avoid the hard stuff, like baby carrots.

As they reached the back door of the courthouse, Bill suddenly stopped walking.

"Ken Palmer," he said. "He took me trout fishing once. Most boring day of my life."

CHAPTER 19

After his encounter with Orlando Cortez in the third-floor catwalk, Foxx reported for duty at the fifth-floor desk. It was a quiet morning, even by the leisurely standards of midsummer. A hand-delivery here, a chambers inquiry there. Foxx attended to these small tasks cheerfully, politely, one might even have said contritely if one knew what was going on in Foxx's head. No one did. Ever. Including Foxx himself, who rarely analyzed what he did after he did it. He believed, like a primitive existentialist, that you were what you did, not what you said, not what you thought, not what you felt, not what you intended—unless what you intended translated into action. He did not think too deeply about why he hung Cortez out a window sixty feet above the trash-littered floor of the light court. What surprised him, or more strictly speaking, troubled him, was the retching into the trash basket. He must have understood something on a subconscious level for his body to react that way.

Twice during the course of the morning he heard the sound of a wheeled trash can rolling on the terrazzo floor, but the sound receded without a custodian ever coming into view. Foxx's lunch relief showed up at the stroke of one o'clock. Foxx rode the elevator down to the rotunda, went out the front door, and angled down the steps to the park on the northwest face of the courthouse.

Along the sidewalk, a row of benches backed up to the edge of the park, and on that row of benches, during every lunch hour in all but the foulest weather, gathered a group of longtime court employees. They came from all strata of courthouse society: law clerks, back-office administrators, court officers, court reporters, data entry clerks, and messengers. They called themselves "the good guys," which Foxx considered self-congratulatory but otherwise not far off the mark.

Foxx was not one of the good guys. Rather than harp on the latest New York sports debacle or purvey rumors about a retirement buyout, he preferred to spend his lunch hours in silent contemplation, sometimes with one of his daily ration of six cigarettes, other times with a joint. But Foxx was not unwelcome on the bench, and so he sat at the edge of the good guys, waiting for their critical mass of experience and personal connections to attract the person he hoped they would attract.

Foxx spotted Sidney Dweck half a block away, bent sideways over his cane, his thick-soled shoes lifting slowly and landing softly on the pavement, each step a distinct set of careful moves. He crossed Centre Street and momentarily swayed at the curb as he decided to aim himself in the direction of the good guys.

Dweck eventually reached the bench. Several of the good guys shifted to make room, but Dweck preferred to stand. He knew each of the guys by name, and Foxx noted how expertly he managed to acknowledge each one. They talked some city politics, some courthouse gossip, and when Foxx sensed the conversation winding down, he got up and circled behind the bench. He intercepted Dweck as he hobbled toward the brass door.

"Do you have a minute, sir?" said Foxx.

Dweck stopped his studied pace. Up close, he looked rather devilish. His chin was sharp, his ears were pointy, his eyebrows curled up at their extremes like a pair of horns.

"A minute is a rather large percentage of the time I have left," he said.

"It's about Calvin Lozier," said Foxx.

"Now, there's a name I haven't heard in a while. What about?"

"Vincent Scannell thought you could help me."

Dweck slightly turned his head and squinted his closer eye at Foxx.

"Those two names together can mean only one thing," he said. He pointed his cane, inviting Foxx to sit on a nearby bench. "So tell me what this is about."

Foxx explained his childhood friendship with Ralphie Rago and his promise to find out who killed Calvin Lozier before Ralphie died.

"People still make those kinds of promises these days?" said Dweck.

Foxx said nothing. He was unconvinced of the strength of his promise, though he thought Orlando Cortez would vouch for it.

"Lozier sought me out," said Dweck. "He wanted to know how to become a judge. I was amused. He seemed to think the process was alchemic and that I was a sorcerer."

"Aren't you?" said Foxx.

Dweck grinned enough to reveal two rather long eyeteeth.

"He was a nobody from nowhere," he said. "He was what the Romans called a *novus homo*. Know what that is?"

Foxx knew but shrugged to feign ignorance. Five years of Latin had imparted knowledge that seemed rudimentary back then, but in the ensuing years had drifted almost completely off society's collective radar screen. It was refreshing to hear Dweck use the term.

"It means someone with no political connections who ran the *cursus honorum* from praetor to aedile to consul."

"Caesar did that," said Foxx.

"Ah, but not everyone is a Caesar," said Dweck, "and Lozier certainly wasn't. But he obviously had a lot of drive and desire, so I took him on as a project. Steered him toward the right political clubs, told him what functions to attend, which asses to kiss, which asses weren't worth kissing. He did everything I told him, and he did it with a smile.

"Now, for city judgeships, we have our own *cursus honorum*. You do all that scut work and then you get a shot at running for lower civil court. The election itself doesn't matter, because there is only one rule here in Manhattan: The Democrat always wins. What you need is the nomination. Once you get the nomination, you're on the lower civil bench. You don't piss all over yourself, after two or three years, you get appointed as an acting Supreme Court justice. Once you're there, you start working for a full Supreme Court nomination. Could take you a few years, but usually everyone who helped nominate you for the civil court slot will help nominate you for the Supreme Court slot."

"So that's the *cursus honorum*," said Foxx. "Lower civil, acting Supreme, and then Supreme." He had known these terms for years but never distinguished among them. For him, a judge was a judge was a judge.

Dweck grunted and went on.

"Like anything else, there are good years and bad years. Judges' terms don't run like clockwork, like the mayor or the president. There are lots of judgeships. There are lots of judges who don't fill out their entire terms. They retire, they move on to the next step, they die. So the terms get skewed. Some years there are lots of judge-ships up for grabs, some years not. The year we are talking about was as lean as it gets. Only one lower civil slot was open."

Foxx's cell phone buzzed in his shirt pocket, but he ignored it.

"Lozier didn't have a prayer getting that one slot," said Dweck. "He knew it, too. He also understood my conditions for helping him. Work hard, run with class, lose with dignity, pick yourself up and run again. The next year promised to be a better year. There would be several lower civil slots at stake, and he would be per-ceived as the good soldier who ran a good campaign the year before and was patiently waiting his turn. That counts for something.

"The nominating convention was early in September, and in early June, Lozier started talking like he had the nomination in the bag. I listened and I listened, and after about a week I finally sat him down and said, 'I don't know what you think has changed, because I don't see any different outcome in September.' And he said, 'Lots changed.' So I said again that nothing had changed and that I kept my ear pretty close to the ground so if anything did change, I would know. He just smiled and said, 'You'll know when the time comes.'"

Foxx sensed someone standing to his left, close enough to block the sun. But he was too interested in what Dweck was telling him to bother with someone invading his personal space.

"I'm not a dirty tricks kind of guy," Dweck continued. "It doesn't work in this context anyway. You're not trying to poison the electorate against your opponents because there is no electorate, just delegates who will control the nominating process year after year."

"So what changed?" said Foxx.

Dweck started to answer, then looked past Foxx at the exact moment that Foxx sensed movement to his left.

"Officer Foxx."

Foxx turned to see two court officers looming over him. They were big guys, guys who weren't assigned to 60 Centre, because if they were, Foxx would have known them. They struck identical poses, feet slightly apart and arms slightly akimbo because their hands rested on their belts close enough to finger their sidearms and their billy clubs.

"Are you Foxx?" the closer officer said.

"Yes," said Foxx.

"You need to come with us," said the other officer.

"And that would be where?" said Foxx.

"Captain Kearney's office."

"I'm due back there in ten minutes," said Foxx. "I'm posted at the security desk."

"This can't wait."

"And what's 'this'?"

"Not for us to say," said the closer officer.

"You can do this the easy way or the embarrassing way," said the other officer.

"What's the embarrassing way?" said Foxx.

"We disarm you and cuff you."

Foxx got up from the bench.

"Do you have a card?" he said to Dweck.

Dweck took his wallet from his lapel pocket and handed Foxx a card.

Foxx slipped the card into his shirt pocket, where his phone buzzed once as a reminder that he had a voice mail.

"I'll call you later," he said.

The two officers flanked Foxx as they walked into the courthouse through the brass door, up a flight of stairs to the north wing of the lobby, then through a catwalk and a public corridor to the elevators in the rotunda. There were still a few minutes left to lunch hour, so the rotunda was empty. An elevator opened immediately, and they rode up to the fifth floor.

Captain Kearney stood waiting in the open door to his office. He wore his brown suit. His arms were folded across his chest.

"Thank you, men," he said to the two officers.

They both mumbled and then one said they would wait outside. Kearney let Foxx pass, then closed the door. He went behind his desk and sat down, but didn't invite Foxx to sit.

"What possessed you to hang Orlando Cortez out a window this morning?" he said. "Never mind. I don't want an answer. Save it for your disciplinary hearing."

Kearney held out his hand. "Shield and firearm. Now."

Foxx opened his holster guard, lifted out his pistol, and placed it on Kearney's desk. Then he unpinned his shield and set it down next to the pistol.

"You are banned from the building," said Kearney. "Those officers will escort you to the locker room. Leave your uniform and equipment belt in your locker. Do not remove any court property. I advise you to call the union and I suggest you pray that this doesn't go any further."

"Like what?" said Foxx.

"Formal criminal charges," said Kearney.

The two officers escorted Foxx to the locker room. They waited at a not-so-discreet distance as Foxx changed into his street clothes, hung his uniform and equipment belt in his locker, and spun the padlock. They walked him out the back door and watched from the top of the steps as Foxx reached Worth Street.

Foxx did not look back. He passed Judge and Barbara Lonergan, walking arm in arm as they returned to the courthouse. He didn't acknowledge them, and they acted as if he didn't exist. He remembered the voice mail after he turned out of sight.

"It's me," Bev's voice said in his ear. "Just a heads-up. Two officers from central administration are coming to detain you. Call me."

Foxx erased the voice mail and pocketed the phone.

———

The union of which Captain Kearney spoke was the court officers' union, and its office was conveniently located within sight of the courthouse in a nondescript building just west of Broadway. The door was marked by a large decal in the shape of a shield, and beyond that door was a small waiting room. The receptionist was a feature that Foxx hadn't anticipated, and she ran down a litany of possible reasons for one of the rank and file to disturb her day.

"Grievance," she said, "uniform allowance, benefits—"

"Benefits," said Foxx.

"Medical, dental, optical, legal—"

"Legal," said Foxx.

"Could you be more specific?"

"I need a lawyer."

"For what reason?"

"Isn't that between me and my lawyer?"

The receptionist told Foxx to wait and the wait was mercifully short and the lawyer Foxx met at the end of the wait seemed competent.

"You're speaking figuratively, of course," the lawyer said halfway through Foxx's story. His name was John Jaffrey.

"No, I'm speaking literally," said Foxx.

"You hung the custodian out a window?"

" 'Hung' may be an exaggeration," said Foxx. "Dangled, maybe?"

"Is there a distinction?"

"Probably not."

"Why?" said Jaffrey.

"He thwarted me."

"In what way?"

Foxx finished the story.

"You're investigating an old murder?" said Jaffrey. "By what authority?"

"None," said Foxx. "I know this sounds crazy. But Cortez knows something, which means that other people likely know something, too, and if I don't get back into the courthouse soon, it'll be too late. Ralphie Rago, the guy in jail, is dying."

Jaffrey leaned back and drummed the top of his pen on the legal pad where he had stopped taking notes several minutes earlier.

"The quickest way for me to get you back in is to go through the union, and even that can take weeks," he said. "If I'm forced to take this to court, it could take months."

"I don't have that much time," said Foxx.

"And I'm not a magician," said Jaffrey.

———

Foxx left Jaffrey and phoned Bev as soon as he hit the street. He walked and talked for several blocks while recounting the whole story.

"I can't just make a few phone calls and get you reinstated," said Bev. "If anything, I might get a call to investigate this stunt of yours."

"Wouldn't be the first time," said Foxx.

"I'll do my best," she said, "but don't expect much."

"Thanks. And do you have anything on Lozier?"

"You mean his murder?"

"That, yeah, and anything else."

"Do you have a few minutes?"

"I have all day at the moment."

"Call you back," said Bev.

Foxx found himself on a bench in the park across the street from the courthouse. Twenty minutes later, his phone lit up with Bev's avatar.

"Nothing about the murder," she said. "Not surprising, because a murder wouldn't be a matter for the inspector general. But . . ."

"But what?" said Foxx.

"I need to be careful with this. Let's just say that Mr. Lozier was well known to this office."

"How so?"

"Remember, this was well before my time, so I'm just going by the files."

"Files? Plural?"

"Two, to be exact," said Bev. "Sexual harassment claims."

"Ah yes," said Foxx. "Rago's lawyer told me about Lozier's reputation around the courthouse."

Bev was silent.

"You still there?" said Foxx.

"I'm here," said Bev. "I'm trying to decide what I can say, and all I can say is that the complaints weren't brought against Lozier. They were brought by Lozier."

"Say again?"

"You heard me, Foxx. He brought sexual harassment claims against two different women."

"When?"

"A couple of years before he got killed."

"What happened?"

"Not over the phone, Foxx. You want to come down and visit, you can read the files. But before you get too excited about people with a motive to kill Mr. Lozier, neither complaint ended in his favor."

CHAPTER 20

Barbara began to shake the moment Bill mentioned Ken Palmer, and she was still shaking after settling Bill into his chair, loosening his tie, and watching him drift off into his nap. She was not sure whether she was scared for him or, somehow, scared for herself. The shakes certainly would not go away.

She peeked into Larry's office. He was working at his desk and though he had changed out of his gym clothes, his cheeks still showed the high color from his boxball game.

"Would you lock the entry door, please?" Barbara said, then added, "It's stifling in here, and I want to keep all our doors open."

Larry got up and threw the dead bolt. Barbara went back to her desk and opened a search engine on her computer. She straightened her back, laid her fingers on the keyboard, and typed in some search terms. Kenneth Palmer—murder—upstate New York.

The first hit was an article from a newspaper called the *Delaware County Democrat*. This wasn't an online publication but a scanned version of a hard-copy paper. On the first page, above the fold, was a story headlined ATTORNEY MURDERED WHILE TROUT FISHING.

"Oh my God," Barbara blurted.

"You okay?" Larry called in.

"Fine," Barbara said. "Sorry."

She began to read.

Longtime Delaware County lawyer Kenneth Palmer was found dead late Thursday afternoon on the Upper Beaverkill just south of Morton Hill Road. According to his secretary, Betty Prusha, Palmer had taken the day off and was trout fishing on a private section of the river owned by a client. Prusha became concerned in the early afternoon when several calls to Palmer's cell phone went unanswered and he had not responded to any of his messages. "He hated cell phones," she said, "but he always answered and he always returned calls."

A sheriff's deputy drove to the river and found Palmer's body hung up on a fallen tree about thirty yards downstream from where his car was parked. He also found a local teenager sitting on a rock and holding Palmer's fly rod.

The sheriff's department confirmed that Palmer last made a phone call at 9:37 A.M. to Simcoe's Garage. He reported to the owner, Darwin Simcoe, that he had a flat tire and asked that Simcoe send someone out to change it. Simcoe stated that he sent a man out there and that the man returned half an hour later, having changed the tire. State police are searching for the man, whom Simcoe described as a drifter looking for odd jobs. Meanwhile, the teenager, whose name is being withheld due to his age, is being questioned.

The second hit was another article from the same newspaper, dated one week later. The county medical examiner had determined that Palmer died from drowning and that marks on his neck indicated that he had been forcibly submerged. After several days of questioning, the teenager found with Palmer's fly rod was arrested and charged with murder. His name was Luke Godfrey. He was eighteen years old, and therefore of the age of majority. He suffered from Down syndrome and was the foster son of Buck and Sarah Cannon, who owned a bed-and-breakfast. There was no mention of the man who changed Palmer's tire.

Barbara found no other articles, which to her did not mean that nothing was happening, just that the court case was in that non-newsworthy phase between arrest and trial. She got up and went to Larry's doorway. She watched him work, but withdrew before she was tempted to say anything. Some things, she knew, were better left buried.

CHAPTER 21

Daniel Kaplan—Kappy to his friends, his partners, and the roughnecks who worked for him—never forgot a face. Names, he wasn't so good with. But what were names other than marks on a page or sounds in the ear? Faces were something else entirely. They were infinite in their variety, with differences so subtle as to be indescribable. But you didn't need a facility with words to recognize a face. The mind could do that in ways that seemed almost impossible to perceive.

They were out on the pool deck of his house, in the hot tub. The lights were low, three candles flickered in amber jars, and billions of stars powdered the sky above this isolated hilltop. Kappy had spotted her across the bar in a roadhouse down near Livingston Manor. He recognized her immediately despite the number of years since their one, unsuccessful date. He had been a bumbling young lawyer, she the hands-down hottest court reporter in the county. Her marriage was long gone, as was his first career. He was a fracker now. A big-time fracker. A mother-fracker, he liked to say. If a woman laughed at that, it meant something.

"Another drink?" he said.

She drained what was left in her glass and floated it across the trembling water to him on a tiny life preserver. She had big hair, the ends wet where the water lapped around her shoulders.

He set the glass on the deck, then slid his foot along the inside of her thigh and toed the crotch of her panties. "I expect to find these off when I get back," he said.

He went inside through the sliders and crossed the brilliantly polished hardwood floor to the big white tiles of the kitchen. He mixed her another margarita, going lighter on the tequila because he liked his women tipsy, not drunk, and the hot tub always enhanced the effect of alcohol. Finished, he went into the study, unhooked a framed photo of the Milky Way from the wall, and tapped a small mound of coke onto the glass. He wouldn't share this with her, just the way he wouldn't go heavy on the tequila. If anything would be true in his life now, it would be the women he bedded.

As he snorted the four lines, he thought he heard a car door slam and an engine ignite. The sounds made no sense, and because they made no sense, he discounted them.

On his way through the kitchen, he shed his bathrobe, peeled off his wet boxers, and grabbed the drink from the counter. He felt the coke pressing in his nostrils, behind his eyes, against the roof of his mouth. Yes, he thought, imagining her naked and waiting in the hot tub.

He stepped onto the deck and waited a moment for his eyes to adjust to the darkness. The water rippled the surface of the hot tub in the perfectly symmetrical pattern that occurred only when no one was there. He crossed to the deck rail and looked down at the end of the driveway. Her car was gone. He felt suddenly foolish in his nakedness and his expectations, and then his head exploded.

Kappy awoke facedown on something soft. He thought it was flesh—her flesh—but it smelled like rubber and chlorine. His head pounded. His mouth tasted of blood. He coughed, and grains of coke dropped onto the back of his tongue.

He tried to move but couldn't. His hands were behind his back, his legs bent up at the knees. He was hog-tied.

He opened his eyes and saw that he was on a raft. A blue inflatable raft. Just like the one he bought at the start of the summer. The raft began to spin. With great effort, he lifted his head enough to see the pool deck move slowly past and then the back of his house and then a man crouched at the edge of the pool. The man grabbed the raft and beached a corner on the deck to stop the spinning. Then he pushed up from his crouch and sat on a chair.

"Good evening, Mr. Kaplan," he said.

Kappy grunted.

"Remember me?" The man was just a silhouette against the lights glowing beyond the sliders.

"Can't see you," said Kappy.

The man looked over his shoulders as if to assess the ambient lighting. Then he leaned forward and played a flashlight on his face.

"How about now?"

Kappy squinted. The drinks and the coke and the blow to his head had addled his brains, but not enough to affect his ability to recognize a face. The man got up and shoved the raft back into the pool.

"I'm sorry," said Kappy.

"Sorry for what?"

The raft was in the middle of the pool, spinning slowly in the gentle current from the filter pump. The man walked along the deck at just the right speed to stay in Kappy's sight. One hand pressed against his hip, holding something Kappy couldn't make out.

"I read about it in the papers," said Kappy. "The name rang a bell."

"Rang a bell," said the man.

"It was a long time ago."

"Not for me. It's like yesterday. You could have done better."

"I did pretty well," said Kappy.

"In the beginning."

"Yes, if you remember. Then the family hired that big-city lawyer."

"I told you, I remember everything. It's like yesterday to me."

"Then you remember how he sweet-talked the judge and how

the judge just got swept away. Hell, it was my first case. I did pretty damn good for my first case."

"Your first case, but my only case," said the man. "There's no handicapping system. You don't get points for being the underdog. You don't get a medal for punching above your weight class."

"Yeah, well, if you've been paying attention, what I tried to do then is done every day now. We were ahead of our time."

"I have been paying attention. And unfortunately, time is something you never get back."

The man raised his arm. In the dim light, Kappy recognized the square muzzle of a pistol.

"No!" he yelled.

The man pulled the trigger. There was no report, just a sharp hiss. Something clipped the rubber near Kappy's face, and a jet of air blew on his cheek.

The man pulled the trigger several more times, riddling the raft with pellets. A few stung Kappy in the back.

"You can't do this!" Kappy screamed.

"I already did," said the man.

"But that was years ago," said Kappy. The raft was quickly deflating. Water ran in the grooves between each of the ribs. "There's no connection."

"How can there be no connection?" said the man. "Everything proceeded from that. Everything."

CHAPTER 22

Reading and then rereading the newspaper accounts of Ken Palmer's murder should have allayed Barbara's fears. Yes, Bill had known Palmer, actually had spent a day fishing with him, perhaps on the very river where Palmer had been murdered. But in this context, Cannon's interest in contacting Bill now seemed less about Bill's slight connection with Palmer than about Cannon's connection with the suspect. Sure it was sad that Cannon's foster nephew (if there were such a relation) had been arrested for the crime. But how often did the police, or whatever passed for the police in a place like Delaware County, make a mistake about a crime so clear as this one? And how did Cannon expect Bill to rectify the situation?

But now, with Bill drifting off to sleep beside her, Barbara could not shake the feeling that something was out there, some beast slouching over a far-off hill to wreak even more havoc with their lives. She slipped out from under the covers and stood beside the bed to make sure that the faint tremble in the mattress would not wake him. Bill's breath caught for a moment, then after a long exhalation resumed its slow rhythm.

She poured milk in the kitchen, added Scotch in the den, and after downing the drink returned to bed.

———

That ancient affair was a largely physical and purely courthouse relationship. No romantic dinners, no weekend dates, no late-night phone conversations. She was surprisingly comfortable with the arrangement, believing that she had invested enough, but not too much. She accepted his claim that he needed to work the political clubs, that he needed to visit and schmooze in every club from Inwood to Battery Park City. The relationships he formed needed constant attention, like seedlings in a cold April flower bed.

But the lunch hours were theirs. They met every day, and when the weather turned too cold for the park bench, they moved to his judge's robing room. Twice, sometimes three times a week, he would tap his shirt pocket to show that he had the key. They would finish lunch quickly and head down the stairs. Within minutes after the door closed behind them, she would be supine on the sofa, prostrate on the desk, or astride him on the floor.

Yet outside lunch hour, it was as if they did not exist for each other. When work landed in the steno pool, she tried to grab the decisions from his judge's chambers. She communed with him through his handwriting, which wasn't especially neat but definitely was distinctive. She thought that if she could analyze his handwriting, she could understand the man. But she stopped short of going to the library for books on handwriting analysis. There was no real need. They were crazy for each other, she told herself, because they played each other's song.

Winter thawed into spring, the weeks passing in a cycle of lunches in the robing room and love in the room at the bottom of the stairs. She was mildly troubled that there was no public face to their relationship, slightly more troubled when the weather turned warm enough to return to the park bench and he still insisted on the robing room. But she understood the time constraints. He had a difficult job on top of the even more difficult crusade to become a judge.

Sometimes he stood her up. She would wait in the catwalk corridor near the robing room door, her lunch bag clutched in her hand. She would listen for his feet on the stairs, a sound as distinctive and as personal as his handwriting. Even more so than his handwriting, the sound described him as neat, precise, energetic. And on those days when the footsteps never came, there was little she could do. She couldn't call chambers or knock on the chambers door. She simply folded her disappointment into her heart and found an alcove or an empty courtroom where she could be by herself.

He always apologized profusely, always tried to atone for standing her up, not in any material way but in a way she found more valuable—he opened his dreams to her. And so it happened, in the room at the bottom of the stairs. They were bent over the desk. Her feet were on the carpet, her toes still curled. He breathed into the hollow of her neck.

"What should a judge look for in a wife?" he whispered.

She rolled around to face him.

"Get off me," she said.

They moved to the sofa, still naked. She tucked herself in a corner, hugging her knees to her breasts. He sat sideways, one arm extended along the back of the sofa, his fingers brushing her shoulder.

"Is that a serious question?" she said.

He nodded.

"A judge needs a wife who understands him," she said.

"Does that mean the wife needs to have a law degree?"

"A law degree would be shared knowledge," she said. "Understanding isn't always based on shared knowledge. Shared knowledge can get in the way of understanding. If I knew the law, I might wonder why you were so perplexed by the case you had on trial. I might resent you being in a bad mood because, under the same circumstances, I might not be in a bad mood. But if I understood you, truly understood you, it wouldn't matter whether I knew the law or not. I would accept that you had responsibilities I could not fathom."

"Sounds like you've thought about this," he said.

"I have," she replied.

Though they never returned to the topic again, that brief discussion hovered in the air whenever they were together. Alone in her bed at night, she would trot it out in her memory to parse every word and interpret every inflection. A month passed, then a second. Summer was approaching, and the work that the campaign entailed took an obvious toll. He seemed exhausted, stressed, pressed for time. She could not only see it in his eyes or hear it in his words, but read it in his work, as well. His decision drafts became shorter and more perfunctory.

They saw less and less of each other. They met for lunch only when he had the key to the room at the bottom of the stairs. There was an urgency in his lovemaking. Sometimes their clothes didn't even come off. She probed, asking if anything was wrong, whether there was anything she could do to help. He only told her to be patient. Everything would work out.

She began to doubt what they had between them. That discussion, now months in the past, was like a pebble dropped in a pond. The waves that spread out from its center were losing their intensity. Then, in early June, something happened. Or didn't happen. For three consecutive days, she waited in vain in the corridor outside the robing room. For three consecutive days, no decision drafts came down from chambers. When it became apparent on the third day, a Friday, that she would not hear his footsteps on the stairs, she reached for the robing room door. Surprisingly, it wasn't locked. She peeked in carefully. The room was empty, the judge's desk clear. The wall fan hummed, rattling slightly at each end of its sweep.

She stepped inside and crossed to the courtroom door. The courtroom was quiet and empty. She went to the robing room desk and lifted the phone to call chambers. She hung up on the first ring.

She passed a lonely weekend that was all the more desolate because she had no way to reach out to him. No phone number, no address. Those details never had seemed necessary, and now suddenly they were.

Again on Monday morning, no decision drafts arrived from chambers. Yet she still waited at the robing room door as the one-o'clock hour approached. It was insane, she knew, to hope for a different outcome. But then she heard his footsteps on the stairs. She embraced him, and he embraced her. They kissed long and deep, their most public display of affection that still was witnessed by no one. He lifted the key from his pocket and jiggled it as if ringing a bell. Two minutes later, he unlocked the door to the room at the bottom of the stairs.

There was a self-absorption in his lovemaking, a detachment, a definite sense that she could have been anyone. He finished quickly, stepped back, pulled up his pants. She sat on the desk, her bra and skirt pushed together around her waist. She hugged herself, frightened by the sudden chill in the room.

It was then that she knew, but still she picked and probed until she forced the words out of him.

You never could be a judge's wife.

CHAPTER 23

Foxx arrived at Ralphie's cubicle and found a doctor and a nurse standing on opposite sides of the bed and talking to each other in hushed tones. Ralphie looked more frail and more sunken than he had just three short days ago. The doctor caught Foxx's eye, then came out into the corridor.

"He looks worse," said Foxx.

"Actually, he's looked this way since he came in," said the doctor. "The day you were last here was one of his better days, like a drowning man bobbing to the surface."

"Will he bob again?"

"Hard to tell," said the doctor. "We haven't started a morphine drip yet."

"Will I be told before you do?" said Foxx.

"You will."

"Can I talk to him?"

"Sit down and get close," said the doctor. "He'll hear you better and he won't waste energy trying to talk."

The nurse came out of the cubicle, and Foxx went in. He sat down on a stool and leaned over the bed rail. He could hear the oxygen jetting into Ralphie's nostrils from the clip under his nose.

"Ralphie, hey, Ralphie. It's Foxx."

Ralphie's eyelids fluttered, then parted. His eyes rolled in Foxx's direction.

"Hey, Foxx," he said. The corner of his mouth turned up in a vague smile.

"I met with Vincent Scannell. You remember him?"

"My lawyer."

"He told me about your case and gave me his files to read. There are some things I need to look into. One of them is the room you were cleaning when you found the body. He said the room wasn't really an office but a place where people would have sex. Did you know about that?"

Ralphie grunted.

Foxx pulled back from the rail. The grunt pushed out a horrible stench from deep in Ralphie's chest, and Foxx needed to take a few clean breaths. He understood this was not going to be much of a dialogue, so he needed to frame his questions to elicit answers in the fewest possible syllables.

He leaned back over the rail.

"Ralphie, just listen for a minute. I know that Orlando Cortez rented out the room around the time of the murder. I need to know who used the room back then. Was Calvin Lozier one of them?"

Ralphie nodded.

"Do you know who he used it with?"

Ralphie shook his head.

"Ralphie, I need names," said Foxx.

"I don't know," Ralphie gasped.

The stench washed over Foxx again, and he sat back to take another couple of clean breaths.

"Ralphie, I'm sorry but I need your help. I tried to get names out of Cortez. He refused to talk and then he said something that pissed me off, and I did a stupid thing and now I'm in trouble. So it's really important that you try to remember whatever you can."

Ralphie lay silent and motionless. The oxygen hissed in his nostrils. His breathing stopped, and with it so did the putrid puffs belching out of his ravaged lungs. A long moment passed, and just as Foxx was about to call the doctor, Ralphie sucked air.

"The girls went there a lot," he rasped.

"What girls?"

"Steno pool girls. They liked to latch on to the law clerks who might become judges. The law clerks liked them because they thought they were easy."

The rush of words seemed to exhaust Ralphie. He closed his eyes and turned his head. Foxx held his breath and leaned close to steady the oxygen jets until Ralphie opened his eyes.

"Did Calvin Lozier bring any of the steno pool girls there?"

"Yeah."

"More than one?"

"A few."

"Is that what you meant when you told the police he was a bad man?"

"Yeah."

"Ralphie, do you remember any of their names?"

"No."

"Ralphie. Think. It's important. If you want me to help you, I need names."

Ralphie slowly turned his head. His eyes locked on Foxx and his lips twitched as the taut muscles in his neck and jaw loosened.

"I never knew names," he said. His words came out shaky but strong as he struggled to enunciate. His breath washed over Foxx, but Foxx hung in there not wanting to flinch in case this was the last bob of a drowning man. "Because none of these people ever talked to me."

His head slowly turned away, and his entire body sank deeper into the bed. Again his breathing stopped, and again many seconds passed before it resumed its raspy rhythm.

It was near the end of the one-o'clock hour, the fourth lunchtime since Cannon had tried to contact Judge Lonergan. Each of those hours had started with hopeful anticipation. Each ended in silence.

Now the silence was pervasive. He and Dave had not spoken since yesterday afternoon. An airliner passed overhead. Half a dozen bratwursts sizzled on the grill. Cannon lifted his cell phone off the picnic table and flipped it open to see if a call had slipped in without him hearing it. The screen just showed the time hovering over an image of a midwestern cornfield. Another lunch hour drained away.

He went to the grill.

"Hey, want me to turn these?" he called.

Down below, Dave played the garden hose at the mulch surrounding the new cherry tree. He didn't turn, didn't look up, just lifted a hand to signal okay.

Cannon turned the brats with a pair of tongs. The silence, Dave's distance—if he didn't think so before, it was official now. He had worn out his welcome.

He pressed the brats with the tongs. Flames leaped as the grease hit the stones. Three planes passed over on final approach, marking out three minutes of time. Cannon plunked the brats onto a plate, then shut off the grill.

"Dave," he called down.

He did not wait for a reaction. He took the brats inside, divided them onto two plates already heaped with potato chips and kale salad.

Dave was already at the table, huffing from his climb up the steps, when Cannon came out with the two plates and two beers.

"Thanks," said Dave.

"No problem," said Cannon. "How's the tree?"

"Making it through."

"A lot of work."

"It is," said Dave.

Four planes descended toward Kennedy, marking out six minutes of time. Cannon looked at his phone. It was now past two. He could feel Dave's eyes on him. It was time to hit the road, he thought. Finish eating, then get up and go. Even empty-handed.

The cell phone buzzed. Cannon picked it up and saw RESTRICTED on the screen.

"Hah." He showed Dave. "And you said he wouldn't call."

He answered, listened. He pressed a finger to his other ear as another jet rumbled overhead. He could feel Dave's eyes on him, but the feeling was different now. Not skepticism, not judgment. More like expectation.

The voice on the other end didn't identify itself. It didn't need to. It was familiar, and the words it spoke were unbelievable.

"Where?" Cannon said, and after hearing the answer added, "I know the place."

The call ended, and Cannon put down the phone.

"The judge?" said Dave.

"No," said Cannon. "The Delaware County sheriff. There's been another murder."

CHAPTER 24

Somewhere in the back of Foxx's memory lodged a snippet of a magazine interview he had read during college. In the interview, a famous author opined that secretaries could control the world simply by altering the workflow across their desks—the letters misdirected, the phone message not delivered, the typing job unfinished. The author proved his theory by asking a rhetorical question: What if the orders for the D-Day invasion had been misplaced? Foxx didn't buy the example, which he thought of in Latin terms as *exaggeratio ad absurdum,* but he thought the general premise was valid. His dealings with administrative staff (to use the inoffensive term demanded by modern sensibilities) were not as momentous as the fight to liberate Western Europe. Where did he find a certain medical form, or how did he change his number of tax exemptions were more his speed. He presented these types of requests with an ironic detachment that admin staff found amusing and, thus amused, were only too glad to help.

The administrative offices of 60 Centre were on the seventh, and top, floor of the building. The space was once a refuge for the judges, with amenities like a library, a smoking room, and a dining room staffed with waiters and a chef. Nowadays, the library was a conference room, the smoking room was the chief clerk's office, and the dining room was an open space filled with several desks and file cabinets.

Foxx had phoned from the train on his way back from Valhalla and was transferred from desk to desk until he landed with a personnel and payroll clerk named Natasha.

"What?" she said in reaction to Foxx's request. "How many years ago?"

"Twenty-five," said Foxx.

"Twenty-five!?"

"Or thereabouts."

"And what, pray tell, do you need this for?"

"I can't say."

"Personnel files are confidential," said Natasha.

"I don't care what's in the files. All I want are the names."

"I'll see what I can do," said Natasha.

She was waiting in Foley Square an hour later when Foxx popped up from the subway station. The square was stifling in the midday heat, but she sat on the lip of the fountain where the spray kicked up by the pounding water provided some relief.

Foxx settled next to her.

"What's this?" he said.

"What's it look like?" she said.

It looked like a booklet with a pale green cover, but actually it was a phone directory.

"A phone directory," said Foxx.

"Don't ever let anyone say Mrs. Foxx didn't raise a genius," said Natasha.

"She didn't," said Foxx.

"Look at the year." Natasha tapped a long, curving fingernail on the lower right corner of the cover.

"Oh," said Foxx.

"Now open to the page with the sticky sticking out."

"Ah," said Foxx.

"You said all you wanted was names. Well, there are the names." Natasha got up and smoothed her slacks. She started to walk away. "You're welcome, Foxx."

"Thanks," he called after her.

She waved without turning around.

Foxx opened to the sticky-note page and ran a finger down the list of names that made up the steno pool for that snapshot in time twenty-five years ago. Only one name rang a bell, but it was a very loud bell.

Across Centre Street, in the park beside the courthouse, the last few good guys jawed on the bench. But Foxx wasn't interested in the good guys. He was waiting for one of the old steno girls, who he hoped might answer the questions Ralphie Rago couldn't. He scooted around the fountain lip until he faced the courthouse directly. Lunch hour was beginning, and people were flowing down the front steps.

Five minutes later, his phone buzzed.

"Hey, Foxx." It was Vincent J. Scannell. "You at the courthouse?"

"Where else would I be?"

"Good," said Scannell. "I got something for you."

Cannon couldn't say that he had a theory. He didn't even want to say he had a suspicion. But as he crossed the Whitestone Bridge and barreled north through the Bronx, some thoughts formed of their own accord. Two sightings of the same person. Two points in time and space. In geometry, two points made a straight line.

Point one: On a morning back in April, Cannon pulled into Simcoe's Garage for gas. Two pumps each with two nozzles stood on a raised concrete island. One side of the island was full serve; the other was self-serve. Cannon coasted to the self-serve side and began to pump. A few minutes later, Kenneth Palmer rolled his big old Buick to the full-serve side.

The garage itself had three repair bays and an office that Darwin Simcoe had expanded into a snack counter with a coffee machine, microwave oven, and racks of processed food. Outside the office door was a bench, and on that bench sat a few of the local characters. They weren't employees, just guys Darwin allowed to hang around in the hope they might do something constructive and wangle a few bucks out of the customers. They all were broken in some way, and Cannon knew this one by his limp, that one by his claw hand, that other one by his shakes. Kenneth Palmer stayed in his car. He lowered his window and looked expectantly at the bench. Cannon chuckled to himself. Palmer was a notorious cheapskate, and so no one moved off that bench to pump his gas for him. But then a man who'd been leaning against the plate glass office window ambled in Palmer's direction.

"Fill 'er up, regular," Palmer said, and flashed a credit card like a switchblade.

The man fed the card into the slot in the pump, then pulled the hose around and stuck the nozzle into the gas tank. Cannon watched him. The man had no limp, no withered arm, no palsy. He seemed normal; in fact, he looked quite fit and handsome in a weathered way, with deep lines etching his forehead and cheeks and hair grown out from what had been a neat cut.

Cannon finished pumping his gas and went into the office to pay. As he waited for his change, Palmer's gas tank hit full. Palmer started his car before the man hooked the nozzle back into the pump, then drove away the moment the man handed over his credit card. On his way back to his car, Cannon heard the guys on the bench snickering. Cannon started his car and took one last look at the bench. The man leaned against the window, his head bowed and his hand pinching his eyes.

Something about that pose struck Cannon as vaguely familiar. He dwelled on this frisson in his memory bank for a minute or so, ultimately reminding himself that he had reached the age where everybody reminded him of somebody.

Point two: A few days later, Cannon was heading south on 206 to meet someone for late breakfast at the diner. As he reached the curve near the general store, he noticed an oncoming car. He noticed it because he recognized it as one of Darwin Simcoe's fleet of old junkers. The car had to be thirty years old, a K-car from the mid-'80s. Boxy, rusted around the wheel wells, listing to port on bad springs. Darwin cannibalized these junkers for parts, but until then used them whenever he dispatched one of the local characters to run an errand.

Both Cannon and the other driver entered the curve and hit their brakes at the same time. Cannon didn't normally stare at the faces of oncoming drivers, but he was idly curious about whom Darwin was sending out today. Turned out, it was the man who'd pumped Kenneth Palmer's gas. Cannon didn't give the man much further thought. He still couldn't place him, not that he gave it much of a try. He just assumed the man had to have some defect to haunt the garage, and if it wasn't obviously physical, it must have been mental. Crazy could come in neat packages.

It was later that day when Kenneth Palmer's secretary sent a sheriff's deputy to the Beaverkill when Palmer overstayed his fishing plans and she couldn't raise him on his cell phone. It was the deputy who found Palmer hung up in an eddy and Luke, the eldest and highest-functioning of Buck and Sarah's foster children, thirty yards upstream fishing with Palmer's fly rod.

After Luke's arrest, Cannon went to see Darwin Simcoe. Yeah, Darwin spoke to the sheriff. Called him the moment he heard about Kenneth Palmer. Told the sheriff Palmer had phoned him about a blown tire and would he send someone out to change it. None of the regulars on the bench wanted to move their sorry asses to help the old lawyer, so he sent some guy who'd been hanging around for a few days to change the tire.

"Didn't you think?" Cannon had said.

"It's my job to think?" Darwin had answered. "I told the sheriff that I sent the man to change the tire. He did change it, too, and Palmer gave him fifteen bucks."

"How do you know?"

"He showed me. Couldn't afford a damn candy bar and a soda before I sent him, but he bought a microwave hero and a cup of coffee when he came back. Palmer had his wallet on him with a hundred fifty in it. That fly rod of his was worth twice that."

CHAPTER 25

As promised, Wendy Robinson waited on a bench in front of St. Paul's Chapel with two Century 21 shopping bags pinned between her ankles.

"Hi," she said brightly. "This worked out. Thank you for meeting me."

"No, thank you," said Foxx.

Wendy Robinson patted the empty wood beside her.

"I happened to be down here with my daughter and her friend when Mr. Scannell called me," she said.

Foxx judged her as older than Ellen, and she gave the impression of someone whose looks had improved with age. Sharp features, laugh lines, a touch of crow's-feet. Foxx was a sucker for a face with character, and he would have been a sucker for hers in different circumstances.

"I gave my credit card to my daughter," Wendy continued, "so we may have longer to talk than we need. At my expense."

Foxx couldn't be sure what Scannell had told her, so he explained why he was looking into Calvin Lozier's murder and the two theories he needed to pursue.

"They're probably more like intimations than theories," he said. "Anyway, you link the two."

"You think? What if I don't know anything about either?"

"I'll just accept that and move on."

Wendy flashed a grin. "I'm kidding," she said, and elbowed his arm. Then she darkened. "I was a naïve little woman when I married Calvin. The murder revealed much of what I'd come to suspect about him. Still, it was a shock, and I wasn't willing or even able to talk. Then by the time I was able to talk, nobody cared."

"Aren't there therapists?" said Foxx.

"It isn't the same talking to them," said Wendy. "You never know what they'll throw back at you or what they'll twist to make you believe that everything was your fault. Because, of course, you can get everything you want and if you don't get everything you want, it's because you somehow failed. What I needed was to talk to people who were hungry for gossip. But they aren't around anymore."

Her cell phone rang with a chord from a tune Foxx recognized but could not place.

"Sorry, I need to take this." She listened for a moment, then said, "No, absolutely not," then listened some more, repeated herself, then ended the call.

"Just saved myself a bunch of money," she told Foxx. "I hope, anyway. Well, where were we?"

"We hadn't started," said Foxx.

"Well, then I need to cut right to it," said Wendy, "because I don't have as much time as I thought. I don't remember Calvin very fondly. I don't remember much what attracted me to him. He had opinions, I suppose, a point of view about life. I had none, and when you have no strong opinions and you are in the company of someone who does, that someone becomes very compelling. I never understood what attracted him to me, though at the time I suspected I gave him stability. A place and a person to come home to.

"We met on a blind date, and he told me everything I needed to know in the first fifteen minutes: he worked for the court system and he was going to become a judge. That got him into law school and got him through law school, and now that he worked for the court system, he was close to achieving that goal.

"He was a judge's law clerk. He tried to explain the job to me, but I must have had such a dumb look on my face that he just stopped in mid-sentence and said, 'If you're not a lawyer, you'll never understand what I do.' Well, I wasn't a lawyer, and for the next several years, he never bothered to finish the explanation.

"We dated for three months before we got engaged, then we were engaged for three months before we got married. It was a very small wedding. The judge he worked for married us in his chambers, then we went out for dinner: us, my cousin who stood up for me, a friend who stood up for him, and the judge. It was the only time I ever went inside the courthouse."

"Who was the friend?" said Foxx.

"I don't remember," said Wendy. She checked the time on her phone. "I always had the feeling that I was out of sight, out of mind for Calvin. It wasn't long after we got married that I began to feel I was out of mind even when I was in sight. I mean, he overlooked me, figuratively and literally. We could be out to dinner, not saying very much, him looking around like he expected to spot someone he knew, and then he would focus on me as if just realizing that I was there.

"I rationalized, of course. I told myself he was always working hard, both at his job and at becoming a judge. I was right about that. He was working hard. But later, when I began to suspect the other women, I rationalized that, too. I told myself they were the outlets he needed, and that once he became a judge, all that would end.

"Even then, these women were always just theoretical to me. I never found any evidence, which meant either he was super careful or I was just paranoid. But then came the murder, and on the first night of the wake, I saw all the courthouse ladies lined up to pay their respects and I knew I had been right."

"Did you know who he had affairs with?" said Foxx.

"Anyone, everyone," said Wendy. "At that point, did the specifics matter?"

"It would if one of them killed him."

"I can't imagine anyone mustering the passion to kill him."

"But a good number mustered the passion to have sex with him."

"Doesn't mean they cared. And if they were smart, they wouldn't have. Because he didn't care."

"Except about becoming a judge," said Foxx.

"Right," said Wendy. "If 'turn-on' is the right description, the black robe was his turn-on. But you can't always get what you want."

"Sidney Dweck told me that Calvin thought he was going to win that year. Did he give you that impression?"

"Impression? This is Calvin we're talking about here. He told me about as much about the campaign as he did about his job as law clerk."

"Meaning?" said Foxx.

"Meaning that he probably started to explain the whole idiotic process to me, trailed off in the middle somewhere, and never bothered again. But I did glean—Is 'glean' the right word?"

Foxx nodded.

"I did glean a few things from what he allowed me to see or hear. This was his third campaign cycle. The first two didn't count. They weren't his campaigns. He just put time in working for other candidates. Then he struck out on his own for a two-year time investment. Year one, he worked the political clubs. Year two, well, that would be the year he would work toward a nomination. Sidney Dweck took him on. Calvin did tell me—he needed to be particularly full of himself to tell me anything—he did tell me that Dweck saw it as a charity job because there was no way that Calvin would get the one open slot on the ballot. He'd just be positioning himself for the following year, when there would be several.

"But then I heard something, or overheard something. Calvin and Dweck talked on the phone every night. Mostly I heard nothing because we had an extra room in our apartment that was Calvin's office, and that's where he holed up after he got home from the political clubs. Well, this one night—it was a few weeks before

Calvin got killed, July, maybe late June—Calvin started yelling over the phone. I thought he was having a fight with one of his girlfriends, which would have been surprising enough. But then he said something about 'falling into his lap' and 'this could be his time after all' and something about 'death in Manhattan.'"

"Did he tell you what any of this meant?" said Foxx.

Wendy rolled her eyes. "But I did get a sense that his attitude changed after that phone call. He wasn't investing time anymore. He was expecting to win."

The sky had turned a dusky pink by the time Cannon turned off the pavement and onto the dirt road. From a distance, the hilltop seemed to have been shaved bald to accept the modern monstrosity of a house dropped right on its crown. Nice view, thought Cannon. At least it had been.

A sheriff's department cruiser was parked at the bottom of the driveway. A deputy leaned against the door, but pushed himself off as Cannon got out of his car.

"Rousma up there?" said Cannon.

"You Cannon?" said the deputy. He looked about twenty. "Yeah, he's up there."

He lifted the crime scene tape that stretched across the driveway, and Cannon ducked under. The driveway was steep but leveled off in front of a garage door before continuing to climb to a huge circle edged with decorative stone. The deck loomed above the circle.

"Hey," Rousma called down from the deck.

Cannon hauled himself up the stairs, and they shook hands.

"We pieced together a few things since I called you," said Rousma.

He and Cannon had started as sheriff's deputies on the same day thirty-five years ago. Cannon peeled off a few years later to work for the courts. Rousma stayed. Now Rousma was the county sheriff and Cannon was a retiree with a PI license.

"Seems like Kaplan met a woman at a roadhouse near Livingston Manor," said Rousma. "Came back here and got into the hot tub together. They had a few drinks, and then Kaplan went into the house to fix another round. She stayed in the hot tub. Says that while he was inside, she got this spooky feeling someone was there. She looked around but couldn't see much because Kaplan kept the lights low so they could see the stars. But then she thought she saw someone in the corner of the deck. Now, Kaplan was gone longer than it should have taken him to fix a couple of drinks, so she thought he was playing a trick on her. She called out, 'That's not funny.' The figure didn't move. She called out again, 'I see you,' and now the figure came over, dressed all in black and wearing a ski mask. It wasn't Kaplan. He told her she needed to leave because he had business with Kaplan and didn't want her to get in the way. So she got out of the hot tub, gathered up her clothes, and drove off."

"Just like that?" said Cannon. "Without saying good-bye to Kaplan?"

"She says the man was very persuasive," said Rousma. "She also says she didn't like Kaplan very much anyway. Didn't know what she was doing there. Kinda wanted an excuse to leave, so she took the invitation."

"She was scared?" said Cannon.

"Of the guy in black? Yeah," said Rousma. "Kaplan only skeeved her."

"Did she recognize anything about this guy? Voice, physique?"

Rousma shook his head. "So Kaplan didn't show up at work that next morning. Wasn't answering his cell phone or his house phone. You know what he does, right?"

"Owns a fracking company," said Cannon.

"Right. Lots of things to attend to every day. So about eleven or so, his secretary came looking for him. Found him in the pool."

"Drowned?" said Cannon.

"With a twist." Rousma led Cannon to a large dark green garbage bag lying on the deck near the deep end of the pool. He opened the bag enough to show a folded piece of blue plastic inside. "That's an inflatable raft. It's riddled with pellet holes. Kaplan took a few shots himself, mostly in the flanks and the shins. He was hog-tied. Probably floating on the raft until the air ran out."

"Jesus," said Cannon. He thumbed the raft to gauge the thickness of the rubber.

"I know what you're thinking," said Rousma. "Palmer gets drowned and now Kaplan gets drowned, so if the same guy did both, it can't be your brother's kid."

"Luke," said Cannon.

"Yeah, Luke," said Rousma. "But let me tell you that Kaplan had a special talent for pissing people off. After fracking got banned here, he started horning in across the border in Pennsylvania. Dirty business, in more ways than one."

"So if you're assuming this is business related, why'd you call me?" said Cannon.

"Because I promised I'd call you," said Rousma. "I keep my promises, even when it goes against my better judgment."

CHAPTER 26

On weekends at home, Barbara tried to replicate a weekday in chambers. After breakfast, she and Bill would sit across the kitchen table from each other. Barbara would sort through the week's mail, separating the bills from the junk and the junk from the few legitimate pieces that required her attention. Bill would page through the newspaper. For years, his newspaper of choice had been *The New York Times,* but early in the summer Barbara had added the *Daily News* and the *New York Post* to the morning delivery. She could not fathom what Bill's mind comprehended as he licked his finger and turned another page. He never had been one to share his thoughts while reading. But she believed the larger print and the many color photos in the city's tabloids were more engaging than the stuffy old *Times* for his present state of mind.

This morning, Barbara did not move on to her second Saturday task, which was to fetch the big ledger checkbook and pay their bills by hand. Instead, she fixed herself a second cup of coffee and waited for Bill to finish with the newspapers.

"I want you to do something for me," she said as Bill stood the newspapers on the table and tapped their edges together.

"What's that?" he said.

"I want you to write some checks."

Bill never had learned to type, and during his years as a lawyer and later as a judge, he had done a prodigious amount of writing in the beautiful, looping cursive he had learned from his grammar school nuns. Stick a pen in his hand, and the same muscle memory would infuse his body as when he picked up a basketball.

Barbara sat beside him. She placed a bill next to the check ledger, pointed out the name and the amount, and then prompted him to write. She paid close attention to his hand, how he gripped the pen in the pads of his thumb and forefinger, how the top knuckle of his middle finger pressed in for support. He didn't scratch with his hand, but wrote with his entire arm. His hand glided along the tabletop on the perfectly aligned blade formed by his fingernails.

She marveled at the consistency of Bill's handwriting, the beauty of the flourishes that harked back to a different era. But more important, watching him write, she wondered if she had done him a disservice. If Dr. Feldman were correct, if the theory of the Keystone was based on fine motor movements, then the three-way work process in chambers should be changed. Bill should write out his decisions himself, not pronounce them for her or Larry to scribble down.

Bill wrote out checks for their cable TV, Internet access, cell phones, electricity, magazine subscriptions, and three charities. After he wrote the last check, Barbara handed over the envelopes. With some prompting, he stuffed each one, licked the flap, and stuck on the stamp. More fine motor movements, different fine motor movements.

Finished with the bills, they went out for their usual Saturday morning walk, crossing Fifth Avenue to the park and heading uptown. The sky was gray, the air calm. The leaves on the trees hung heavy and still. But on the sidewalk, all was motion. Joggers, skateboarders, athletic-looking young mothers pushing double-wide strollers. Normally, the excess of motion annoyed Barbara because she needed to keep an eye on Bill. Today, though, the motion had a festive aspect. It exhilarated her, rejuvenated her. For the first time since she had opened that judicial complaint letter, she felt a stir of optimism.

She hugged Bill's arm to her side and swayed with him.

"Bill," she said, "do you remember that trial from last April? The one about the antique car?"

"The Maxwell," he said. "The plaintiff inherited it from his father, tried to restore it himself, then needed to hire a professional to finish the job."

"That's the case," said Barbara. Once again, the contours of Bill's memory confounded her. There seemed to be many hidden chambers just waiting for the right question to unlock them.

"The plaintiff," she said, "was very angry about losing."

"Someone had to lose," said Bill. "He hired the defendant to do the impossible."

"I know," said Barbara. She remembered typing that exact sentence in the post-trial decision. "And now he's filed a judicial complaint against you."

"Against me? Because I ruled against him?"

"That's not exactly the reason, but I'm sure it's at the heart of it."

"I want to fight it," said Bill.

"You are going to fight it. You already have a lawyer to defend you. His name is Arnold Delinsky."

"Do I know him?"

"You wouldn't," said Barbara. "He doesn't take cases to court. He only defends judges against complaints, and no one ever filed a complaint against you before."

"I need to meet him. When can we meet him?"

"Soon, darling." Barbara let her arm drop and laced her fingers in his. "You'll meet him soon."

When Cannon obtained his private investigator's license, he splurged on a set of five hundred business cards. The cards were white on black, with the tiny image of a Civil War cannon in the upper left corner, three fingerprint smudges in the lower right corner, and Cannon Investigative Services lettered in between. Striking, he thought. But in this part of the state, where most people

knew everyone else's business, a licensed private investigator was
something of a joke. He gave out about thirty cards before embar-
rassment overtook him and he conveniently lost the rest.

He still could snoop, though, and he had skin thick enough to
withstand the daggers people stared at him when he started asking questions. So he wasn't surprised, or even very concerned,
when Missy Forsythe's extremely pleasant face hardened as he
crossed the lawn to the steps of her front porch.

"Mornin', Miss Forsythe," he said, trying to strike a folksy tone.
"I believe Sheriff Rousma told you I'd be coming along."

"Good morning," Missy replied, her articulation definitely non-
folksy. "He said a colleague wanted to ask me some questions."

She and a preteen girl sat on a green metal glider. They each wore
shorts and T-shirts and had pink rubber plugs wedged between all
their toes. Their toenails glistened. The girl, with her chin on one
knee, brushed the nail of her pinkie toe with teal blue polish.

"But if you're a colleague, where's your uniform?"

Cannon lifted a foot onto the second step and leaned a forearm
onto his thigh. Since folksy talk didn't work with Missy Forsythe,
maybe a folksy stance would. He worked his shield out of his pocket
and held it up for her to see. It was a gold six-pointed star in a
circular field of blue and the words COURT OFFICER RETIRED etched
in a panel below the circle. Most people tended to see the star and
not the words. Missy was one of them.

"Lacey," she said after Cannon pushed the shield back into his
pocket, "can you go inside please? I need to talk to this man."

Lacey made one final stroke with the tiny brush, then leaned
down to blow on her nails before she slid off the glider and heel-
walked into the house. The screen door slapped shut behind her.

Missy stretched her legs out in front of her and wiggled her toes.
Each one was a different color, the right pinkie the same teal blue
as Lacey's.

"Interesting color combo," said Cannon.

"Do you have kids?" said Missy.

"No," said Cannon.

"My daughter is twelve. I'll do anything to stay relevant in her life. Even paint my toenails ten different colors." She paused. "Am I in trouble with my job?"

"I'm sorry?"

"Sheriff Rousma called you a colleague, you show me a court officer shield. Am I in trouble with my job?"

"Why would you be?"

"I can't think of a reason, not that it matters," said Missy. "So you're not an investigator for the courts?"

"No. I'm retired from the courts. I'm a private investigator now. Licensed. I had business cards at one time. People didn't actually laugh, but close. I found flashing the shield more effective. You work for the courts?"

"I'm a court reporter in Sullivan County. Almost twenty years."

"I was a court officer in Delaware County for thirty."

"But you're here about Daniel Kaplan."

"Yes, but it's not just a professional interest. It's personal, too. Mostly personal."

"Did you know him?"

"I remember him when he was a young lawyer trying to scrape together a practice. But that's not the connection. My brother and his wife, they ran a bed-and-breakfast before the business dried up. Their kids were grown up and gone, so they started taking in kids with Down syndrome as foster children. One of those kids is in trouble."

"The Kenneth Palmer thing?" said Missy. "That's your brother's foster son?"

Cannon nodded.

"So you think that whoever killed Daniel Kaplan also killed Kenneth Palmer, which would mean the boy couldn't have killed Palmer?"

"I wouldn't say 'think,'" said Cannon. "'Think' would mean I have a theory. I don't. All I have is a feeling."

He asked her to recount what she had told Rousma. She did, and it sounded exactly the same as what Rousma told him.

"This thing about 'business,'" said Cannon. "The sheriff thinks it's connected to fracking."

"Like a competitor?" said Missy.

"Or an environmentalist group. Some of them can be pretty extreme in their defense of Mother Earth."

Missy took a deep breath. She pulled her left foot onto the seat of the glider, gingerly tapped her toenails, then unwedged the plastic plugs.

"I don't know what I was thinking," she said. "I dated him once when he was still practicing law. He was impressed with himself to the point of being an asshole. So you might ask what I was doing with him the other night? Well, I'm starting to get concerned about providing for Lacey. You know, college and such. So I ran into him and he started chatting me up and I decided that giving him another chance wasn't a complete waste of time."

"Was he still an asshole?" said Cannon.

"Actually not. He still had an edge to him, but then you probably can't do what he does, or did, without having an edge. At least not successfully. Actually, he was very polite. We were in his hot tub for an hour and he didn't even touch me until he got out to make that last round of drinks."

"Were you scared?"

"Of Kaplan?" said Missy. "Well, that touch gave me second thoughts about the wisdom of going back to his place, but those thoughts disappeared when I saw that man in the corner of the deck."

"Do you remember anything else that man said? Anything at all?"

Missy lifted her other foot and unwedged the plugs.

"No," she said.

"This thing about having 'business' with Kaplan. Could it have been 'old business'?"

"Maybe," said Missy. "I can't say for sure."

From inside the house, Lacey called, "Mom, can you help me?"

"Thank you," said Cannon. "I appreciate your time."

They got up from the glider. Cannon thought Missy would go directly inside, but she called to Lacey that she'd be right in and walked Cannon to his car.

"That thing I said about you having kids," she said. "I hope you didn't take it the wrong way."

"What way is that?"

"That you couldn't possibly understand what it means to have them," said Missy. "But I can see that you do. You're a good foster uncle, Mr. Cannon."

CHAPTER 27

S omething felt wrong about coming here in the morning. He associated the morning with hope, potential, a new beginning. But the morning held none of those for him now. Nothing did. It was over. Everything was over, except for the task he had set for himself. And someday soon, that would be over, too.

It was high summer now. In the orchards behind the main house, a breeze would carry the tangy aroma of windfall apples oozing on the ground. Here in the woods, the air was thick and funky. The trees hung heavy and still. Above them, the gray clouds barely held themselves together.

He pulled the severed wires apart and picked through the swirling brush. On the other side, the ferns had begun to shrivel, the skunk cabbage leaves showed yellow around the edges. He didn't bother to lift his feet. He didn't care about leaving a trail behind. His reason for coming here in the morning was purely related to time. He needed to get on the road.

He opened the gate and went inside the plot. The azalea blooms he saw last visit were long gone. Stone pots overflowing with purple and white impatiens stood beside each grave marker. The grass, still green, grew thin and stringy in the heat. He planned not to linger, not with his time problem, not with the impending rain, not with what almost happened the last time. He went straight to the marker and brushed away bits of detritus that had fallen around the two pebbles stuck to the back of the plinth. He rubbed at the spot where the third pebble would sit, squeezed out a dollop of the slurry, then set the pebble in place. Finished, he went to the foot of the grave and spoke to the boy in his head.

He heard a crunch behind him and before he could turn felt something like a metal rod press into his spine.

"Don't move," said a voice.

He froze.

"Put your hands on top of your head. That's right. Now web your fingers together. Good."

The metal rod pulled away from his back.

"Now turn around slowly."

He did, seeing a man who was grizzled and paunchy and holding a rifle.

"Thought it was you."

"Henry?"

"That's right. It's Henry. Now, don't you move."

Henry circled him, patting his flanks, his chest, his back. It wasn't an expert pat-down, but it was sufficient enough to reveal only a set of car keys and the vial of white slurry.

"All right, you can put your hands down," said Henry. He stepped back but didn't lower the rifle. "You done here?"

"Yes."

"All right, then." Henry lifted the rifle toward the gate as if to say *git*.

He went through the gate first, heard the latch clank shut, felt Henry fall into step three or four paces back and quartered off his right shoulder.

"They still in the main house?" he said.

"Till last year," said Henry. "Divided the year exactly in half. Six months here, six months in Florida. But he took sick down there last winter. Never came back. In a nursing home in Sarasota."

"What about her?"

"Sticks with him. Sends us instructions every day. Used to be by telegram. Now they come by e-mail. I don't expect she'll come back here till he kicks."

They walked in silence until they came within sight of the brush that grew around the wires.

"Stay right here," said Henry. "No. Don't turn around. Just listen. I want you to stand here for the count of thirty while I get my ass back to the main house. I done my job, and if I see anything else, I'll need to do more. Get me?"

"Yeah," he said.

A few moments passed.

"Should I start counting?" he said.

"Not yet," said Henry. "I'm thinking what I want to say. And what I want to say is that most of us believed you. Including me. Got that?"

"I do."

"Good. I been wantin' to say that and never thought I'd get the chance," said Henry. "Now start counting."

CHAPTER 28

After speaking with Missy Forsythe, Cannon spent a dismal afternoon tooling aimlessly in his car: the courthouse, Simcoe's Garage, the turnoff that led up to Buck and Sarah's place. By nightfall, he was back at home with a sackful of fast food and a six-pack of Jenny Cream. Home was a converted efficiency above a garage set back from the road behind an old Victorian. The stairs angled up on an outside wall, and the landing at the top was usable as a deck if he didn't mind tilting back his chair and setting his food on the pressure-treated planks. He did just that.

The thick overcast of the afternoon had drained away into a beautiful evening, one of those rare August twilights where the entire world resolved into high definition with the sky aglow beyond the sharply dark tree line. But Cannon couldn't enjoy it. He ate fast and drank fast, then slammed down the front legs of the chair so he could rest his forehead on the rail.

The self-criticism that began to bubble up as he drove away from Missy Forsythe's now washed over him. Coming from Rousma, the news of Daniel Kaplan's murder had inspired him to believe that Kaplan and Palmer had been murdered by the same person. But Rousma, it turned out, was just offering a courtesy based on decades of friendship, and Missy confirmed everything Rousma said but gave up nothing else that Cannon even could bootstrap into a lead.

So here he was, a full day later, and the intimations he had felt so powerfully were fading like an intriguing aroma dissipating with each successive breath. He didn't know what he was looking for and, even if he did, doubted his ability to find it. A licensed private investigator. What a laugh. What the hell was a license other than a piece of paper? It didn't mean that he had any particular skills, any particular smarts, any ability to deduce penetrating conclusions from disparate facts. And if he thought that riding to Luke's rescue was his pathway back to Sarah, well, he had another think coming.

He popped a second Jenny Cream, drank it down, then lifted a third to consider it in the purple twilight. He remembered his one year at SUNY Cortland and the roommate who taught him how to shoot a beer. You opened a hole in the bottom of a can with a church key can opener, sucked out the air, tilted your head back, and popped the top. The beer shot into your mouth so fast, you needed to swallow like crazy to keep up.

He thought about going into the house and pawing through the kitchen junk drawer. He must have a church key in there somewhere, and the idea of shooting the rest of the six-pack and collapsing into bed to sleep the night away was enticing. But the same psychic inertia that earlier sent him tooling around the county kept him in his chair. He opened the fourth can and took a mighty swig. The thought caught him in mid-swallow, and he coughed the beer all over his belly.

Then he went inside and changed his shirt. He couldn't visit stinking of Jenny Cream.

———

Cannon heard the doorbell ring inside, but heard nothing else. He waited a few seconds for the point when a second ring sounding too desperate shaded into sounding like one last halfhearted attempt before departing. It wouldn't be the first time people cowered behind closed doors, waiting for him to go away. If Rich and Mary Ann Kaukonen did, well, it would mean he reached a new low.

The second ring faded, and just as Cannon was about to peel himself away came a faint metallic clacking. At least someone was on the way, though in this household he could not predict who. A chain unhooked, a dead bolt pulled back, and then the door opened.

"Bobby Cannon," said Mary Ann. She leaned crookedly on her walker.

"Evenin', Mary Ann. Sorry for not calling first."

"Nonsense. The only reason to call would be to make sure he was still awake. And he is, so you're in luck." She was a pretty woman, but afflicted with a spinal problem that twisted her into someone who appeared much older than her age.

"You said it, I didn't," said Cannon.

Mary Ann laughed. She swung the walker around and led Cannon toward the back of the house. She didn't roll it so much as bump it, which made the clacking sounds.

"Rich?" she called. "Company."

"Who is it?" growled a voice from deep inside the house.

Mary Ann reached a doorway, then bumped sideways to let Cannon pass. Rich sat in a chair facing a large TV where a baseball game played without sound. He had a snack table in front of him, his own walker to the side of him, and a blanket on top of him. The jalousie windows were open, and a standing fan swiveled back and forth. The room felt ten degrees cooler than the rest of the house.

"Well, if it isn't Bobby Cannon," said Rich. "What a damn surprise. You want anything to drink? Beer? Wine?"

"I'm okay," said Cannon.

"Good. Because we ain't got any," said Rich. He nodded at Mary Ann, who backed away from the door, her walker clacking into the distance.

Rich had been a longtime court clerk and now was a long-running retiree. Cannon settled onto a small sofa and engaged in some polite small talk before getting to the point.

"I'm looking into something," he said.

"Heard that," said Rich. "Thought it was a while ago."

"It was. Now it is again," said Cannon. "Can you think of any cases where both Ken Palmer and Daniel Kaplan were involved?"

"Can't you? You were in the same courthouse almost as long as me."

"Yeah, but you were in the courtroom. I was sitting at a desk in the lobby. I'd see people drift in and drift out, but I never knew who was fighting who over what."

Rich turned toward the TV. The fan swept back and forth across the room several times. Rich seemed to lose himself in the base-ball game, though there was nothing Cannon could see that was obviously engrossing.

"Get this out of the way," Rich suddenly said.

He meant the snack table that pinned him in his chair. Cannon hopped to it, balancing the table so the plate and coffee mug and silverware would not slide off.

"Now, roll that around," said Rich. He meant the walker, which was designed differently from Mary Ann's. The wheels had wire spokes and rubber tires, the handles had hand brakes, and if Rich reversed himself, there was a seat he could sit on. He gripped the handles and bent himself at the waist, imparting enough momen-tum to roll to a desk in the far corner of the room. Newspapers stacked in tall piles stood on one side of the desk; dozens of file folders stood in smaller piles on the other.

"Kaplan got a lot of assigned-counsel family court work when he started out," said Rich. He sat on the walker seat and bellied up to the desk. "Real low-life stuff. I mean, families? The word conjures up nice feelings, except in family court. Anyway, Palmer was well established in the legal community. He had the atten-tion of our esteemed judges, and they appointed him law guard-ian just about every time there was a kid involved. So you can imagine that Palmer and Kaplan butted heads more than a few times."

Rich went quiet as he opened a file folder and sorted through the clippings inside.

"I suppose this would be easier with a computer," he said. "But the fact is, I don't care what's going on in the world or in the country or even in other parts of the state. I care about what's going on right outside our door. So I read the *Democrat* front to back. I think about each story and then I think behind each story. Then I clip them and sort them. You can see I'm a bit behind."

A few more minutes of silence passed as Rich sifted through clippings. Then he snatched one out, held it up to the light, and pinched a corner in his lips as he rolled back to where Cannon waited on the sofa. He parted his lips, and the clipping sailed perfectly onto Cannon's lap.

The article was about a twenty-five-year-old man who had died of a drug overdose back in January. Cannon read it, then handed it back to Rich.

"So?" said Cannon. "I'm supposed to know him?"

"I thought you might," said Rich.

"I don't."

"Well, Palmer and Kaplan tussled over this one for damn near two weeks. Even went up to the appellate court in Albany before it ended. Craziest damn case you ever heard. This filthy-rich couple from over near Ellenville are raising their grandson because the parents, who were going through a divorce, are both gone in a murder-suicide. The grandson is about five, and suddenly this guy who works for the grandparents files for paternity. Albert Halleck, you remember him, had the grandparents, Kaplan had the guy, Palmer was the law guardian."

"I don't remember any of this," said Cannon.

Rich squinted one eye.

"Then maybe you remember this," he said. "Halfway through the trial, the grandparents fired Halleck and brought in this hotshot from New York City. You were friendly with him. Drove him around one weekend because he was looking to buy some property. Don't think he ever did."

"Shit," said Cannon. "Billy Lonergan was on that case?"

"I guess he didn't talk to you about it while you were driving him around," said Rich. "Would have been improper anyway, seeing as how all those family court cases are closed to the public. Anyway, this young man who died of the overdose, he's the kid from that case."

CHAPTER 29

The outgoing voice mail message was recited in a no-nonsense male voice with a hint of a British accent. If this were an emergency, the caller was to hang up and call 911. Otherwise, the doctor was either on the phone or with a client and would return the call as soon as possible.

Cannon lay his phone on the counter and pushed his coffee cup forward to signal he wanted a refill. The Roscoe Diner was in its August doldrums. The trout streams were low and sluggish. The yearly rush of students and parents to upstate colleges was a week away. The town, which jokingly billed itself as halfway to everywhere, was right now halfway to nowhere.

Cannon waited half an hour, but got the same outgoing message. This time he spoke his name and said he needed to talk to the doctor about a mutually important subject. Then he drained the last of his coffee, dropped some bills on the counter, and headed out to his car. Binghamton wasn't far away. If the doctor called back, he could pull over and talk. If not, he could reach the office in an hour.

The office was in a refurbished building on a downtown street. The door was closed but not locked, and Cannon found himself in a waiting room where no one was waiting. The end tables beside the three tiny couches were devoid of magazines. The desk was devoid of a receptionist. The wall calendar above the credenza was stuck on the month of May.

A corridor led deeper into the office suite, and from that direction came the thudding sound of heavy boxes dropping on a floor. The desk phone rang. After the fourth ring, the thudding stopped and the outgoing message played. It ended with a long, loud dial tone. The thudding began again.

Cannon followed the sound. He passed an office with a desk, chair, and a couch. An empty bookcase stood alone on one wall, and behind the desk several rectangles of unfaded blue paint showed where frames once hung.

"Hullo." In a doorway at the end of the corridor, a man stood with a heavy cardboard box in his hands. He was a few years younger than Cannon, with close-cropped salt-and-pepper hair, a trim physique, and sinewy arms. "You must be Cannon."

"How did you know?"

"Heard your message on that infernal machine. The only other person who phones is the landlord, and he won't leave any."

The man dropped the box. The lid popped off, and Cannon could see it was stuffed with file folders. The man dusted his hands and took three quick strides down the corridor.

"Roger Wetherbee," he said.

They shook hands.

"The voice on the outgoing message," said Cannon.

"Very perceptive. That was recorded several years ago. Have a bit more gravel in my voice now." Wetherbee cleared his throat. "Now, what is this mutually important subject you wished to discuss? Is that a clever way of saying you are a patient?"

"No," said Cannon. "I'm not a patient. Definitely not a patient. But I am looking for access to a file. A forensic file for a court proceeding."

"How old?"

"Twenty years or so."

"Files that old may already be in the rubbish," said Wetherbee.

It finally dawned on Cannon. The empty office, the barren waiting room, the boxed-up files. The doctor was closing her practice.

"What time do you expect the doctor?"

"I don't."

"Is there any way I can speak with her?"

"I'm afraid that's not possible," said Wetherbee. "The doctor passed away."

"When?" said Cannon.

"Memorial Day weekend."

"I'm sorry," said Cannon. "May I ask how?"

"In point of fact, she was murdered."

Cannon felt the world begin to spin. He shouldered into one wall. Groped his way to the office door. Pulled himself inside. Sat himself on the couch. He only half heard what Wetherbee was saying behind him, something about a divorce, her plan to retire, the rent on the office paid only till the end of July, his own tardiness in cleaning out. Something about no good deed going unpunished, which he added with an unexpected touch of mirth. Cannon lowered his head between his knees until the spinning stopped.

"Are you all right now?"

Cannon lifted his head and saw Wetherbee staring at him from the doorway.

"Can you tell me the circumstances of her murder?" he said.

"I can tell you what the authorities told me," said Wetherbee. "Maxine drove to her summer house on the Friday of Memorial Day weekend. Sometime late in the afternoon on Sunday, a neighbor noticed that the front door of her house was open. She called in and found Maxine lying on a chaise on her deck. She was dead and apparently had been for approximately twenty-four hours. Manual strangulation, the authorities said."

"Not drowning?" said Cannon. "What I mean is, the deck wasn't a pool deck?"

"Good heavens, no," said Wetherbee. "She was positively phobic about water. Stayed away from anything deeper than her ankles. Even in the bathtub. Why?"

"I'm a private investigator, and I'm looking into what I believe is a series of murders. In April, a lawyer named Kenneth Palmer was forcibly drowned while trout fishing. Last week, a former lawyer named Daniel Kaplan was bound and left to drown in his swimming pool. They were involved in several cases together. But one case in particular also involved Dr. Rosen as a court-appointed forensic psychologist. I was hoping to talk to her about it."

"There's still a room full of files," said Wetherbee. "Help me sort through them, and you're welcome to the file if we find it."

woman's garish hat, a man's tattered sport coat, a teenager's inappropriate hairstyle. If he stared long enough, the frayed filter between his mind and his tongue would let go, so Barbara would preemptively hustle him outside.

But this Sunday morning was like a Christmas carol in August—all was calm and all was bright. Bill seemed especially sharp, especially focused on the Mass. During the sermon, he held Barbara's hand on his lap and gently squeezed whenever the priest made a particularly poignant statement. He knelt throughout the long Eucharistic Prayer without fidgeting once, took communion, and sang the recessional hymn in a voice that was off-key and loud, but not excessively so.

Barbara wondered whether this behavior was directly linked to yesterday's fine motor exercise of writing checks. The thought filled her with hope that Bill not only would withstand the threat of the judicial complaint but also that he might actually get better.

It was a feeling she hadn't allowed herself for a very long time.

———

Barbara could not remember the exact day Judge Lonergan entered her consciousness. She might have heard one of the girls talking about him. She might have typed one of his decisions, her fingers stumbling on their first encounter with L-O-N-E-R-G-A-N. But she surely remembered that day just before Christmas when he swept into the steno pool, telling all the girls they were doing a great job and handing out boxes of expensive chocolate. He was so tall, so handsome, so gregarious, so just plain nice. She was smitten.

The steno pool was dark in the dead of winter. The sun never rose high enough to touch the light court outside its bank of dusty, slop-painted windows. But she could see the sunlight at the top of the mine shaft. Bertha was gone from the steno pool—no great loss because they were no longer on speaking terms—and Barbara hoped a judge would notice her. Judge Lonergan was at the top of her wish list, so whenever the court officer dropped

CHAPTER 30

The Lonergans regularly attended Mass at Holy Trinity Church until the Sunday in late June when Bill acted out during the relative quiet of the Eucharistic Prayer. Barbara pretended to be ill the following week, and she would have fabricated more excuses in the weeks to come if Bill had not insisted on returning. On one level, Barbara did not want to risk a second public scene. But on another, she thought that his insistence was a good sign. He still was aware when Sunday rolled around, still appreciated the comfort of ritual, still believed in the tenets of his faith. She also understood the need to preserve the core of Bill's being, and the law and his religion represented two huge slabs of his personal bedrock.

And so the Lonergans became nomads of their faith, attending Mass at various churches and never the same church twice in a row. For Barbara, Sunday mornings at church became an extension of weekdays at the courthouse, something she needed to manage and war-game to avoid anything more than the most casual human contact. She would time their entry to coincide with the start of the Mass, guide Bill to an empty pew, and occupy him until the ritual took hold of Bill's attention. Still, he would drift, and Barbara needed to be aware of the signs. Sometimes he would fidget; other times he would stare at someone in the congregation. Barbara knew what the staring meant. Bill would have fixated on something—a off work from the chambers floors, she pulled out the Lonergan decisions for herself.

Then it was summer, just before the start of the August term. Steno work was slow. Half the judges took vacation in the July term, while the other half, which included Judge Lonergan, took vacation in August. The officer came in one morning and, instead of dropping a pile of work onto the table, handed Barbara an envelope addressed in beautiful cursive to *Ms. Barbara Frisbie, Stenographic Department*. Inside was a note written in that same cursive. *I would like to speak with you. Say 1:45 today? My chambers?*

It was the tone of the note, not its content, that impressed her. He "would like" not "want" or "need" or "must." It was "speak with" not "talk to." She knew enough about judges to understand that this was no nebulous request, no opening offer in a negotiation. She was expected in his chambers at 1:45. But the delivery of this request was so gentle, so graceful, so unfailingly polite.

Judge Lonergan's secretary, a thin middle-aged woman with the nervous mien of a chain-smoker, led Barbara into the judge's office. The judge looked up from his desk, a pair of half-glasses low on his nose. His face was red, his hair white-blond, his nose bigger than she remembered from his Christmas sweep through the steno pool, but a nice fit to his broad face. He waited for his secretary to close the door, then stood up and clasped Barbara's hand in both of his. They were square hands, attached to strong wrists. She remembered thinking that if she never saw this man again, she always would remember his wrists.

"I have a problem, Ms. Frisbie. . . ."

And during the momentary pause before the judge spoke his next word, her mind fabricated an entire scenario. She had made some subtle mistake in typing a decision. She had omitted a small word—"not," perhaps—and the result was that the outcome of the decision was totally changed. Despite the polite note and the friendly demeanor, the blame would be on her head.

". . . My secretary's husband is taking a job out in Illinois. She'll be leaving me the first of September. I wonder if you would be interested in working for me."

She stammered, more out of relief than surprise at the offer. The judge, it seemed, read otherwise.

"I know it's a big move," he said. "You leave the pool, they hire someone else, and if things don't go well here, there is no going back. But you should consider this. I've been on the bench for almost four years. I have ten years left in this term. I'm forty-six years old. I'm in excellent health. I plan to run for reelection. And I tend not to like change, especially in the people who work for me."

She did the math. Ten years left in this term. Fourteen more if he won reelection. Twenty-four years. Then she relaxed enough to venture a tiny joke.

"Do I need to stay the entire time?" she said.

"Only if you wish," said the judge. "You don't need to tell me right now. Take a day or two to think. But while you're here, I'd like you to meet someone. She may ask you some questions, but don't fret. It's not an interview, more like a get-acquainted session."

The judge buzzed the intercom. A moment later, the door opened and a woman walked in. She was tall and elegant, with golden blond hair and clear skin. She sat in a chair beside Barbara, took a cigarette from a gold case, and tapped the filter.

"Ms. Frisbie," said the judge. "Meet Jill Hayward Lonergan, my wife."

She could see that she had nothing in common with Jill Hayward Lonergan, not looks, not clothes, not age, not the obvious aroma of money that seemed to permeate the air around her. But as they shook hands, she had the uncanny certainty that she was looking at her future self.

———

There was a particular feel to the weekend before the last week before vacation. The upcoming week would be extremely busy, with lawyers urging that their cases be decided before the judge slipped away for an entire month. Still, in the serene quiet of the Sunday morning before that frenetically busy week, Barbara could feel the pull of vacation. Flashback images of vacations past returned unbidden to her mind: packing, tipping the day porter for trucking their luggage to the curb, the Town Car pulling up, Bill telling everyone they were doing a great job.

Fresh out of Mass (Bill had shaken the priest's hand at the steps and told him his sermon was "brilliant"), the pull of vacation locked on to Barbara's psyche. In less than one week they would be gone. In one week, almost to the hour, they would be checking in at the Keystone. It would be a very different type of vacation, she knew, but a vacation just the same.

Barbara hooked her arm around Bill's as they turned onto Broadway. It was a particular type of New York morning, quiet in a way that only a New Yorker could appreciate. Yesterday's mugginess had blown away, and now even that breeze had faded. The sky was a cloudless blue. Traffic passed in a whisper. Barbara felt a surge of optimism, not only about her immediate plans but about the rest of her life as well. And so, rather than head directly home, she suggested they stop for breakfast.

They sat in a window booth in a diner Barbara never would have considered except for her optimistic mood. The general hush that had fallen over the city seeped into the diner. The other customers conversed in whispers. The waitresses whisked up and down the aisles as if they wore slippers. Even the sizzling from the grill seemed muffled. The Lonergans ordered. Barbara smiled at Bill, and Bill smiled back. He slid a hand across the table, and she laid her own in his. They did not speak, and for once, Barbara did not interpret the silence as a symptom of dementia but as a comfortable companionship borne of their years together.

The food came, scrambled eggs for her, a vegetable and cheese omelet for him. They released their hands and began to eat. It was then that the first specter appeared at the edge of Barbara's optimistic vision of the future. She could take Bill to the door of the Keystone, but she still needed to coax him inside. It was a detail she had sloughed over, and now it hit her with full force. How would she get him inside the door?

Barbara withdrew into herself, as she did so many times in these last few months when the reality of Bill's condition played out in some near-future event. She envisioned Dr. Feldman at the door, two burly aides lurking to the side, Bill's trusting smile curdling into apprehension, then fear, then betrayal. She heard herself speak soothingly to him, but she could not form the actual words to assure him that everything would be all right.

The thud came from a great distance. It shook the table, but not enough to disturb her reverie. Then came a second thud, louder now, and a more urgent shake of the table.

"That man," someone said.

Still, Barbara remained in her own thoughts. Then came a third, even louder thud. Bill's glass fell over, and iced tea splashed onto Barbara's skirt.

She looked up. Bill pointed to his throat, a stricken look on his face, his mouth moving but making no sound. His fist banged the table so hard, the saltshaker toppled. He stood up.

Barbara jumped out of the booth. Bill leaned over the table, his face flushing a deep red, his eyes big in their sockets.

"Breathe, Bill, breathe," said Barbara.

His mouth trembled, but no sound came out.

Barbara knew instantly. It was that damn omelet. She told the waitress to hold the cheese, but there it was leaking out on the plate. She needed to get behind Bill, but there was no room. Four people sat in the adjoining booth. They all looked in Bill's direction, but seemed confused by what was happening.

"Get out!" Barbara yelled, grabbing at the two people seated on the bench that backed up against Bill's. They quickly slid into the aisle, and Barbara jumped up.

Bill stood in the cramped space, bent sharply at the waist, his face almost touching the table, his body shaking horribly. Barbara braced herself on the bench and worked her hands around Bill until she could web her fingers. She needed to lift him higher.

"Bill!" she yelled. "Push yourself up. Push yourself back."

Her chin pressed against his spine. Tears streamed from her eyes. She couldn't see, so she didn't know whether it was her panic or his willpower, but he slowly rose up from the table.

She had leverage now. She balled her hands into fists and yanked back sharply. Once, twice. On the third yank, Bill coughed. Something thwapped onto the table. A large plug of broccoli and melted cheese.

Barbara pressed her chin against the side of Bill's neck.

"Bill," she whispered.

He was panting, gloriously panting. And groaning, beautifully groaning. She loosened her grip and let him sink back onto his bench. She looked around. Everyone in the diner stared at her.

"He's okay," she said. "He's okay."

She jumped off the bench and adjusted her skirt and blouse.

The manager came over. "I called for an ambulance," she said.

"You . . ." Barbara stopped herself. "Thank you, but it wasn't necessary."

"Well, they're on their way."

Barbara recalled the serenity of the streets, the whispering traffic. The ambulance would be here in a few minutes. She listened, but heard nothing yet.

The manager drifted away.

Barbara whispered in Bill's ear. "Do you feel better?"

He pointed to his throat. "It hurts."

"It will go away," she said. "Can you walk?"

He grunted yes.

Barbara quickly calculated the tab. Doubled the tip, then tripled it. She could hear a distant siren as she laid fifty dollars on the table.

"Hey, you can't leave," the manager called.

"Thank you," Barbara called back.

On the sidewalk, she listened for the direction of the siren.

"It's a fast break, hon," she said, and tugged Bill in the opposite direction.

CHAPTER 31

T he sun lit the dust on the windshield, and beyond the glare, Buck Cannon sat in his old cane rocker on the porch. Beside him, on a three-legged stool, stood a sweat-beaded pitcher of lemonade. Buck held a glass on his lap. He was clean-shaven, with sharp features and deep lines running back from his eyes and permanent dimples at the corners of his mouth. His moccasins were flat on the floorboards, and the tendons in his bare ankles twitched as they gave a slight rocking motion to the chair. He peered through the windshield long enough to meet his brother's eye, then immediately turned his gaze to the field of Queen Anne's lace that sloped down to the road.

Cannon fingered the ignition key. At another time, seeing this sort of welcome from Buck, he would have thrown the car into reverse and patched out in a spray of gravel. But today he needed to swallow back the mix of guilt and longing and anger for the greater good. And so, taking a breath to prepare himself for his older brother's passive resentment, he killed the engine and pulled himself out of the car.

Buck hardly reacted as Cannon climbed onto the porch and settled into a matching rocker. He kept his squinting eyes on the field as if he expected something to materialize on the road beyond, but his ankle twitched harder and rocked the chair through a few more degrees of arc.

"Hey," said Cannon.

Buck nodded.

They sat in silence for a while, Cannon resisting the inevitable pull from inside the house. In the trees, the cicadas chattered. On the porch, the floorboards squeaked beneath Buck's rocker.

"What time is he getting here?" said Buck.

Cannon looked at his watch. "Soon."

"I don't see the point of this."

"The point is this, Buck. Just because you won't accept help from me doesn't mean I can't help you."

"If you think this evens things out."

"I don't. Nothing has. Nothing likely ever will. Put it away, Buck. We're adults here."

From inside the house came the sound of thudding footsteps. The screen door burst open, and a boy wearing oversized khaki shorts and a striped polo shirt threw himself at Cannon.

"Uncle Bobby, Uncle Bobby," he said.

He buried his face in Cannon's gut, then climbed onto his lap.

"I love you, Uncle Bobby," he said, his eyeglasses askew.

"Let me fix these." Cannon pressed the glasses back into place, though the boy's nose had hardly enough bridge to balance them.

"I love you, Uncle Bobby," the boy said again, and planted a wet kiss on Cannon's cheek.

"I love you, too, Max," said Cannon.

Max let out a braying laugh, slid down from Cannon's lap, and ran back into the house. The screen door slapped shut behind him.

"Hear that?" said Cannon. "Tell me he says that to everyone."

"I'll say no such thing," said Buck.

Cannon stood up. He'd sat, talked, listened. He'd let Buck take his shots rather than rush headlong into the house. Now the shots were over, the sullen silence had descended, and the pull overcame him.

In the kitchen, Sarah stood at the stove, where two frying pans sizzled with oil. She forked a browned chicken tender onto a plate. Grease spread through a paper towel.

"Hello, Robert." She pecked his cheek. No one else called him

Robert, and the formality was oddly intimate. Still, she slid out of his groping embrace and turned back to the stove.

"Buck cordial to you?" She laid three more chicken tenders into the pan.

"Buck is Buck," said Cannon.

"Well, you're here and you're making progress."

"With Buck? He didn't even ask what I found out. Does he care?"

"Of course he cares."

"What about you?"

"You're a good man, Robert."

Cannon grabbed a beer from the refrigerator and went back onto the porch. Buck glanced his way long enough to spot the beer, then jumped his rocker to face in the other direction. Cannon popped the top and took a long pull.

The cicadas went still, and the sound of a distant car rose in the sudden silence. Buck heard it, too. He got up from the rocker, walked to the edge of the porch, and leaned against a post. At first, only the dust was visible, swirling along the valley floor. Then the car itself flashed a glint of sunlight. It swung onto the bottom of the long uphill drive, the gold letters of SHERIFF coming clear well before the car pulled up beside Cannon's. Rousma got out, tossed his hat onto the front seat, then shook out his legs as he walked to the steps.

"Afternoon, Buck." Rousma nodded at Cannon. "Bobby."

He stood with one hand gripping the rail as if waiting for an invitation. He must have seen something in Buck that escaped Cannon because he stepped up onto the porch. Buck sat down, uninterested.

"Your meeting," Rousma told Cannon.

Cannon called into the house for Sarah. She came out a minute later, wiping her hands on her apron.

"I have something," said Cannon.

———

Foxx began calling Sidney Dweck on Friday afternoon. The office phone rang into voice mail, and Foxx left a message about wanting to continue their conversation. Dweck didn't return the call, so after hours on Friday evening, Foxx tried his cell. This call went directly into voice mail, and Foxx left the same message. Dweck didn't return that call, either, and at odd times over the weekend, Foxx kept trying but left no further message. Finally, just after noon on Sunday, Dweck answered.

"Sidney Dweck," he said.

Three syllables, and Foxx immediately heard a difference in Dweck's speech. "Sidney" now began with *sh* and "Dweck" ended with a short *e* rather than a hard *k*. But before Foxx could speak, a distant voice said, "Give me that," and after a few thuds, that voice grated in Foxx's ear.

"This is Mrs. Dweck. Who's this?"

"My name is Foxx," said Foxx.

"I don't know any Foxx."

"I know Mr. Dweck from the courthouse."

"Everyone knows Mr. Dweck from the courthouse."

"We had a conversation the other day. I need to ask him a couple of questions."

"Well, you can't. He is not well. He had a stroke."

Dweck spoke in the background. He wanted to know who was on the phone. His wife said it was someone named Foxx. Dweck demanded the phone. His wife refused. Dweck demanded again, and she must have handed it over because Dweck said, "Hello," and in the background she said, "I should become a widow because you want to talk."

"Hold on, Foxx," said Dweck. He muffled the phone and when he came back, the background noise was gone. "What happened the other day?"

"Never mind me. What happened to you?" said Foxx. "A stroke?"

"Nah, just a mild TIA," said Dweck. "My voice slurred, my left side went weak. Get 'em all the time and always bounce back. But my secretary, God bless her, called EMS before I could stop her."

"Good thing she did," said Foxx.

"Says you. I'm the one in the hospital. But I'm almost completely back. How do I sound?"

"Fine," Foxx lied.

"Damn right. What about you? Last I saw . . ."

Foxx was on his porch. Through the window, Ellen sat at the kitchen table with the Sunday papers.

"It was nothing," said Foxx.

"Didn't look like nothing to me," said Dweck. "When I heard your message, I figured you needed my help."

"I do, but not for that," said Foxx. "I spoke to Wendy Robinson on Friday."

"Who's that?" said Dweck. "Never mind. Wendy. Must be Calvin's widow. She remarried?"

"With a daughter going to college."

"How'd you find her?"

"Scannell," said Foxx. "And she was only too happy to talk. Seems like living well really is the best revenge, even when the object of your revenge is dead. She didn't know much about the campaign. Calvin kept her mostly in the dark. But she shed light on one thing."

"Which was?" said Dweck.

"She remembers a phone call around the time you said Calvin's attitude about the campaign changed," said Foxx. "She remembers it because she overheard it and she overheard it because Calvin was yelling and Calvin never yelled on the phone, at least not when he was talking to you."

"I remember a phone call like that," said Dweck.

"Do you remember what it was about?"

"I do."

Dweck said nothing else. Foxx could hear him breathing into the phone. A bell rang. A doctor was paged over an intercom.

"Are you going to tell me?" said Foxx.

Dweck sighed. "First off, you need to know I never was a dirty-tricks kind of guy. Not then, not ever."

"Okay," said Foxx.

"Like I told you the other day, my plan was that Calvin should lose with dignity and set himself up for the next year. Now, the way things stood at the time, in a straight-up delegate vote, Calvin would have come in a distant third. But he knew, because I told him, that if one of those two folded, he might siphon off enough votes to force a second or a third ballot. If that happened, well, then anything was possible.

"Apparently, we had a campaign volunteer who had gone to college with one of those two front-runners. He supposedly had a photograph that would be political death for the person in it."

"What kind of picture?" said Foxx.

"If I knew, I wouldn't tell you," said Dweck. "But I don't know, and that's the God's honest truth."

"What do you think it might have been?" said Foxx.

"Don't know," said Dweck, "and don't care. But think about it. How many of us wouldn't be embarrassed by the things we did in college?"

"So what happened?"

"The first thing that happened is I refused to discuss it. I wasn't about to be a party to using it, and he wasn't about to let the opportunity go by. So we were at an impasse. He was in no rush. Whatever this photo showed would be most effective at the convention, so I bided my time. I helped Calvin the best I could, legitimately, that is. And when the convention rolled around, I planned to resign. But then, well, that became a moot point."

"Who were the two candidates ahead of Lozier?" said Foxx.

"The name of one escapes me, which means he didn't stay in politics," said Dweck. "But you know the other one. He's the AJ at 60 Centre."

———

"It all started with a paternity case," said Cannon. "Not the standard variety where a mother goes after a guy so he'll own up and help raise their child, but one where the guy tries to prove paternity.

"Now, I didn't see any of this directly. Rich Kaukonen was actually in the courtroom. My post was in the lobby, and I do remember the lawyers and clients coming in and leaving. I just didn't know what it was about at the time. Rich told me the whole story last night.

"The man who claimed paternity worked as a pilot for a rich family named Van Gelder, The Van Gelders had a son, and the son married a young woman from the Netherlands who came to the States to work as an au pair. The parents were dead set against the marriage, probably because they thought the woman was a gold digger. But the son married her anyway. Eventually, though, he filed for divorce, and it was during the divorce that the wife started seeing the pilot. At least, that's what the pilot claimed. And then she became pregnant.

"The divorce proceedings took a long time. There was a lot of money involved, so the lawyers were milking it. And then came the pregnancy, which complicated matters, although the question of paternity never was mentioned. The baby was born—it was a boy—and almost another year passed before the lawyers finally worked out a settlement on maintenance and property distribution, along with custody, visitation, and child support. The night before the judge was to sign the judgment of divorce, the son killed his wife and then himself. You all with me?"

Buck said nothing. Sarah muttered something about a vague memory. Rousma sucked his teeth.

"The Van Gelders had legal custody and raised the boy on their estate," said Cannon. "About five years later, the pilot came out of the woodwork and hired a lawyer to file a paternity suit. The Van Gelders fought it, of course, but the pilot's lawyer, a young guy right out of law school, argued that there was this new DNA test that was easier and more accurate than any blood test for proving paternity. We take it for granted now, but back then it was too new for the courts to buy into.

"The judge surprised everyone by ordering the test, but before it could be done, the law guardian, that's the court-appointed lawyer for the boy, filed a motion to reargue, and the Van Gelders, who didn't like to lose, fired their lawyer and hired this big shot from New York City. The judge reversed himself and canceled the DNA test. The trial continued, and the pilot lost. He took an appeal, and lost that, too. That was the end of the paternity suit.

"The pilot didn't exactly go away. He haunted the boy for a couple of years. He sent gifts and sneaked onto the estate property to visit with him. But finally, the Van Gelders got an order of protection, and he disappeared. That was all about twenty years ago. Then, last January, that young boy died of a drug overdose."

"What's all this got to do with Luke?" said Buck.

"Ken Palmer was the law guardian," said Cannon.

"So what?" said Rousma. "Ken Palmer was the law guardian for lots of kids around here."

"Right, but you remember me telling you that the day before Palmer was murdered, I noticed someone hanging around Simcoe's Garage and then the next day I saw that same person driving back to Simcoe's Garage around the time Darwin sent someone out to change Palmer's blown tire. I didn't know where I knew him from. Now I remember. He was the pilot."

"We didn't know he was a pilot, but we know his name," said Rousma. "Tom Kehoe."

"How the hell did you know?" said Cannon.

"We talked to him."

"When?" said Cannon. "Where?"

"Day after the murder. At the garage."

"Darwin said he didn't know his name."

"He didn't," said Rousma. "But some of his—ahem—workers did."

"You mean Swayze, Reid, and Berkeley?"

"They're the ones. Talk to them?"

Cannon shook his head.

"Should have," said Rousma. "They didn't just know his name.

They knew he was staying at the campground near Spring Brook. And that's where he was, living out of his car."

Cannon shook his head.

"You think I'd rule out a suspect without looking him in the eye?" said Rousma. "He seemed down on his luck, but not shady or dishonest. I questioned him, and he answered without a hitch. Drove out to change the tire, got fifteen bucks in return, spent seven on food at the garage, still had eight in his pocket."

Cannon looked at Buck and then at Sarah. Buck gazed out across the field like he'd heard enough and was waiting for the noise to stop and everyone to leave so he could return to his rocking. Sarah dropped her eyes, then coughed the kind of cough that masked a whimper.

"He could have lied," said Cannon.

"He could have at that," said Rousma, "but I asked the boys at the garage whether they took note of him when he got back from changing that tire. They did because while he was gone, they laid bets on what Palmer would give him. Now we know Palmer was killed in the water, not up on shore and then floated down the river. So the killer would've been wet, too. They said Kehoe wasn't. Pants were dry and kind of dusty, which was consistent with getting down on his knees to loosen the lug nuts."

"What about Daniel Kaplan?" said Cannon. "He was Kehoe's lawyer in the paternity case."

"Yeah, well, half the state of Pennsylvania probably wanted Kaplan dead, and we got two persons of interest we're looking into."

"But Palmer and Kaplan were both on that paternity case," said Cannon.

"So? Palmer and Kaplan probably locked horns twenty times before Kaplan had the good sense to quit lawyering."

"What about this?" said Cannon. "The judge in the paternity case ordered a forensic psychologist to examine the boy, the pilot, and the Van Gelders. Now, this isn't normal practice in a paternity suit, but that New York City big shot I told you about sweet-talked the judge into ordering it. I read her report. She recommended that it was in the best interests of the boy for him to stay with the Van Gelders. Her report was none too kind to the pilot. Basically thought he was crazy. She was murdered on Memorial Day weekend."

"Drowned?" said Rousma.

"Strangled," said Cannon. "But does that matter? All three were connected to the paternity case, and all three have been murdered. Now, what are the chances of that? So what I want you to do, Sheriff, is reopen your investigation into Ken Palmer's murder."

"I can't do that," said Rousma.

"Why not? You're the damn sheriff. You can do whatever you want."

"I need a reason."

"I just gave you three."

"No," said Rousma. "What you gave me are three people murdered over a four-month period and some guy connected with some court case from a long time ago. I can't do it. I don't say I don't want to do it. I can't do it. Sorry, Buck. Sorry, Sarah. And yes, Bobby, sorry to you, too."

Foxx told Ellen about his latest conversation with Sidney Dweck, which brought her current on his investigation except for the bit about hanging Orlando Cortez out the window, his suspension, and the possibility of criminal charges. They tried to imagine what type of photograph would cause the political death of a candidate for a civil court judgeship in the New York City of the 1990s. Naturally, the possibilities pointed toward sex, which led to their having sex, which ended the conversation without arriving at any solution. Ellen barely had enough time to shower, dress, and scoot down to Artie's for the dinner shift.

Foxx sat alone on the porch and stared out beyond the boatyard to Hart Island and the crumbling brick facade of the old Reformatory Prison. His father had worked there many years as a cook, riding out in the morning and back in the evening on a prison launch. Foxx often stared out at the prison when he needed to settle his mind in the hope that some sort of inspiration might take root. Today, there was nothing.

His cell phone buzzed on the plastic table beside the daybed. The union was calling.

"Foxx here," said Foxx.

"John Jaffrey." It was his lawyer. "You must have friends in high places because I just got a call from your union delegate. You've been partially reinstated."

"What does that mean?" said Foxx.

"Report to work as usual tomorrow. You'll find out from Captain Kearney."

Cannon sat in the dark on the landing outside his door. He had his feet on the rail and his chair tipped back as he drank a Jenny Cream and listened to the highway traffic invisible beyond the trees. A day that started out with such lofty hopes crashed in a fiery tailspin. Rousma schooled him but good in the science of detection. A private investigator might be exempt from all those constitutional amendments that restricted a sheriff's freedom to probe. But you still needed to work a case step by step, not hurl yourself forward with grand leaps of supposition. He'd simply assumed that Rousma never heard the name Thomas Kehoe or bothered to track down the drifter who hung out at Simcoe's Garage before leaving town. The smug set of Buck's jaw as Rousma reversed his cruiser away from the porch was bad enough; the disappointment in Sarah's eyes was worse.

So now he had another plan, one that did not involve the detection skills he plainly lacked. This one was harsh, cruel, and cynical. And that was if it worked. If it didn't work, well, he was no worse off than he was now.

A car pulled into the driveway below him. The engine shut off and the headlights went out and the door opened and shut. A few seconds later, the stairs shook.

"Hi," said Sarah. She looked gray in the darkness.

Cannon tipped forward. He set the beer down, but it fell over and spilled some before he righted the can.

"I brought you some fried chicken tenders. We weren't none of us very hungry after you and the sheriff left. Not even Max."

"I'm not done yet," said Cannon.

"That's not what I meant. I meant we had leftovers. Nothing else."

"I know what you meant, Sarah. Rousma may be correct in what he said today. But I'm right, too. I'll prove Luke couldn't have done it."

Sarah backed down the first couple of steps, then turned.

"I'm leaving at first light tomorrow," Cannon called after her.

Sarah stopped on the stairs, one foot lower than the other, her hand on the rail.

"Back to New York City."

"Again? Your last trip didn't accomplish anything."

"I know," said Cannon. "But this one will."

CHAPTER 32

I never feel like I need a vacation until I start getting ready to go on vacation."

Bill said those words to Barbara one week before the very first time she would see chambers close for summer vacation. Barbara was surprised. The phone rang incessantly, hand-delivered letters steadily streamed to the security desk, and lawyers buttonholed the judge in the corridors, the lobby, even on the street. The requests, whether telephonic, written, or face-to-face, were all the same: *Please decide my case before you leave.*

Barbara, still the judge's secretary rather than Bill's wife, was surprised at how hard he worked during that last week before vacation. He would not allow her to stay beyond five o'clock, but he remained at his desk for three, four, sometimes five hours, pounding out decisions in his beautiful script. She wondered why he, a judge, would feel obligated to grind so hard when he should have been winding down. It took a while—a couple of years, really—to understand that the lawyers, not the citizens of Manhattan, were his true constituency. And Bill Lonergan, the consummate politician, aimed to please.

After they married, when they were no longer simply judge and secretary but also husband and wife, she thought she might have some sway. But Bill could not be swayed. He actually had practiced law, he reminded her, and knew what it was like to be on the bar side of the bench, dealing with impatient clients while waiting for decisions to come down from on high.

Barbara acceded to this work ethic. She no longer left at five
o'clock, but stayed with him until he finished what he set out to
finish. As they trekked home in the heat of those summer nights,
she told herself she had fallen in love with a good and decent man.

Now, however, things were different. Bill had neither the will
nor the stamina to work like hell during the week leading up to
vacation. Sure, the three of them, Larry included, would knock out
their daily quota of decisions. But Barbara's main task would be to
fend off the many requests.

Yet, as they arrived at the courthouse that Monday morning,
even the prospect of constant entreaties did not dampen Barbara's
spirits. Bill not only looked crisply dapper in his gray suit, but also
seemed to be in his best mental state in several weeks. She inter-
preted the choking incident, scary as it had been, as a sign that
things would get better if only because they could not get any worse.

Foxx made sure he arrived at the courthouse early enough to show
that he appreciated the efforts made on his behalf. The locker room
was fairly empty. The few other officers getting ready for the day
nodded at Foxx, then returned to conversations that were abnor-
mally hushed, even for the early hour. Foxx closed his locker
and spun the padlock. Without his pistol, his equipment belt felt
unbalanced, and he unconsciously hiked it several times as the
elevator climbed to the fifth floor.

Captain Kearney waited at the security desk. He held Foxx's
shield but not his pistol.

"I don't know how you arranged this," he said. "I know you have
friends, but it still surprised me."

"Surprised me, too," said Foxx.

Kearney grunted. "Anyway, I talked to the head custodian. We've
taken precautions to make sure you and Cortez don't cross paths.
He will not work in any of the chambers. You are to confine yourself to the fifth and sixth floors. If you want to leave for lunch,

take the public elevator down to the rotunda and go out through the front door. Cortez leaves at three thirty. He'll be long gone by the time you go to your locker."

Kearney handed over the shield and stood silently while Foxx fixed it to his uniform shirt.

"You know the drill, right?" said Kearney.

Foxx nodded.

"Good. I didn't want to embarrass either of us by saying it out loud." Kearney stepped backwards, began to snap off an about-face, then steadied himself. "A word to the wise. I've heard there have been some rumblings about retribution. You might want to take precautions."

"I will," said Foxx. "Thanks."

Kearney now snapped off his about-face and walked to his office with his hands clasped at the base of his spine. Foxx settled behind the desk, which felt much different from last week. The drill Kearney had mentioned was simple. Not only could he not carry his pistol, but he also could not involve himself in any confrontation, physical or verbal. If a confrontation began to brew, he needed to retreat and call for backup. Quite a comedown for an officer whose baleful stare was a potent weapon.

Soon enough, the officers began to float up from the locker room. The courthouse was like a living organism, and rumors spread as quickly and efficiently as the secretions of an endocrine gland. This was especially true of the court officers, whose blue uniforms and quasi-military job description created their own form of isolation within the greater courthouse community. Few met Foxx's eye as they scratched their name on the sign-in sheet. Most glanced at his empty holster.

———

Midmorning relief allowed Foxx the few minutes of freedom he needed to climb a set of back stairs to the sixth floor. The book on Bertha was that she was the laziest and grumpiest secretary in the building. The fact that she had retained her job for so long meant one of two things: either she had a godfather somewhere in the upper reaches of the court system, or she knew where the bodies were buried. The first would be a verifiable fact; the second was just an expression. Foxx hoped for the latter rather than the former.

The entry door to chambers was open. Bertha sat at her desk, holding a compact at eye level as she brushed powder onto her generous cheeks. She looked up from the tiny mirror as Foxx crossed the threshold.

"Well, well," she said. "Are you here to appeal your sentence to Judge Patterson?"

"No," said Foxx. "I'm here to ask you some questions."

"And if I don't answer, you'll hang me out a window?" said Bertha.

"Not exactly," said Foxx. The old phone directory was rolled up in his back pocket. He pulled it out and tossed it onto the desk, spinning it so that it landed with its pale green cover facing Bertha.

"Mean anything to you?" he said.

"Like what?"

"Like the year on the cover. The same year Calvin Lozier was murdered."

"Okay," said Bertha. "And?"

"The wrong guy went to jail for the murder, and that means everyone in this phone directory is a suspect."

"Number one, there can be suspects only if there is an investigation," said Bertha. "And number two, why do you care?"

"Ralphie Rago is an old friend," said Foxx. "He says he didn't do it. He asked me to look into it. I'm beginning to believe he's right."

"You're a little late to that dance, aren't you?" said Bertha.

"Some things take time to coalesce," said Foxx.

"Is that why you hung Orlando Cortez out the window?" said Bertha.

"Ralphie's lawyer told me that Cortez arranged the use of something called the boom-boom room. That's where Lozier was killed."

"The boom-boom room," said Bertha.

"The lawyer tried to squeeze Cortez to show that other people besides Ralphie had access to the room, but Cortez resisted and the trial judge was no help. I tried a different approach."

Bertha handed the directory back to Foxx. He thought she was ending the discussion. Instead, she looked at the phone console, then nodded toward the door. Foxx went out into the corridor with Bertha right behind him.

"He's on a phone call," she said, meaning Judge Patterson. "Gives us a few minutes, but not many."

"A few minutes is all I have," said Foxx.

"I don't like Cortez," said Bertha. "He looks at me funny whenever he comes in to clean chambers, like he knows something I don't, which not too many people in this courthouse can say. Now, what do you need to know?"

Foxx quickly told her what Ralphie told him about the boom-boom room and the mutual interest between the law clerks and the steno pool girls.

"Not all the steno pool girls," said Bertha.

"What about the boom-boom room?" said Foxx. "Is my information correct?"

"Oh, there was a room, all right," said Bertha. "Lots of people knew about it, and I'm sure that more claimed to use it than actually did. But it wasn't called the boom-boom room. Not then. Not before the murder."

"Did you ever use it?"

Footsteps squeaked. Bertha looked at where the corridor angled, waiting to be sure the footsteps headed elsewhere.

"No," Bertha said firmly. "Never."

"Did you know anyone who did?"

"No. Not that anyone would admit it. But definitely not. One of the other girls and I went looking for the room one lunch hour. This was maybe four or five months before the murder. All we knew was that it was at the bottom of a back stairway, and you know

how many of those there are. We found it on our third try. Whatever the room was, it sure wasn't soundproof."

Another door opened and closed, this time in the other direction.
Bertha held her breath until those footsteps faded.

"I take it you don't know who was inside."

Bertha shook her head.

From inside chambers came the click of a latch and the creak of
a door swinging open. A moment later, Judge Patterson appeared
behind Bertha.

"Wondering where you went," said the judge. He nodded at
Foxx, then added to Bertha, "When you are done," and stepped
back into chambers.

Foxx opened the phone directory to the steno pool page.

"Are any of the other girls still working here?" he said.

Bertha took the directory from Foxx. She lifted her glasses and
held the page close to her right eye. "Just one other," she said, and
pointed at a name.

"Don't know her," said Foxx.

"Sure you do," said Bertha. "She goes by her married name now.
Lonergan."

CHAPTER 33

They were almost at the end of their second circuit of Columbus Park when it happened. Barbara was feeling optimistic, excessively optimistic, the kind of optimistic that, like pride, preceded the fall. But she could not have foreseen this exact type of fall.

During their morning work session, Bill had ruled on seven motions and, with Larry's prompting, had written three other decisions in his own hand. It wasn't just that Bill had worked so long without fading into disinterest. There was a decisiveness in his demeanor, a confidence, dare she say, a verve that she had not seen in months. For once, she did not need to scatter birdseed to get him through the morning.

At the start of the walk, Bill barely glanced at the basketball players. Instead, he tucked Barbara's hand in the crook of his elbow and walked her up the east side of the park on Mulberry Street. They talked, they joked, they even flirted to the point that Barbara toyed with the idea of going back to chambers and locking themselves in Bill's office.

Whatever reservations she had about the Keystone's theory were diminishing fast. Two days of forcing Bill to write rather than idly page through newspapers or stare at birds boiling against the window seemed to have a beneficial effect on his mental state. The prospect of him spending thirty days in the Keystone's intensive therapy now seemed very promising. Maybe his brain actually did have the capacity to repair itself.

Coming down the west side of the park, they reached a fork in the sidewalk. The right fork hugged the street, while the left cut between the iron fence that ran along the soccer field and a triangular garden patch thick with tall clumps of ornamental grasses. Barbara could see Larry beyond the soccer field, playing boxball on an asphalt square. Closer, nestled among the grasses, was a park bench. A small, elderly man sat on the bench, and as they drew close, the man jumped up.

"Damn you!" he yelled.

Bill stopped, then reared back to avoid the open-handed round-house the man swung at his jaw.

"You fixed the trial! Now you fixed my complaint!"

The man swung another roundhouse, but Bill ducked that one, too. Barbara stepped in front of Bill and, as the man wound up for a third swing, she rammed her purse into his chest. The blow knocked him back onto the bench, but he jumped up quickly and dived toward Bill.

Barbara, stumbling, watched what happened next unfold in slow motion. The man hunched low, his legs churning, his shoulder aimed at the most vulnerable part of Bill's body. He launched himself forward, but just before he cracked Bill's knees, a shadow sliced between them and absorbed the impact.

Barbara's perceptions returned to regular speed. The shadow resolved into a bigger man who wrestled the little man to the ground.

"Go," the bigger man told Barbara. "I got him. Go."

Barbara dragged Bill toward the courthouse while a crowd of children and teenagers stared through the park fence. From behind her came the muffled sounds of a struggle. She hoped the bigger man was restraining the little man, though she dared not turn her head.

Bill staggered. He tried to throw Barbara off as if he wanted to

break free and run, but Barbara held on tight until Larry dashed
through the gate and grabbed Bill's other arm.

"What the hell was that?" said Larry.

"I don't know," said Barbara. She turned around, but both men
were gone. "Let's get him to chambers."

———————

Back in chambers, Barbara closed herself and Bill into Bill's office,
but not for the reason she in her naïve optimism had planned just
a few minutes earlier. Bill shook uncontrollably. Barbara managed
to peel off his suit jacket and sit him in his chair. He pitched forward, his arms wrapped across his belly, his head bobbing. He tried
to speak, but managed only to grunt. She knelt in front of him,
held his hands, pressed her forehead against his.

"Take a deep breath, Bill," she said. "Slow down."

He obeyed. She could feel the tension leaving his hands, his
forehead pressing harder against hers as he relaxed his spine. She
slowly stood up and laid him back in his chair.

"What was that?" he said, his words perfectly formed now.

"Mistaken identity," she said, though she realized now that the
little old man was the same man who had filed the grievance against
Bill. As for the other man, the Good Samaritan who intervened, she
had not a clue.

She fetched the birdseed. Though she had promised herself not
to feed the birds—not today, maybe not ever again—this was an
emergency, and in an emergency, you reached for the comfort of
the familiar. She jerked up the window, spread the seeds on the
sill, and jammed the window back down. Within seconds, a small
bird with a wine-colored breast landed.

Barbara went out through her office and peeked at Larry, still in
his sweaty boxball attire. She pressed a finger to her lips and closed
the door.

Arnold Delinsky answered his phone quickly. Barbara began
her story and, despite Delinsky interrupting with three "My God's"

and one "You gotta be kidding me," finally recounted the entire incident.

"And you're sure it was Andrew Norwood?" said Delinsky.

"Not at first," said Barbara. "I didn't care who he was, frankly. I was trying to protect Bill. It was afterwards that I remembered him from the trial."

"And this other man?" said Delinsky.

"Just a passerby. He knocked Norwood down, leaned on him to keep him from getting up, and told me to get Bill out of there. I dragged Bill for half a block before I turned around. They were gone."

"This certainly is a first for me," Delinsky said after an audible sigh, "a physical confrontation between a complainant and a client."

"Does it change anything?"

"You mean, can I get the complaint dismissed because Norwood attacked the judge? No, the process already has started and needs to run its course."

"I want to get Bill out of here now," said Barbara. "Not wait for the end of the week."

"Not a bad idea," said Delinsky. "If Norwood tried this once, he could try it again. And you may not be so lucky a second time in the Good Samaritan department."

———

Hand-deliveries arrived during the traditional one-o'clock lunch hour, and by two o'clock the black box on the fifth-floor security desk often was filled with envelopes. The lunchtime relief officer did not handle the deliveries, just pointed the messengers to the box and then nodded as if to say *drop 'em*. When the regular officer returned at two, the first order of business was to sift through the envelopes and bind each judge's deliveries with a thick rubber band. Some chambers automatically sent someone out shortly after two to collect the mail. Others waited for a call from the officer at the desk.

Foxx called Judge Lonergan's chambers at 2:05. A few minutes later, Larry Seagle arrived and rooted through the black box for Judge Lonergan's mail. Larry still wore his T-shirt and gym shorts. His athletic eyeglasses clung to his head, and the elastic band running from earpiece to earpiece cut into his springy gray-brown hair. Foxx knew little about Seagle beyond his habit of playing box-ball in Columbus Park at lunchtime. Most of the officers seemed to give him a wide berth that, herd mentality aside, probably meant something, though Foxx didn't know exactly what.

Seagle tucked the mail under his arm. His sneakers squeaked and then the fire door banged. Silence ensued, which Foxx took as a sign that his chances of encountering Barbara Lonergan, née Frisbie, without walking down to chambers and knocking on the door hovered in the slim to none range of the probability meter. But then, a few minutes later, the door banged open again and, rather than the squeaks of Larry Seagle's sneakers, Foxx heard the smart tapping of Barbara Lonergan's heels on the terrazzo floor.

She did not stop at the desk, not to throw back a misdirected letter or to double-check that Seagle had picked up all of Judge Lonergan's deliveries. Instead, she strode right past Foxx and down the corridor.

Foxx got up to follow. Ladies' room, he thought as she punched through the fire doors. But he saw enough through the slowly closing door to see her pass the ladies' room. The corridor then angled, and at that angle was a set of stairs. Barbara started up, and Foxx broke into a run to catch her.

"Mrs. Lonergan," he said.

She stopped, squeezed the handrail, then slowly turned.

"Is there a problem, Officer?" she said.

"No," said Foxx. "I need to ask you a question."

"About what?"

Foxx moved up a step. At his most baleful, he could stare someone into saying something they didn't mean to say or answering a question they never intended to answer. But he needed to lock on to the person's eyes. Barbara Lonergan did not move. He climbed another step, but still fell short of eye level.

"Something from a long time ago," said Foxx.

"How long?" said Barbara.

"Twenty-odd years," said Foxx. "It involves a good friend of mine. Ralphie Rago. Name ring a bell?"

"No," said Barbara.

"How about the boom-boom room?"

"The what?"

"The boom-boom room. It was a—"

"The name says it all, sir," said Barbara. "And I don't have the slightest idea what you are talking about. Now, if you will excuse me, I have a meeting with the administrative judge."

––––––––

Barbara made it up to the sixth-floor landing before the shakes overtook her. She gripped the handrail, pressed her other hand to her chest, and tried to will her heart to stop thumping. First Bill gets attacked on the street by a lunatic, and now this court officer asks her this question. And it wasn't just the question itself that frightened her but the way he asked it, the look in his eye like he already knew the answer. The boom-boom room. Yes, she had heard about it. But like so many things, the name was hung on the room only later, years later. And there was only one person who could have told that officer what he was asking.

Bertha sat at her desk, writing on a legal pad. She looked up just enough to make eye contact, then looked back down. Barbara saw that the door to Judge Patterson's office was closed and that the door to the law clerk's office was open and the law clerk nowhere in sight. She walked up to Bertha's desk.

"Good afternoon, Bertha," she said.

Bertha muttered under her breath, still writing.

"I said, good afternoon, Bertha."

Bertha shrugged. "So who cares," she said, not looking up.

"Bertha, look at me."

Bertha kept writing.

"You need to look at me, Bertha."

Bertha lifted her head, and Barbara slapped her. It was a perfect slap—a hard crack as flesh met flesh.

"What the . . ." Bertha blubbered, covering the four distinct finger marks that rose on her cheek.

"You know exactly what it's about," said Barbara. She shook the sting out of her hand.

"What's going on here?" Judge Patterson stood in his doorway.

"Nothing," said Bertha. She twisted in her chair and pretended to sneeze.

The judge stared doubtfully at Bertha, then turned to Barbara.

"You need to see me?" he said.

Barbara nodded. She could feel herself start to tear up. The judge stepped aside, and Barbara went into his office. He glanced once more at Bertha, then closed the door.

Barbara sat on the sofa and immediately started to cry. The judge settled beside her, some distance between them until her crying intensified and he slid over. She leaned against him, and he hugged her in the loose, perfunctory way she knew so well.

"Bill . . . ," she said, and sobbed even harder.

"What about Bill?" said the judge. "Did something happen to Bill?"

She nodded, then shook her head into his shoulder.

"Yes? No?" the judge said. "Which is it?"

He let go, and Barbara sat upright. A couple of deep breaths, and she was composed enough to speak.

"Bill had a grievance filed against him," she said.

"Oh," said the judge. "Is it related to his . . . ah . . . situation?"

"No," said Barbara. "It comes out of a trial he held in April, before his condition arose."

"He'll fight it, correct?" said Judge Patterson.

"We retained Arnold Delinsky, and a hearing in front of a

commission attorney is scheduled for the first week we are back from vacation."

"And how is Bill bearing up under this?"

"Very well," said Barbara. "He's shown even more signs of improvement over the last few days. And he will receive intense therapy over the vacation. So I have to say, I was feeling good until just a few minutes ago."

"Oh?" said Judge Patterson.

"Someone attacked Bill as we walked around Columbus Park."

"Physically attacked?"

"Yes. It was the man who filed the grievance. He tried to hit Bill. Twice. Luckily, Bill ducked out of the way. I knocked the man down. And then a passerby helped."

"Are you sure it was the same man?" said the judge.

Barbara nodded. "He yelled something about fixing the trial and fixing the complaint."

"We need to report this to the police."

"No," said Barbara. "No police. They would need to interview Bill, and right now he couldn't handle that. I want to leave for vacation immediately so Bill can rest and get the help he needs so that he can put an end to this grievance once and for all. With your permission, of course."

Judge Patterson stroked his beard.

"I know that's asking a lot," said Barbara. "I know we will leave an army of angry lawyers behind."

"They'll live," said Judge Patterson. "You need to do what you need to do, for Bill's sake and for your own. I can handle any emergency on Bill's behalf, as long as your law clerk is available to explain any issue I may need to act on. You just help Bill get well and get past this grievance. We need him here."

"Thank you," said Barbara. She almost choked on the words.

They hugged lightly and then stood up from the sofa. Barbara started toward the door, but Judge Patterson touched her shoulder.

"I saw what you did to Bertha," he said. "I pretended I didn't, but I did. You slapped her. Why? Something she said?"

Barbara nodded, but said nothing else.

"She has a sharp tongue." He rubbed away a track left by a tear. "Anything I should know about?"

"No," said Barbara. "Something personal. It was stupid. I shouldn't have. But after what Bill just went through . . ."

"That's understandable. And I'm not going to order you to apologize or mediate a truce. But I can't have the two of you angry at each other."

CHAPTER 34

The big man grabbed a fistful of shirt at the back of Andrew Norwood's neck.

"Let me go!" Norwood yelled.

He planted his feet, but the big man lifted him off the sidewalk and hurried him across the street. A flatbed with a crane was parked along the back of the criminal courts building, and the big man used it for cover so he could look back at the aftermath of what he just had prevented. In the distance, the woman and a short man were helping the tall old gent toward the intersection at the end of the park.

"Let me go!" Norwood yelled again.

He flailed his arms, but could not reach the big man, who held him at a much longer arm's length.

"I'll let you go if you promise not to hit me."

"Why would I hit you?" said Norwood.

"Why would you hit that old gent?" said the big man.

"Wouldn't you want to know?"

The big man let go of Norwood, who ran neither from him nor at him, but simply fixed his shirt and then his pants with an attitude of meticulous dignity.

"This way," said the big man.

Norwood followed. They walked past the crane to the parking lot that separated the criminal courts from the Manhattan Detention Complex, then headed west on a street so narrow and lined by buildings so tall the sun rarely hit the pavement. Across Broadway, the big man suddenly stopped, yanked open a door, and pushed Norwood inside.

———————

Cannon didn't know what the hell was going on.

It started out like a routine tail job. He picked up Judge Lonergan and his secretary as they exited the rear door of the courthouse. Cannon had not laid eyes on Bill Lonergan in over twenty years, but he still was tall in stature and athletic in his movements, as you would expect of a former basketball star who almost made it in the pros. He still was sharply dressed and impeccably groomed, as you would expect of a successful lawyer who ascended to the bench. His hair was white and thick, and his face, which Cannon remembered as outsized even in relation to his height, seemed to fit him better now than in his middle age. But something Cannon did not expect was the obvious intimacy between the judge and his secretary. And then the explanation suddenly came clear: she was his secretary and his wife.

The Lonergans walked around the block-sized park between the criminal courts and Chinatown, and Cannon followed their meandering pace at twenty yards. He doubted they would make him. The sidewalk was crowded enough that he constantly needed to sidestep people, Mrs. Lonergan had met him only briefly, and the judge had not seen him since he grew his mustache and his gut.

The attack came so suddenly that Cannon did not completely comprehend what his eyes fed his brain. But there it was, happening right in front of him. A gnomish old man leaped out of a duck blind of tall grass and ran at the judge. The judge jumped back, and then his wife stepped forward and slammed her purse into the man's chest. The man fell back, but caught himself on a park bench. He pushed off, aiming his shoulders at the judge's knees. The judge's wife stumbled, and for a moment Cannon thought that the little man would tackle the judge. But then someone stepped in between.

Kehoe, Cannon realized. It was goddam Kehoe.

The judge's wife and a man wearing athletic gear quickly dragged the judge to safety while Kehoe wrestled the little man into submission. Cannon felt a combination of elation and confusion. Kehoe obviously was pursuing the judge, but why did he just save the judge from this angry little man? And who was this angry little man? An accomplice? Or just another man with a vendetta against Bill Lonergan?

Cannon hung back, watching. The judge, supported by his wife and the man in athletic gear, crossed Worth Street to the courthouse. Meanwhile, Kehoe dragged the little man in the other direction. He pinned him to a truck, spoke to him sternly, then pulled him away. Cannon followed. Kehoe and the little man rounded the criminal courthouse and headed west until they went into a bar near Broadway.

Cannon slipped a blue plastic oblong from his pocket and pressed it into his ear. It looked like an old Bluetooth device, but it actually was a sound amplifier. He adjusted the volume, then went into the bar.

———

The bar was dark and dismal, cool, almost empty, and smelling of hops.

"I don't drink," said Norwood.

"Well, I do," said Kehoe. "And I need one."

They claimed stools away from the taps and the few scattered midday drinkers. The bartender ambled over at the same time that a waitress dropped a menu in front of a man who had seated himself in a booth. He was a heavyset man with a walrus mustache and plastic eyeglasses. An old-style Bluetooth device hung blinking from his ear.

Kehoe ordered a pint of beer. Norwood, reluctantly, ordered a seltzer.

"So why did you attack that old gent?" Kehoe said after the bartender set down the drinks.

"What gent? Gent is short for gentleman. And he isn't."

Kehoe lifted his pint glass and watched Norwood over the rim as he took a long pull.

"Aw, it's a long story," Norwood said. "You probably don't want to hear it."

"Try me."

Norwood nipped at his seltzer. The fizz made him cough.

"You sure?" he finally managed to say.

"Sure as shootin'."

"Haven't heard that expression in a while," said Norwood. He took another sip, stifled the urge to cough, and thought about where to begin.

"When I was a boy," he said, "my father had a 1925 Maxwell. Every Sunday he would take me to the county airfield in that car. There was an observation deck and an ice cream stand, and he would buy me an ice cream cone and we would watch the airplanes take off. My father never got rid of that car. He kept it in the garage, but as the years passed, it started to deteriorate. I got older, and he started talking about the two of us working together to restore the car. I wanted to restore it with him, but life kept getting in the way. Or rather, I let life get in the way. By the time I came around, he already was too sick.

"He left the car to me when he died and he put in his will that I should restore it because he would be watching me from above. The estate lawyer said I didn't need to obey the will. He said my father was going senile and that he wrote that paragraph into the will to placate him. Legally speaking, it was a wish, not a command. Well, he didn't know the history, and I couldn't be so cavalier about what my father wished.

"At first I tried to do it myself, but I kept screwing up. So I hired a mechanic who specialized in restoring vintage cars, then shipped the car and all of its parts to his garage. He told me it would take three months. But the three months stretched to six and then to nine, and whenever I asked to see where he was at, he always had some excuse. One day I just showed up cold at his garage. He hadn't done a goddam thing, and the little he did actually made it worse.

"So I sued him. The judge on the case was that old man. Judge Lonergan. Judge William Lonergan. My lawyer said he was a good judge and a nice guy. Well, Judge Lonergan did seem like a nice guy. Actually, the way I saw it, he was too nice a guy. All he cared about was telling jokes and bullshitting with the lawyers, especially the defendant's lawyer. I kept telling my lawyer that the judge seemed too cozy with the other side, but my lawyer kept saying, 'That's just Judge Lonergan. You'll see. He's the fairest there is.' Except he didn't know what I overheard on the last day of the trial. The judge called us in for a settlement conference, but me and the defendant were just too far apart. We left the conference room, but then the judge called the lawyers back in. As the door was closing, I heard the judge say, 'C'mon, fellas, it's only an old car.'"

"That must have hurt," said Kehoe.

"You don't know how much it hurt," said Norwood. "The judge thought the case was a joke and I was some crazy, eccentric guy, not someone who got screwed trying to close a very important circle in his life."

Norwood took a big slug of seltzer and wiped his mouth with his arm.

"I know. You think it sounds crazy. You think I sound crazy."

"Exactly the opposite."

"Really?"

"I understand that something important was taken from you by someone who didn't understand its true value to you. How did the case turn out?"

"He dismissed it. Said I had no cause of action."

"Did you appeal?"

"That costs money, and as an elderly gentleman on a fixed income, that's money I don't have. But I found another way. I filed a complaint with the Judicial Conduct Commission."

"What can happen with that?"

"Best-case scenario for me is he gets thrown off the bench. But I'm not banking on that. The hearing was supposed to be today, but he got a delay until after his vacation."

"How long is that?"

"A month," said Norwood. "Damn, I've never been so frustrated."

"It's only time."

"Well, I don't have the luxury of time. I'm getting older, you know."

"So am I."

"But I'm further along," said Norwood. "And I'm not a well man."

"You looked pretty agile to me earlier."

Norwood laughed, but without mirth.

"What were you going to do? Kill him?"

"No," said Norwood.

"I didn't think so. At least you have the Judicial Conduct Commission looking into this. You need to let the process play out."

"But he's already manipulated the process against me."

"Don't descend to his level. Keep your integrity. If you lose, you'll need it."

They sat in silence for a while. Then Kehoe quickly drained off his beer and took a small square of paper from his wallet.

"What are you writing?" said Norwood.

"My cell number. You start feeling like you might do something stupid, give me a call."

"Are you some kind of therapist?" said Norwood.

"You might say that."

————

Back in chambers, Barbara barely glanced at Larry and immediately went to check on Bill. He was still slouched in his big chair and he still was asleep. A muscle beneath his eye twitched, then stopped, twitched again, then stopped. It was a nervous tic she realized she hadn't seen in a while, since Memorial Day, in fact, when his accident pushed him into his mental tailspin. She always thought he was outwardly confident but inwardly nervous, as if his public stance forced him into public action despite private misgivings. The eye tic had been evidence of his real mood, and she wondered if its return meant the attack had affected him more profoundly than she thought. She combed his hair with her fingers, fixing the part where it had come undone. The tic stopped, and he smiled faintly.

She went back into Larry's office. Rather than sit, she stood with her hip against a corner of the desk, her arms folded.

"There's been a change of plans," she said. "We're leaving for vacation."

"Now?"

"We're leaving for home now. We'll leave for vacation tomorrow."

"But you can't close chambers," said Larry. "Not this week. Lawyers are waiting for decisions on motions. We promised—"

"Yes, and you well know about lawyers waiting for decisions, don't you?"

"Seriously?" said Larry. "You seriously just said that to me?"

"I'm sorry," she said. "I understand your point."

"It's not exactly debatable."

Barbara lifted her hands. She honestly did not believe that she said what she said.

"I truly appreciate all you have done these last few months. But you must understand that my husband's well-being is paramount. I'll do whatever it takes to keep him safe. And right now that means getting him out of harm's way."

"Harm's way?" said Larry. "Was that something you expected to happen? Is it something you think might happen again?"

"No," she said. "It was totally random and probably a case of mistaken identity. But I'm not taking any chances. I'm not going to spend the next four days looking over my shoulder for him."

"But you can't just leave like this."

"I can, and we will," said Barbara. "I already talked to Judge Patterson, and he gave his permission."

Bill began to cough, ending the discussion. Barbara walked back to her desk, but rushed into Bill's office when the coughing intensified. She sat him upright, leaned him forward, and rubbed his back. The coughing subsided.

An hour later, Barbara waited with Bill while the officer assigned to the judges' entrance went out to Worth Street to hail a cab. Even this simple decision wasn't easy. She had considered going to Captain Kearney and asking him for an escort home. Kearney would have spared "the personnel and the vehicle," meaning a pair of court officers and the black sedan used mostly to ferry Judge Patterson to and from meetings at central administration. But she was hesitant to let Kearney know that something had happened to the judge, and she did not want the officers to see Bill in this state. Casual greetings at the back entrance to the courthouse were one thing, thirty minutes of constant contact and observation in a sedan was something else. No, she needed the anonymity of a cab ride, but could not risk the time it would take to hail a cab themselves. That crazy little man could still be out there, watching. And she couldn't bank on the big man coming to Bill's rescue a second time.

The officer came back inside and told Barbara he had found them a cab. Bill thanked him and told him he was doing a great job, though not with his usual gusto. As Bill climbed into the backseat, Barbara mouthed "not feeling well" to the officer. The officer nodded. He closed the door after her and rapped the roof. As the cab pulled away, a curious thought rose unbidden in Barbara's mind. She wondered if they ever would see the courthouse again.

CHAPTER 35

With the Lonergans gone, Larry finally peeled off his sweaty T-shirt, exchanged his athletic eyeglasses for his wire-rimmed bifocals, and buttoned himself into his suit. Bertha was on the phone when he walked into Judge Patterson's chambers. She was speaking low, with her hand cupped around the mouthpiece. She lifted her head and signaled with her eyes that he could go right in. The judge had warned Larry to watch himself around Bertha. *Knows the ropes,* he had said. *Doesn't miss a trick.* And so Larry had been careful. He would knock rather than barge in, sit straight rather than slouch in a chair, speak rather than bark. Today, though, he forgot the protocol. He didn't knock, and then lost the doorknob on the backswing, causing the door to slam.

"Larry," said the judge. He was editing a decision and looked up over his reading glasses.

"What the hell is going on?" said Larry.

"Sorry?"

"You know what I'm talking about."

The judge dropped his pen, then tossed his reading glasses onto the desk.

"Barbara asked permission to get the judge out of town a few days early," he said. "I gave it."

"But why?"

"You know what happened. You saw what happened. Do you

think my giving or not giving permission would have any bearing on what Barbara wanted to do?"

Larry grunted. Barbara Lonergan was a mama lion, Judge Lonergan her cub.

"Look on the bright side, Larry. You get a few peaceful days in chambers. The judge gets a few extra days to prepare. Barbara gets her husband safely out of town. Everyone benefits."

"What does the judge need to prepare for?" said Larry.

"You don't know?" said Judge Patterson.

"Obviously not."

"The man who attacked the judge today filed a grievance against him."

"A Judicial Conduct Commission grievance?"

Judge Patterson nodded.

"Damn," said Larry. "A real grievance? Complaint and all?"

"Sounds like it."

"About what?"

"Conduct at a bench trial. Before your time."

"You know he won't get through a grievance hearing without hanging himself," said Larry.

"Barbara thinks he can. She has a plan."

"What plan?" said Larry. "Aw, what the hell does it matter? She didn't think it important enough to tell me. Did she even tell him?"

"I only heard about this a little while ago myself," said Judge Patterson. "She didn't get into that, but she did tell me she enrolled the judge in a facility that she believes will prepare him."

"I don't know what you see from up here," said Larry. "You might see our statistics, but you don't see him. He's bad. He's around the bend. I see it every day."

"And Barbara sees more of him than either of us," said Judge Patterson. "If she thinks this program will work, who are we to say otherwise?"

Midafternoon quiet at the security desk. The air was motionless. Heat seeped through the mini blinds that hung in the lobby windows. Foxx slouched in his chair, the fingers of one hand beating out the drumline of a tune playing in his head. The desk phone rang. He slowly leaned forward and saw on the readout that the call was coming from Judge Patterson's chambers.

"You blabbed."

"And hello to you, too, Bertha."

"You told her what I said."

"First off, Bertha, you didn't tell me much of anything other than that Barbara Lonergan worked in the steno pool back then. Second, I didn't mention you at all. And third, she denied knowing anything about the boom-boom room."

Bertha mumbled under her breath.

"What was that?" said Foxx.

Bertha mumbled again.

"Bertha."

"I said she's a damn liar."

"What does that mean? She knew about it? She used it? What?"

"We need to talk."

"So talk."

"Not over the phone," said Bertha. "Can you come up here?"

"When I get relieved. That'll be sometime between three thirty and four. What did she say to you?"

"Very little," said Bertha. "But enough."

Foxx's relief did not arrive at three thirty or even three forty-five. Then, just before four, Foxx heard the fire door open. One of the ladies' room attendants ran toward him.

"Please," she said, huffing. "Something happened. She's hurt."

"Who?" said Foxx.

She tugged his arm. "Come now. Quick."

The rules of engagement flashed through Foxx's mind, but since it sounded like someone was in trouble rather than causing trouble, he got up and followed the attendant to the ladies' room.

"In here," she said.

She pushed through the door, and Foxx barreled in behind her. A woman lay facedown on the floor, one arm pinned under her stomach and the other flung over her head. Green disinfectant leaked from a spray bottle onto the tiles.

Foxx crouched beside her and pressed two fingers against her neck. Her pulse felt strong.

"Give me a hand," said Foxx.

The attendant crouched between the unconscious woman and the three stalls. The stalls were empty, each of the big old wooden doors slightly open.

"Make sure her head is okay," Foxx said.

As he rolled the woman over, he saw one of the stall doors quiver. He thought nothing of it until the unconscious woman's eyes snapped open and she said, "Surprise." The stall doors pulled back, and three men rushed out. Two grabbed Foxx under the arms and pulled him to his feet. The third, Orlando Cortez, planted himself a few inches from Foxx's face and smiled.

"Hello, dickhead," he said.

Foxx said nothing.

"Get out," said Cortez.

The two women ran from the ladies' room, slamming the door behind him.

Foxx twisted his shoulders, testing the strength of the two men, who were custodians he knew by sight but not by name. He didn't like what he felt.

Cortez again planted himself in front of Foxx. Not so close this time, more like an arm's length. He didn't smile, he didn't speak, and then without any fanfare, he punched Foxx in the gut.

Foxx doubled over. His vision darkened. A thin cord of saliva leaked out of his mouth, held for a moment, then pulled free and hit the floor.

The two men straightened Foxx up, and Cortez punched him in the gut again. The men straightened Foxx up a second time, and

Cortez punched him for a third. The fourth punch landed slightly higher, just below Foxx's sternum. The air rushed out of his lungs. The two men did not straighten him up this time. Instead, they lowered him to his knees, then twisted him to the floor.

Foxx lay on his side, fighting for breath. The last thing he heard was the scraping of metal on metal. The last thing he felt was a blast of hot air. The last thing he saw was Cortez opening the window that overlooked the light court.

Then he blacked out.

———

Cannon expected Kehoe and the little man to separate as soon as they hit the sidewalk. But they stayed together, heading east across Broadway and then north on Centre Street. Cannon stayed half a block behind, buffeted by swells of tourists heading downtown toward Wall Street, the Battery, and the Statue of Liberty. The traffic light stopped him at Canal Street, and by the time he crossed, the two men already were pulling out of a parking lot in a car driven by Kehoe. Cannon wanted to flag down a cab, jump into the backseat, order the driver to follow that car. But there were no cabs to be found, and so he watched Kehoe's car disappear into the uptown traffic.

Cannon reached Dave's house by midafternoon. Dave sat on his deck, sipping iced tea while down below, the garden hose pumped its inevitable water into the mulch around the cherry sapling. Cannon sat down, drank a glass of iced tea, and collected himself. There was something strangely quiet about the neighborhood, and he eventually realized that the wind had shifted the day's landing pattern elsewhere.

Dave listened skeptically to the idea that brought Cannon back to town. But Cannon sensed a definite arousal in Dave's interest when he described the attack on Judge Lonergan.

"And you're sure it was Kehoe?" said Dave.

"Positive," said Cannon.

"But if he saved the judge from that little guy, doesn't that go against your theory?"

"No, because it's consistent with his MO," said Cannon. "I listened to every word they said."

"How'd you manage that?"

Cannon slipped his Bluetooth-looking device from his shirt pocket.

"It's called the big ear," he said.

"Came with your private eye kit?" said Dave.

"Very funny, but it works. The little guy has some beef with the judge. That's what led to the attack. Kehoe tried to talk him down. Did a pretty damn good job of sympathizing with him."

"But you're convinced Kehoe intends to kill everyone who's connected with that case?"

"Everyone who isn't already dead," said Cannon. "Judge Lonergan is the only major player left alive. Unless he wants to go after the Van Gelders themselves."

"What about you?" said Dave. "You were part of that trial, weren't you?"

"Me?" said Cannon.

"Yeah, you. You were the first face Kehoe saw every time he walked into the courthouse."

CHAPTER 36

A groggy Foxx offered no resistance as Cortez's two compatriots flipped him onto his stomach. One pressed a knee against his spine and bound his hands behind his back while the other bound his ankles with lengths of clothesline Cortez sawed off with a four-inch blade. Cortez, meanwhile, measured out the distance between the windowsill and the pipes that ran from the middle of the three toilets into the wall. He then added three feet for knotting and ten feet to create some suspense.

Cortez tied the end of the rope to the toilet pipes. He knew nothing about which knot would best hold a 160-pound man hanging at a distance of thirty feet. He didn't quite care, and when he finished the knot and yanked it tight, he used his blade to cut a gash halfway through the rope.

The two men stood Foxx upright as Cortez slapped him awake.

"See how you like this, dickhead," he said.

He climbed onto the radiator and pushed the window up one last inch.

"Give him here," he said.

The two men lifted Foxx, Cortez grabbed his shirt, and they all fed him through the window until gravity took over and the clothesline scraped across the window frame. Cortez poked his head outside. Ten feet down, the foreshortened Foxx swung against the sunbaked brick ninety feet above the light court floor.

"Have fun, dickface," he said.

He jumped off the radiator, dusted his hands, and ushered the other two out of the lavatory.

Foxx did not know the exact physiological effects of hanging upside down for an extended period of time. All he knew was that his stomach hurt like hell and the hot sun seared every square inch of exposed skin.

He took stock of his predicament. Cortez and his boys hadn't dropped him out the window; they'd hung him out the window, which meant they intended to scare him rather than kill him. But the difference between intent and result could be meaningless. It was late on an August afternoon. Almost half the courthouse workers were out on vacation. Those who remained often ducked out early.

Foxx squinted against the glare. He counted seven visible windows in the light court, seven possible vantage points where someone could spot him. Every one of those windows had their blinds closed tight against the bright heat. Officers who made the day's final sweep of the courthouse didn't necessarily include the light courts in their observations. The custodians might look out, but then again, three custodians hung him here.

First he heard the scraping of metal on metal. Then he felt a tremble in the clothesline. He opened his eyes. After hanging almost motionless for a time, he was swinging again. But it wasn't the slow, stately back and forth like the pendulum of a grandfather clock. It was more staccato, as if someone kept snapping the line.

Suddenly, he felt a lurch. He moved upward. Not far. Barely an inch, if that. Then he felt a second lurch, and now a brick that had been level with his eye was two inches below.

A slow rhythm developed. He felt a tremble, then a lurch, then another brick sank an inch or two below eye level. The progress was slow and steady, never more than two inches at a time. At one point—he estimated he had risen halfway to the window—the lurches stopped and the slow swinging began again.

"Hey," he called. "Don't quit now."

There was no response. But after a moment he felt the tremble, then the lurch, and then he was moving upward again.

Finally, his feet snagged on something. He couldn't see, but from its position and feel, he thought it was the windowsill. He hoped it was the windowsill. A voice muttered "dammit." Nothing happened for a while; then he dropped several inches. His stomach flipped.

"You still there?" he called.

No answer came. He hung motionless, his nose pressed against the hot brick.

"You didn't leave, didya?"

Still no answer. He tried to twist himself and curl his neck at the same time. But he could not get a good look at anything beyond his waist.

Then came a tremble and a lurch. The rope moved, but he went down instead of up. This wasn't help, he thought. This was Cortez. Checking on him. Or worse.

But no second tremble came. No second lurch dropped him deeper into the light court. Two hands grabbed his feet and twisted them as one might turn a steering wheel. Foxx twisted himself in the same direction. His chest rubbed against the brick wall, then his shoulders, and then finally his back. He had turned 180 degrees, and now his back was flat against the bricks.

After a moment, he lurched upward. His heels cleared the windowsill, and then he could bend his knees. He heard panting inside the ladies' room, and though the rope still pulled at his ankles, he kept his knees sharply bent over the sill. He was that far inside and did not want to give up his newly won territory.

Two arms wrapped around his shins. The arms pulled, and his butt scraped across the edge of the sill until he leveled off, teetered for a moment on the base of his spine, and then tumbled inside.

He bounced off something hard—the radiator, he instantly realized—and then landed on the floor.

"Sorry," said a voice.

Foxx shook his head and focused his eyes.

"Bertha?" he said.

"Who else were you expecting? Captain Kearney?"

"How long was I out there?"

"How would I know? It's after five."

"Geez," said Foxx. "More than an hour. How'd you find me?"

"I didn't. I waited for you to come up and talk. When you didn't, I decided to leave. This is the ladies' room closest to chambers. I saw the rope." Bertha took a pocketknife from her purse. "Move."

Foxx rolled sideways, and Bertha sawed through the knot that bound his hands. Then he rolled back, and she sawed through the knot at his ankles. He could see now that the rope led back into the middle stall and that Bertha had wrapped the slack around the length of the wooden door as she hauled him up.

"I coulda died out there," he said. He patted his cheeks, which raged with sunburn. His mouth felt parched.

"Cortez, right?" said Bertha.

"And two other custodians, not to mention the ladies who tricked me into coming in here."

"Always a sucker for the ladies," said Bertha. "And it's not that you coulda died out there. You woulda died out there."

She got up, then reached a hand down and pulled him to his feet. She wasn't just a meaty, buxom, middle-aged lady. Her arms and legs were solid muscle.

"Look at this," she said. She unwound the clothesline off the door, then bent it where Cortez had sawed the gash. Less than a quarter of the fibers were still intact.

"I was praying it wouldn't break right in front of me," she said.

"Good thing you did," said Foxx.

They left the ladies' room. Bertha immediately crossed the corridor to the stairs.

"You don't plan to report this to Kearney, do you?" she said.

Foxx shook his head.

"I didn't think so." She started up. "Judge Patterson's gone for the day. We have chambers to ourselves."

They sat in the judge's private office, which had twin sofas set at right angles in one corner. Bertha gave Foxx a bottle of cold water, which he drank down in big swigs, pausing only to rub the raw spots on his wrists and ankles.

"I'd put something on your face, too," she said.

Foxx got up. Amid Judge Patterson's diplomas and bar admissions was a framed photo showing the judge's swearing-in ceremony many years earlier. Foxx's reflection in the glass was clear enough to prove Bertha's point.

He sat back down.

"So?" he said.

"So," said Bertha, "I told you that the only person still around here who worked in the steno pool the year of Calvin Lozier's murder was Barbara Lonergan. Now I want to tell you the rest."

"Does that mean you know who killed him?"

"I'll tell you what I know, and you can decide what to think."

"What changed your mind?" said Foxx.

Bertha waved his question away.

"My father was the personal attorney for the city council president," she said. "He wanted me to find a job, I wanted to find a husband, so he pulled a few strings and got me into the steno pool. I started the same day as Barbara, and believe me, she was nothing like what she is now. She looked like a waif and was as meek as a mouse. So like all polar opposites, we had an attraction for each other. As friends, of course.

"We started eating lunch together, then we started going out to meet guys together. She slowly began to primp herself up and emerge from her shell. I dated a few of the guys I met, but nothing ever lasted. She dated no one, like she was saving herself for someone who'd never come her way. But the funny thing was, as things turned out, with all the looking we did outside the courthouse, we both ended up meeting someone inside the courthouse."

"Calvin Lozier?" said Foxx.

Bertha shook her head. "Fact was, we were both seeing guys for months before we each caught on about the other."

"You were both seeing Calvin Lozier?" said Foxx.

"Will you shut up?" said Bertha. "No, we were not both seeing Calvin Lozier. We were both seeing guys and we were both seeing them in the boom-boom room. A lot. There were weeks on end when it seemed that if I wasn't there at lunch hour, then she was. And vice versa. It was so obvious. Stupid obvious. One day, she'd come back to the pool after lunch looking flushed and mussed and satisfied. The next day, I'd come back looking the same way.

"Finally we both got tired of the secrecy. I don't remember if she approached me or I approached her, but we confessed our affairs to one another."

"Who had Calvin Lozier?" said Foxx.

"She did, but I never knew that for a fact. I can only say that I didn't."

"Who did you have?"

"Well, now you're jumping ahead again," said Bertha. "We'd each been sworn to secrecy."

"Calvin Lozier was married, wasn't he?" said Foxx.

"Yes, he was, but we only found out after the murder," said Bertha. "No, the secrecy was because these two guys were both running for judge, actually trying to win the nomination for the only seat in play that year."

"And they thought word of an affair with a steno pool typist would kill it?" said Foxx.

"I don't know what her guy thought, but mine was adamant," said Bertha. "Anyway, we talked all around who was who, and things were fine until summer."

"The summer Lozier was killed?"

"Yes," said Bertha. "The murder was in late August, but in early June, something happened with Barbara. First thing I noticed was that she didn't come back to the steno pool from lunch one afternoon. Next day she came in looking like, what's that old expression, like someone rode her hard and put her away wet. I dragged her out of the steno pool and into an alcove. She didn't want to talk about it, but I kept at her until she told me that her guy broke up with her because he didn't think she would make a good wife for a judge."

"Come again?" said Foxx.

"You heard me," said Bertha. "He couldn't see her as a judge's wife. Now, I knew a bit about politics. I had connections then and I still have connections now. I knew who was getting that nomination, and it wasn't Lozier. I also knew, because I wasn't stupid, that my guy was interested in me for one thing only. And it wasn't what happened in the boom-boom room."

"He needed your connections," said Foxx.

"Exactly. I didn't care. I needed some fun out of life, and I needed to make my own connections, too. But, Barbara, well, she was still a naïf at heart. She really believed she was in love.

"Well, a little deeper into the summer, my guy broke up with me. It wasn't a surprise, because I knew I was disposable once the nomination was in hand. I didn't care because along the way, I picked up some information about him that would come in handy one day. Then came the murder. We were kind of insulated in the steno pool, so word filtered in slowly. First, we heard there was an assault. Then someone was hurt. Then someone was killed. Then that someone was a law clerk. I was sitting next to Barbara when word came it was Calvin."

"How did she react?" said Foxx.

"She got up and left the pool," said Bertha. "We didn't see her for three days."

"She was in mourning?" said Foxx.

"If she was, it was private. See, the murder was the first shock. The second was the revelation that Calvin was married. I mean, he must have slept with two dozen women in the building. Law clerks, secretaries. There were even a couple of judges who fancied him. Personally, I couldn't see it, but there it was. Once the word got out, the wake and the funeral drew lots of gawkers. I didn't miss a minute of any session, so I know that Barbara didn't attend.

"Anyway, the convention came and my ex got the nomination. Six weeks later, he was elected judge. It was then, in the period between getting elected and being sworn in, that he began to see Barbara. It didn't last long. There were reasons I kind of suspected then and won't go into now, but it pissed me off and we haven't been friendly ever since."

"Patterson was your ex, right?" said Foxx.

Bertha nodded.

"So why do you work for him?"

"Why not?" said Bertha. "It's a job, and he's a decent judge, and I told you I needed to make my own connections. So he's it. Our time together was so long ago and so brief, it's almost like it never happened."

"Then why are you not friendly with Barbara?" said Foxx.

"Ask her, not me."

"And why did you open up about this? I never would have thought to question you again."

"Because when Barbara came up this afternoon to see the judge, she slapped me across the face. I knew it was because you'd asked her about the boom-boom room, and I knew that she knew you only knew to ask her because of me."

"Why did she slap you?"

"That I don't know. But there is a kind of weird relationship between Barbara and Judge Patterson that goes beyond their brief fling all those years ago. She visits, and they talk behind closed doors. I haven't been able to figure it out, but it may have something to do with Judge Lonergan or it may have something to do with Larry Seagle."

"The law clerk?" said Foxx.

"Yeah," said Bertha. "Last spring Judge Lonergan's law clerk up and quit, which surprised lots of people because she'd been with Judge Lonergan for so long and he was such a pleasure to work with. I know that Judge Patterson put Larry Seagle in touch with Judge Lonergan."

CHAPTER 37

Foxx's evening commute back to City Island had many varia-
tions. A taxi ride was the rarest, but with his face still afire,
his wrists and ankles chafed, and his spine overstretched, he
decided to splurge. He had much to ponder, and he needed to get
back home as quickly and comfortably as possible and have at it.

The cab was stuck in traffic near the Thirty-fourth Street heli-
port when Foxx's cell phone buzzed.

"Foxx." It was the nurse from the prison medical block. "It's
time."

"He died?" said Foxx. His stomach clenched.

"No," said the nurse. "But he's taken a turn. He is now in a phase
when we say the patient is actively dying."

"What does that mean?"

"It means that bodily functions and organ systems are shutting
down. You need to make some decisions."

"Like what?" said Foxx.

"Like what we should do and what we shouldn't do."

"How long does he have?"

"Hard to say," said the nurse. "People who are actively dying can
last for hours, days, sometimes a week."

"I need to know about him."

"I have no idea. Sorry."

"Keep him alive as long as possible," said Foxx. "I need to see
him one more time. And I need to talk to him."

"He can't talk anymore. The morphine drip—"

"I don't need him to talk to me. I need to talk to him."

"Then you best get here right away."

"I can't," said Foxx. "I have nothing to tell him yet."

"This is not a game," said the nurse. "We are on his time, not yours."

"I agreed to act as his proxy. So now I'm acting. I want you to do everything to keep him alive. Everything."

He stabbed the phone to end the call and looked out the cab window. A helicopter rose off the pad, rocking side to side until it lowered its nose and sped down the East River.

Foxx punched in another number and waited for an answer.

"You still there? Good. I'm on my way."

The inspector general's office suite was in the central administration building, which stood where Beaver Street met Lower Broadway, just south of the Wall Street bull. The IG's private office had windows that looked out over the Battery, into New York Harbor, and across to the Statue of Liberty. Theoretically, anyway. Those windows had thick, daylight blotting drapes, which Foxx never had seen parted.

Bev sat behind her desk, hovering on the edge of the cone of light a high-intensity lamp aimed at a pile of paper. A conference table formed a T with the front of her desk. Foxx took a seat in the right corner. From this angle, he saw only her huge glasses, her blunt features, the suggestion of thick hair.

"Did you enjoy your first day back on the job?" said Bev.

"More than you can imagine," said Foxx. He knew that Bev suffered from migraines, which she counteracted with the daylight blotting drapes and the seancelike ambience. He sat in silence, grateful for the darkness because he didn't need to explain his own haggard appearance.

Bev leaned into the light.

"To what do I owe the pleasure of your company?" she said.

"I need to know about a law clerk named Larry Seagle." He spoke offhandedly, not looking up.

"Why do you need to know about him?"

"Not sure yet," said Foxx. "He works for Judge Lonergan. I don't see them as a pair."

"You and me both," said Bev.

She snapped her intercom, whispered some orders to her secretary, then leaned back into the darkness. Several minutes passed while Foxx patted his cheeks, rubbed his wrists, arched his back. Eventually the door opened and shut, allowing him a stroboscopic glimpse of Bev's secretary carrying a file folder. She set it down on the edge of the desk blotter, then left the office.

Bev's hand reached out into the light. She opened the folder briefly, then let it fall shut. "Seagle's had just about every problem under the sun," she said. "Drugs, alcohol, suspicion of fraud. Yet every time one judge has enough of his antics, another one lines up to hire him. His last escapade was the worst. He was working for a judge with a high-volume assignment in Kings County. Got behind in his motions and started hiding the oldest ones in a locked file cabinet. You know how judges need to report their undecided motions at the end of each quarter? Well, Seagle prepared clean reports for his judge, and the judge signed off on them. Then some lawyers who had been waiting over a year for their motions to be decided complained to the judge. The judge looked into it, and Seagle's whole scam unraveled. He hadn't broken any criminal laws, just flouted a bunch of court rules. So the case came here."

"Nothing stuck?" said Foxx.

"Actually, everything stuck," said Bev. "He was banned from working for the court system for twenty years, which would have put him well into his dotage."

"So how does he end up working for Judge Lonergan?"

"Under our deal he couldn't be hired as a staff attorney by the courts. But we couldn't stop a judge from hiring him as a law clerk because that is a personal appointment. Not that I didn't try. Soon as I caught wind that Judge Lonergan intended to hire him, I shot off a letter suggesting he appoint someone else. He never answered my letter, which bothered me because I knew of Judge Lonergan's reputation and I couldn't see why he would consider someone like Seagle. Are you asking because you think he's involved in Lozier's murder?"

"Was he even around then?" said Foxx.

"He's been around forever," said Bev.

CHAPTER 38

The sky was almost full dark by the time Kehoe pulled onto the gravel patch behind the house. Dinner was long over by now, and he could tell from the windows on the upper floors which of the other boarders were in and which were out. The pregnant couple waiting to close on their new house were in, as was the newly divorced middle-aged man with the consumptive cough and the vampire pallor. The young medical-supplies rep was out, as she had been the previous two nights, wining and dining doctors.

He walked around front, then crossed the lawn to the steps. It had been a long day, and he was tired now. Missing dinner didn't bother him. Avoiding the others actually was an unintended benefit. The husband was sickeningly attentive to his wife, as if she couldn't carry a baby and chew gum at the same time. The divorced man was bitter as hell. Either get over it or do something about it, Kehoe wanted to scream at him. But that would just provoke a coughing jag and ruin everyone's night. The sales rep, well, he hadn't actually spoken to her, but she oozed self-absorption. No, tonight, he just wanted to get to his room and go to sleep.

The house had a wide front porch. One side was screened in; the other was open to the air and the bugs, of which this town seemed to have millions. He slapped a mosquito on his arm as he reached for the door.

The lights were low inside. In the common room, the TV

flickered without sound. At the end of the hallway, light from inside the kitchen outlined the swinging door. He stood still for a moment, letting the strap of his backpack drop from his shoulder to his elbow as his eyes adjusted to the dimness.

"Welcome back," said a voice.

She stood halfway up the stairs, one hand clutching the handrail. He blinked her into better focus and saw that she wore a light-colored caftan. Her other hand held a wineglass.

"Thank you," he said.

She came down the stairs with a processional air, her hand gliding along the rail as one foot and then the other took turns reaching for the next step.

"Hungry?" she said.

He wanted to say no, but could not get the word out.

"I saved you a plate." She reached the bottom of the stairs. Her hand stayed on the rail while she took a sip of wine, then rose as if to touch his face before she thought better and let it drop to her side.

"This way," she said, and headed down the hallway to the kitchen.

He followed, too tired to resist. She pushed open the door, and the light rushed out at him. She was barefoot, he could see. The caftan hugged her hips. Her hair, down instead of pinned up as it was during the day, was a pleasing mix of gray and blond.

"Still hot in here from earlier," she said.

A wall fan over the stove whirred.

She opened the refrigerator and poured herself a bit more wine.

"How about you?" she said.

"Just water."

"Sure." She filled a glass from the faucet, then lifted a plate covered with aluminum foil from the stove top. "Let's go out to the porch. It's much cooler there."

The screens muted the harsh light from the streetlamps. Like wearing sunglasses, he thought as he settled into a chair. She opened a snack table in front of him, produced silverware from a small sideboard, and lifted off the foil.

"Voilà," she said.

She sat on the love seat, then swung her legs onto the other cushion. The move pulled the hem of her caftan up above her knees. She crossed her ankles. He caught himself staring. She had nice legs.

"How was your day?" she said.

"I took a walking tour of the Financial District," he said, "then broke away for lunch in Chinatown." He forked a chunk of chicken into his mouth and chewed it down. "Then I saved a man."

"From what?"

"From another man."

"A mugging?" she said.

"No. It was more than that."

He told her about coming upon one old man attacking another old man and a woman he took to be the wife of the victim trying to protect her husband. He explained how he separated the two men and immobilized the attacker until the wife could drag her husband out of harm's way. Then he recounted how he took the man to a bar, sat him down, and listened to his story. Because he knew there had to be a story.

"The man turned out to be very angry at the other man for doing him wrong," he said. "It was kind of sad, really. He feels he was treated unfairly, and from what he told me, he probably was. But everyone is treated unfairly at one time or another, and only some get twisted by it."

She listened, rapt, sipping her wine. Whenever he looked away to cut another piece of chicken or to lift his water glass to his lips, he sensed her eyes drinking him in. He had felt this interest when he first arrived, when she led him up the stairs and showed him to his room. And now, well, maybe he would see where this went. Or maybe he wouldn't.

He finished the food and the story at the same time. She got up from the love seat, lifted the snack table away, swung one leg over his knees, and sat facing him on his lap.

"Is this okay?" she said.

"It's surprising."

She backed off his lap, crouched on the floor, and separated his knees.

"I'm full of surprises," she said.

This time the cab returned Foxx to City Island without anyone buzzing his cell phone. He paid the fare and let the cab circle around him, tires crunching on the sandy pavement, before he trudged up the front steps. The daybed on the porch tempted him, but he resisted. He unlocked the door and turned on the kitchen light.

He took off his clothes, doused the lights, and crawled under the covers. Despite the heat of the humid night, he felt a chill. It was the same chill he would feel after a long day at the beach. At least the chill felt mildly pleasant. His spine felt like he'd spent the afternoon on a medieval rack.

He didn't think he had fallen asleep, but suddenly Ellen was in bed.

"Hey," she said.

"Hey," he grunted. She felt cool alongside him.

"You okay?" she said.

"Fine."

Her finger brushed his forehead. "Do you have a fever?"

"Nah," he said. "Too much sun."

At home, Barbara was busy, thankfully busy because she did not want to think. She needed to get Bill situated, arrange for tomorrow's car service, fix their dinner, and then pack for their monthlong stay in the country. In the past, Bill always had packed for himself. He was no help this time, but on the other hand, he needed little for the Keystone beyond underwear, slippers, and several sets of warm-up suits. Luckily, he felt comfortable in warm-up suits. He usually lounged in them during the winter, so he had three in relatively good shape. He also had a fourth in mint condition—an official New York Knicks warm-up suit she had bought for his sixtieth birthday. Bill never wore it, because the very idea of a man his age in professional basketball warm-up togs made him feel like a wannabe. She corrected him, saying he never was a wannabe but a shoulda-been. There was a huge difference between the two.

She planned to take this warm-up suit along because she wanted the staff to know that Bill had been a professional basketball player, at least until that career-ending injury in his first exhibition game. People always seemed to have an outsized regard for professional athletes, even more so than for judges.

The packing exhausted her, and it was past midnight when she climbed into bed beside Bill. Mission accomplished, she thought, as sleep immediately overcame her.

She popped awake in darkness. No, she thought, as she read the digits on the alarm clock. *3:15*. Not tonight. Not now.

She got out of bed, gulped down a Scotch and milk cocktail, and got back into bed. No avail. Dammit, she thought. Her last bout with insomnia lasted several weeks after Bill's accident. She would wake up with uncontrollable dark thoughts playing a continuous loop in her head. Eventually, she adjusted. Bill's condition became the new normal, and undisturbed sleep followed. The grievance could have caused another spate of sleepless nights, but hiring Delinsky and arranging for the Keystone quelled her subconscious fears.

Now came the attack and the disquieting thought that someone who wanted to hurt Bill was out there. She got out of bed and shuffled silently and alone through the darkened apartment. The living room windows looked down on the street. She stood at the window, her eyes closed and her hand raised. She understood now that something had awakened her and called her out of bed, not to drink the Scotch and milk but to look out this window. Slowly, her fingers insinuated themselves between the drapes. Her other hand joined in, and after a deep breath she spread the drapes apart. Then she opened her eyes.

Across the street, a figure stood behind a tree. For a moment, she thought it was the man who had saved Bill from that nasty little runt. But when she blinked, the figure transformed itself into a shadow thrown by the headlights of a passing car.

Barbara went back to the bedroom and climbed into bed. Bill's breath caught, held, then started again. Only then did she realize that she was holding her own breath as well. She rolled over and pulled the sheet tight across her shoulder. Even the illusion that someone was out there watching over them comforted her. She fell asleep within a minute.

CHAPTER 39

Foxx arrived at his fifth-floor security post the next morning with a semblance of a plan, which was several steps above his usual method of winging it, which is what he had done when he caught Barbara Lonergan yesterday afternoon.

He had drifted off to sleep last night with many scenarios running in his head. Later, he woke up with one scenario that had sorted itself out from among the others. He would approach Barbara in a way that was honest—"I'm trying to help a dying man rest easy"—but firm—"I know you and Calvin Lozier had a relationship. I know he broke it off with you. I know he was a jerk. I need to know everything you know because no one else knows as much."

Ellen lay beside him, gently snoring. He nudged her awake.

"Not now, Foxx."

"No, I need to talk."

The sheets rustled and the mattress creaked as Ellen sat up.

"What?"

"I don't need your irony right now," said Foxx. He explained what he wanted her to do.

"Play the part of Barbara Lonergan?" said Ellen. "I never even met her."

"Tighten your ass and stiffen your lips," said Foxx. "That'll put you in the right frame of mind."

Ellen played the role well enough for Foxx to feel moderately prepared. Now, sitting at the desk as the last few officers signed the captain's clipboard, he was thinking about how to set up the encounter. Going to chambers would be messy with the judge and Larry Seagle in adjoining offices. Waiting for Barbara to come out to the desk was too chancy. The best plan would be to call chambers and say that someone was at the desk to see her. It was the plan he decided to use until Captain Kearney clapped his hand on his shoulder.

"Judge Lonergan and the wife are gone," Kearney whispered confidentially. "Might be some irate lawyers. Let the staff handle all inquiries."

"I thought they were here till Friday," said Foxx.

"They were but now they're not. I heard this directly from Judge Patterson. He gave them his blessing."

Cannon sat on a bench with a clear view of the street-level brass door on the northwest face of the courthouse. Some discreet reconnaissance had revealed that this door was the judges' entrance and that the two bright orange cones standing curbside on Worth Street marked the spot where judges alighted from their rides.

His elation over finding Kehoe had faded overnight, leaving him with his customary confusion over what to do next. Clearly, Kehoe was circling, and Cannon, somehow, needed to be there when Kehoe finally struck. Cannon needed to know where Judge Lonergan lived, but even Dave's attempts to find the address came up empty. Still, the judge needed to come to the courthouse, and so Cannon decided to pick up the trail there.

He waited as eight o'clock became eight thirty and eight thirty became nine. When nine thirty came, he pushed himself off the bench and trudged up the front steps to the main entrance. He followed the same route as he had last week, into the rotunda, up the elevator, and around the circular hall to the corridor that led to Judge Lonergan's courtroom.

The corridor was jammed with lawyers again, and rather than shoulder his way through, Cannon waited until the courtroom opposite Lonergan's opened and the lawyers drained away like water in a bathtub. As he reached the door to Judge Lonergan's courtroom, he could see the windows were blotted. It was a common trick, he knew, to thwart prying eyes. But one of these cardboard squares doubled as a sign that read: COURT RECESS TILL SEPTEMBER 8.

Cannon bumped the doors with his elbow, but the dead bolt held fast.

"Shit," he said.

He knew the drill and took the elevator to the fifth floor. The same officer as last week, the one with the silver hair and intense eyes, sat behind the desk. His hair was just as silver, but his eyes were less intense, almost sleepy.

"I was just at Judge Lonergan's courtroom," said Cannon. "There was a sign on the door about being in recess till September."

Foxx shrugged.

"I need to know if that means the judge is on vacation."

Foxx slowly leaned forward and picked up the phone to call chambers. Larry Seagle answered.

"Got someone here asking if the judge is on vacation," said Foxx. He covered the phone. "You were here last week, weren't you?"

Cannon nodded and stated his name.

"His name is Cannon," said Foxx. "He was here last week."

Foxx listened, then relayed the response to Cannon.

"The sign means what it says, he says. The judge is on vacation."

"Does that mean a true vacation?" said Cannon.

"He wants to know if that means a true vacation," said Foxx. He listened, then told Cannon, "If you're asking whether he's out of town and unavailable, the answer is yes."

"Can I find out where?" said Cannon.

"You hear that?" Foxx said into the phone.

He held the receiver away from his ear. Cannon could hear squawking, small and indecipherable.

"He says he can't say," said Foxx. He hung up the phone.

Cannon went out of the courthouse and into the park, feeling he had been treed but good. He sat on a bench and hung his head. The idea of using Judge Lonergan as bait to catch Kehoe had been his last best hope. Now, unless Kehoe happened to show up, that hope was gone.

He sat up straight and tilted his head back. There was nothing left to do but go home, confess to Sarah that his plan had turned to naught, wait for Judge Lonergan to turn up dead, then go back to Rousma with his theory proved but useless in a court of law.

He straightened his head and blinked because he couldn't believe his eyes. He blinked again, but nothing changed.

When Foxx's midmorning relief arrived, he made a beeline to Judge Lonergan's chambers. The entry door was unlocked, as was the custom at 60 Centre Street, and Foxx entered without knocking, as was not strictly proper but was marginally acceptable since the door opened into the law clerk's office and Foxx, at least to the untrained eye, looked like he belonged.

Larry Seagle sat behind his desk as if he expected a boxball game to break out. He wore a T-shirt rather than a dress shirt and his bug-eyed athletic glasses rather than his tiny round spectacles.

"Casual Tuesday?" said Foxx.

Larry forced a laugh.

"Are you here about that Cannon fella?" he said. "Barbara warned me he could be trouble."

"I took care of him," said Foxx.

"Oh," said Larry. He looked down at the work on his desk, then back up at Foxx with a puzzled expression. "Then what can I do for you?"

"You can tell me where the Lonergans went."

"I thought you took care of that fella."

"I did."

"So who wants to know?"

"I do. I need to talk to Barbara Lonergan."

"You can talk to her when she gets back in September," said Larry.

"It can't wait."

"It'll have to," said Larry.

"I said it can't." Foxx summoned his baleful stare.

"Do you want her phone number?"

"No. I need to talk to her face-to-face."

"About what?"

"That's my business."

"Hey, last I looked, you're only a court officer and she's a judge's wife."

Foxx's baleful stare softened into a patronizing smile. He sat on the edge of Larry's desk.

"I may be only a court officer, but I also work for the inspector general, who happens to be very interested in why a judge like Judge Lonergan hired a law clerk like you."

"A judge's law clerk is a personal appointment," said Larry. "You know that."

"I know," said Foxx. "But sometimes force can be brought to bear on a judge."

"Like what?"

"Well, I know the IG wrote a letter to Judge Lonergan and asked that he not appoint you. Judge Lonergan never answered."

"He didn't need to answer," said Larry. "He already made up his mind. So why should he waste his time?"

"Because not answering a letter isn't like Judge Lonergan, which makes me wonder if he even saw the letter," said Foxx.

"I don't know what you're talking about," said Seagle. "If there was a letter from the IG, and I don't know that there was, it went to the judge before he hired me. Is that what you want to talk to Barbara Lonergan about?"

"Actually not," said Foxx.

"Then what is it?"

"It has nothing to do with you."

"Then why can't you tell me?"

"It would make a difference?"

"Depends on what it is," said Seagle.

"I'm looking into the murder of Calvin Lozier," said Foxx. "He was a law clerk who worked in this building. He was murdered down in the basement in a room called the boom-boom room."

"I heard something about that," said Seagle. "Some janitor got put away for it. Why does the IG care?"

"She doesn't," said Foxx. "I do. That janitor is a friend of mine. He's dying in prison and he wants to know who really did it."

"And you think Barbara knows?" said Seagle.

"I don't know what she knows, if she knows anything at all," said Foxx. "But she's one of the few people who worked here when the murder occurred."

"That doesn't mean anything."

"In her case, it does," said Foxx.

"But you can't tell me."

"I already told you too much."

Seagle ripped a sheet off a legal pad and began to write. Foxx glanced at the wall behind the desk.

"I didn't think you were old enough," he said, "and that's a compliment."

"Old enough for what?" said Seagle.

Foxx pointed at a framed diploma.

"To have graduated from college then," he said.

Seagle folded the sheet and handed it to Foxx.

"It's in the Berkshires. Their vacation home. They left a couple of hours ago. You turn up there, you better have a good explanation. You didn't get this from me."

———————

Cannon stood up. He adjusted his belt and re-tucked his shirt, tightened his glasses and patted the tufts of hair behind his ears. If working as a private detective taught him anything, it taught him that he needed to have a story. The story that he needed right now formed in his mind as he crossed the park to the angry little man who had attacked Judge Lonergan.

"Andrew Norwood?" he said.

Norwood looked up from his park bench. An automatic smile flashed on his face, then faded.

"My name is Robert Cannon," said Cannon. He opened his wallet just enough for Norwood to register his retired court officer badge. "I want to talk to you about Judge Lonergan, specifically the grievance you filed against him with the Judicial Conduct Commission."

"Who says I did?"

"I say," said Cannon. "And you not only filed a grievance, you also attacked Judge Lonergan yesterday."

Norwood stood up, but Cannon shoved him back down. He sat beside the little man, his bulk wedging him into a corner, his hand clamped on his scrawny forearm.

"I'm not a cop, Mr. Norwood," said Cannon. His tone turned soothing. "I'm not here to arrest you or discipline you or even scare you. In fact, I kind of like that you attacked the judge."

"You do?"

"He needed to be shaken up a bit."

"He did?"

"He feels too comfortable, don't you think?"

"He does?" said Norwood. "I mean, he does. But why do you care?"

"Because I'm on your side."

"You are?"

"I'm part of a watchdog group looking into favoritism on the part of the Judicial Conduct Commission. We've been tracking your grievance."

"I thought grievances are confidential," said Norwood.

"They are," said Cannon. "But there are people who believe that the commission is like the fox watching the henhouse."

"Really?" said Norwood. "Like who?"

"People who've gotten tangled up in the law, then gotten burned by judges. It doesn't just happen to little people, and when big people get burned, they usually do something about it."

"I still don't understand how you know."

"We've managed to infiltrate the commission," said Cannon. "We have people on the inside."

"Like who? Brundage?"

Cannon said nothing.

"Don't tell me." Norwood smiled. "That receptionist?"

"I'm not at liberty to say," said Cannon, though he arched his eyebrows to imply that maybe he would. "I have a problem, Mr. Norwood," he continued. "I'm part of a two-man team assigned to you and your case. You met the other man yesterday. Thomas Kehoe. He stopped your assault on the judge."

"Him?" said Norwood. "He didn't say anything about that. I thought he was just passing by."

"He wasn't. He was watching you," said Cannon. "And the fact that he didn't tell you means that he was doing his job well."

"But you told me," said Norwood.

"That's because I need your help, Mr. Norwood. I'm up a tree. My job is to observe the judge to see if I can spot anything that bears on your grievance."

"Like what?"

"Like anything," said Cannon. "You'd be surprised."

"So what's the problem?" said Norwood.

"I was just at his courtroom. He's already left for his vacation and won't be back for a month."

"So it's true," Norwood muttered.

"What's true?"

Norwood explained how the commission's investigative interview was to be this week, but that the investigating counsel, this Brundage he mentioned earlier, allowed the judge to adjourn it until after his vacation.

"Shoulda been yesterday," he said, "today at the latest. You want to know why I attacked the judge? That's why. I thought the delay was bullshit."

"Maybe it is and maybe it isn't," said Cannon. "That's what I need to find out. But I can't find that out if I can't find the judge. Everything I see, he's not in the courthouse. So maybe he's really away on vacation. I need to know where."

"I might be able to help you with that," said Norwood. "See, the thing that got me mad during the trial was how the judge was always schmoozing with the lawyers. Well, one thing he kept talking about was saying how he couldn't wait for Memorial Day to get away to his country house. It's in the Berkshires."

CHAPTER 40

The dream seemed real. It always seemed real to some degree, but this time his slow ascent to wakefulness did not disabuse him of its reality. In this version of the dream, everything that had happened hadn't happened, and everything that never happened did happen. The divorce had gone through. Norman had not wigged out. He and Greta got married. They moved away with their boy. He found work, good work, and when they were financially stable, Greta renounced Norman's child support payments. There was no paternity suit.

He opened his eyes, still locked in the logic of the dream. Greta stood at the mirror, turning her head from side to side as she hooked her gray-blond hair behind her ears. Her sturdiness had aged well, her broad back, her ample ass, her strong thighs. She turned away from the mirror, showing him the full frontal, and that was when the dream drained away.

"What time is it?" he said.

"Almost seven." Olga sat in the crescent of space between him and the edge of the mattress. Her bare leg touched where his knee poked out of the sheet.

"Early," he said.

"House rules say breakfast is from seven to nine."

"Don't you make the house rules?"

"I do, which means I need to follow them or look like a fool. Unfortunately, this current bunch are all early risers." She probed the space between his legs. "I see you are, too."

She stepped into a pair of gym shorts, worked a T-shirt over her head, and tied up her hair. Her tiny suite of rooms was just off the kitchen, and soon he could hear bacon sizzling on the griddle and smell coffee in the air.

He rolled onto his stomach and burrowed his head under a pillow. Olga was not the first woman who reminded him of Greta. But she was the first he had taken to bed and not felt the morning-after disappointment that came with chasing shadows. It was more than just the physical similarity. She seemed to have the same calm demeanor and the same understated strength.

He could see himself staying here for the second chance few people ever got. He had done enough. He had slain the principal demons in his life, the ones who claimed just to have been doing their jobs but who obviously harbored great personal animosity toward him. Interloper, they called him. Opportunist. Gold digger. The rest, well, taking care of them would set the world right. But not taking care of them would not betray his son's memory. He could live with himself.

He turned onto his side. She was right; he was an early riser. And right now, he hoped that breakfast would not last very long.

He could stay here.

No one ever would catch him. Too many years had passed for anyone to notice. He had been too careful.

Breakfast ended. The other boarders scattered. Olga brought in a tray. Breakfast in bed.

He could stay here.

After breakfast, they made love. After making love, they showered together. After their shower, Olga cinched her bathrobe and went to clean the kitchen. He offered to help.

"No, you stay here," she told him.

Yes, he thought, he could stay here.

While she was in the kitchen, his cell phone rang.

"Why didn't you tell me?" said a voice.

"Who is this?"

"Andrew Norwood, that's who. Now, why didn't you tell me?"

"Tell you what?"

"That you didn't just happen to be passing by," said Norwood. "That you're not a therapist."

"I don't know what you're talking about."

"Stop it," said Norwood. "I know all about the watchdog group. I talked to your partner."

"My partner?"

"Yeah, he told me all about it. How you were watching me because I looked like the kind of guy who'd do something stupid. Glad I didn't disappoint you."

"Andrew, will you calm down for a minute and explain, because I don't have any idea what the hell you're talking about."

"Okay, okay," said Norwood. "I was sitting outside the courthouse when this guy comes up to me and says he wants to talk to me about Judge Lonergan. He said he was part of this watchdog group that studies how the Judicial Conduct Commission investigates judges. He knew all about my grievance. He said he knew that I attacked the judge yesterday. He said that you and he were assigned to my case. He was watching the judge while you were watching me."

"What was his name?"

"Cannon," said Norwood. "Frank, maybe. No. It was Robert. He said he needed help because the judge left town for vacation and he needed to know where. He figured maybe I knew since I was stalking the judge yesterday."

"That's true? The judge left for vacation?"

"That's what he told me," said Norwood. "Hey, shouldn't you know this?"

"Well, obviously I don't."

"I told him the judge has a vacation house in the Berkshires. That's all I know."

"Why are you at the courthouse, especially after yesterday?"

"Habit," said Norwood. "You get to be my age, there isn't much to fill your day. Why aren't you watching me?"

"How do you know I'm not?"

The phone thudded as if Norwood muffled it.

"I don't see you anywhere," he said.

"I'm kidding, Andrew. Actually, I trust you. But I need to make sure this wasn't someone giving you a line. Describe Cannon for me."

"He was taller than me, but still short. Heavyset, with a walrus mustache and glasses. Sixtyish."

"That's my partner."

"So everything he told me is on the level?" said Norwood. "And you, your group, you're really on my side."

"Everything is true. We are on your side, but you weren't supposed to know that. Damn that Cannon. You're not even supposed to know we exist. Now I need to know you won't talk to anyone about this again."

"Me?"

"You won't, right?"

"No, of course not," said Norwood.

"And you're not going to follow the judge up to the Berkshires, are you?"

"No. I won't." Norwood snorted. "I can't even if I wanted to. I don't get around like I used to."

"Good. You just be patient like I told you yesterday. Your grievance will come out all right."

Barbara did not know how Bill would react to a long car ride. Aside from the drive back from the Berkshires at the end of the holidays, his longest rides since his accident had been in cabs between the courthouse and home, where the tight urban scenery and the stop-and-go rhythm seemed to entertain him. At least he never acted out in a cab as he did, say, in church. So rather than follow their usual high-speed route up the interstate, Barbara instructed the driver to take an old highway that was now a rural byway. The scenery was quite lovely, really, with quaint towns, rolling hills, and neat farms.

Bill was antsy at first, but settled down and finally dropped off to sleep. Barbara drifted, too. Halfway through the trip, Bill moaned. Barbara instinctively reached out to touch him. She felt something wet and popped awake to see a dark spot blooming in the crotch of his khakis. She could smell urine.

"Oh, honey," she whispered.

Bill opened his eyes briefly, then settled back into his nap. Barbara looked out the windows. On one side, a hill rose steeply to an apple orchard. On the other, cornfields rolled toward distant hills. A road sign flashed past, showing that the next town was two miles ahead. Barbara sat back nervously.

She opened her purse and scribbled a list of items on a tiny spiral pad. One mile passed, and the landscape changed from orchards and cornfields to the outskirts of a rural town. A blinking traffic light marked the entrance to a small shopping center. Barbara told the driver to turn in.

"Would you mind?" she said after the driver nosed into a parking space. She pressed the list and a folded one-hundred-dollar bill into his hand.

The driver headed into a store, and Barbara got out of the car. She left the door open to let in some air and paced until the driver returned toting two shopping bags. He set the bag at Barbara's feet, then handed over the change, which was almost fifty dollars.

"Would you mind getting coffee for about fifteen minutes?" she said. He could keep the change.

Back in the car, Barbara worked quickly. She stripped off Bill's khakis and boxer shorts, scrubbed him with baby wipes, then dried him with paper towels. She rolled him onto the dry side of the backseat and scrubbed the damp leather with more baby wipes. Then she dressed Bill in fresh boxers and a new pair of gray sweatpants. By the time the driver returned, the wet clothes were tied up in a plastic bag and barely a trace of the baby wipe scent lingered in the air. The driver discreetly said nothing about Bill's new outfit. Nor did he react when they were under way again and he locked eyes with Barbara in the rearview mirror just as she wiped a tear from her eye.

————

Cannon was beyond the northern suburbs when his phone finally rang. He pulled off the road to answer, less out of respect for the law than out of respect for logistics. His ancient clamshell required one hand to hold the lower part steady and another to lift the lid. Even then, the shells were so thin and his fingers so thick that the whole damn thing could fly out of his hands.

"Got paper and pencil?" said Dave DiLallo.

Cannon unzipped his carry case and wrote down every word Dave said.

"How'd you get it?" said Cannon.

"I know a guy who knows a guy who works in a land records office in western Mass."

"Thanks," said Cannon.

"You're welcome," said Dave. "Don't get yourself killed."

An hour and a half later, Cannon turned off a country road and slowly climbed a narrow dirt-track driveway that rose between two stands of trees. At the top, the trees opened up to reveal Judge Lonergan's country home. A fieldstone house and a red barn faced each other from opposite sides of a circle. A flagpole stood in the center of the circle, and a man driving a tractor mowed the grass inside the circle. Cannon immediately backed down the driveway and swung onto the road. His mind spun with thoughts of what to do next. The man on the mower hadn't seen him; that was good. But he needed to get a better look at the layout.

He drove to a small roadside picnic area he remembered passing on his way in. The trees were tall, the brush thick, and the tables empty. He parked so that his car would not be visible from the road, then walked three-tenths of a mile back to the Lonergans' spread. Luckily, not one car passed him on the way. He could hear the tractor as he climbed the driveway. The man had finished with the circle and now mowed a large swath of grass beyond the house. Cannon slipped into the trees and picked his way behind the barn. There was a back door, unlocked, and he went inside.

Cannon quickly took inventory: a car, a golf cart, small piles of dried grass clippings where he assumed the tractor would be parked, a workbench, tools. The front doors were open, and he could see the house across the circle. The door and all the windows were shut down, which meant the Lonergans had not yet arrived.

A set of stairs led up to the hayloft, which Cannon found not to be a hayloft any longer. Rooms had been framed out and wallboard tacked up, but the renovation was a long way from finished. He walked to the front windows, careful not to get too close. He had a perfect view of the driveway, the circle, and the house.

The tractor came into view, its blades raised like wings. It turned onto the circular driveway and headed toward the barn. The motor thrummed louder, and then the tractor itself rattled as it bumped through the barn door. The engine cut. Boots thudded on the wide-planked floor. The barn doors squeaked closed, and then the wooden hatch slammed down.

Cannon drew closer to the windows and watched the man cross the circle to the house. He was tall enough and lanky enough to resemble Kehoe. But he wasn't, Cannon was sure. The man went inside the house, and one by one opened the windows.

Cannon went down the stairs, out the back door, and retraced his path to his car. He knew exactly what he would do.

CHAPTER 41

Jack the caretaker had filled the refrigerator with fresh produce and cold cuts, so Barbara had much to work with lunch-wise. She made turkey sandwiches and a salad, and the three of them, Jack included, ate at the kitchen island. Jack caught them up on the news about town, as well as what work he had finished and what still needed to be done. Bill seemed well enough engaged, and Barbara doubted that Jack noticed anything amiss. But lunch was short, and as long as Bill nodded at the right times, uttered a few pleasantries, and didn't say anything ridiculous, he could bring off an encounter with an acquaintance without arousing any suspicions. If only the grievance hearing could be so quick and casual.

After lunch, Jack went out to trim the shrubbery in front of the house and Barbara led Bill into the sunroom. The sunroom overlooked a back lawn that Jack had cultivated to attract birds by cutting flower beds where low shrubs and late-summer perennials now grew. Bird feeders stood on wooden posts.

Barbara sat Bill in a chair and pushed an ottoman for him to lift his feet. Outside the window, glass feeders hung from the eaves. A hummingbird hovered, its wings invisible.

With Bill situated, Barbara went back to the kitchen and phoned the Keystone.

"Dr. Feldman, please," she said, and the receptionist transferred the call. The doctor's line rang and rang; then the receptionist cut in and explained that the doctor may have left for the day.

"Will she be in tomorrow?" said Barbara.

"Yes. Is there anything I can tell her?"

"No," said Barbara. "Thank you."

She looked in on Bill, who already had fallen asleep. She considered waking him up for a bathroom break, but decided he had wet himself not because he fell asleep but because he fell asleep in a car. The chair in the sunroom did not vibrate or purr.

She went out to the front porch. She could hear the metallic click of Jack's hand clippers, the twitter of distant birds, the buzz of a honeybee as it backed out of one purple hosta flower and nosed into another. The air smelled of cut grass, and for a moment she felt happy.

"At least until tomorrow," she muttered.

She clopped down the steps. Jack's clippers stopped, and she sensed him watching from among the shrubs as she crossed the circle and headed toward the barn. She remembered how she found it that first year—peeling, sagging, leaking—and how she imposed upon Bill to refurbish it. She lifted the latch, swung open the doors, smelled the dirt and grass and oil that seemed permanently ingrained in the ancient planks. The smell faded as she climbed the stairs. At the top, she clutched the handrail and surveyed the work. Jack had made much progress. The walls were up, the rooms, hallways, and closets completely framed and trimmed.

She had come up with the plan to convert the hayloft into a guesthouse almost three years ago. There had been many sets of plans, but she finally settled on one that she and Bill could afford and that Jack could execute. She was happy to see it had reached this stage. She had a month to paint the walls and pick out the carpeting. This, she realized now, was how she would spend her time while Bill stayed at the Keystone.

She went back down the stairs. The one problem that had not been solved yet was finding guests to populate the guesthouse. Together, she and Bill had many acquaintances but virtually no friends. It was a problem among the judges she had come to know, a separation from the rest of the population that came with the black robe. Bill had spoken about it early in their marriage. He was accustomed to forging close friendships—his teammates, his law partners—but the bench was a lonely place. Always gregarious, he learned that a lighthearted superficiality suited his new role, and so he socialized by telling jokes and asking questions that demanded no answers. Barbara needed more, but for years, Bill— the true Bill she lived with and loved—had been enough. She wasn't so sure she could handle the new Bill.

———

Foxx banged out of the courthouse and made it up to City Island before Ellen's lunch shift ended at Artie's.

"You're leaving now?" she said.

"I need to," said Foxx.

"If you have only a couple of questions, why don't you just call her?"

"They aren't questions she would answer over the phone. I need to confront her."

Ellen dangled the keys, then pulled them back. "Tonight?"

"Depends on when I get there," said Foxx.

"Tomorrow?"

"At the latest."

She dropped the keys into his hand.

Foxx was at his house, packing a travel bag, when the call came. He listened, said he would get there ASAP, then ended the call.

"Goddammit," he said.

Foxx got to the medical block by midafternoon. The lights in Ralphie's cubicle were dim, and the cubicle itself seemed different. As Foxx dragged a stool close to the bed, he realized what had changed. Most of the equipment was gone. The one remaining monitor measured only the heart rate and the oxygen levels. A scrawny, gravity-powered IV tree stood in place of the thicker, digitized model. Two bags hung from opposite branches, one large and clear, the other small and yellowish. This was it. No more bobs to the surface, no more arrows left in the medical science quiver. Ralphie was on his way out.

Foxx sat on the stool and leaned over the bed rail. Ralphie's eyes were closed. Oxygen hissed in his nostrils. His breath whistled mournfully between his teeth. Somehow, it didn't smell as putrid as it had the other day.

"Ralphie," said Foxx.

Ralphie did not react. Foxx lowered the bed rail and jumped the stool closer.

"Ralphie," he said into Ralphie's ear. He rubbed a knuckle against Ralphie's cheek. It felt as dry and as thin as onionskin.

"It's Foxx, Ralphie. Can you hear me?"

Again, Ralphie did not react. Foxx looked at the monitor. Ralphie's heart still beat. His lungs still distributed the oxygen jetting into his nose. Foxx leaned back to take in Ralphie from head to toe. One hand lay limply on his chest. The other lay at his side, palm up, fingers curled. Foxx pressed a finger into the palm. Ralphie's fingers closed weakly around it.

"Ralphie," he said. "It's Foxx. Squeeze my finger if you can hear me."

Nothing happened.

Dammit, thought Foxx. He slipped his finger out of Ralphie's hand, then he got up and looked out into the corridor. The nurses' station was vacant. The only voices sounded far away.

Foxx went back and shut off the morphine drip. He knew that morphine was used not only to manage pain but also to help respiration. He stood at the bedside, watching the monitor and listening to Ralphie's low whistle. When he was certain that Ralphie's breathing would not stop, he sat back down on the stool.

He waited thirty minutes before resting his finger again in the palm of Ralphie's hand.

"It's Foxx. Squeeze if you can hear me."

This time, Ralphie squeezed.

"I'm working on it, Ralphie. I'm starting to see the things you couldn't see and find out the names you never knew. Do you understand?"

Ralphie squeezed his finger.

"I have a few answers. But not the answer to your question. I still need to talk to one of the steno girls. She could be the key. Her name was Barbara Frisbie. Did you know her?"

No squeeze from Ralphie.

"You don't know her?"

A squeeze now.

"She dated Lozier up until a couple of months before the murder."

Ralphie released Foxx's finger. He flapped his hand on the mattress, then lifted it up and pointed at his chin. The oxygen whooshed and Ralphie's breathing whistled, and then Foxx understood what he meant. He lowered his ear to Ralphie's mouth.

"Who?" Ralphie gurgled.

Foxx moved his mouth close to Ralphie's ear.

"I'm sorry. I don't know right now."

———

Cannon returned to the Lonergan place after buying equipment and provisions at three separate stores. He dumped everything into the weeds behind the roadside ditch, stashed the car at the picnic area, then walked back. The stuff was light, but he still needed two trips through the trees and brush to lug it to the barn.

He set up on the second floor, piling his food and water and unrolling his sleeping bag in the largest of the closets. He set the camping chair some distance from the windows and decided against using his binoculars until twilight, when there would be less chance of a stray reflection flashing off the lenses. Still, the Lonergans' presence was obvious to the unaided eye. The front door of the house was wide open and the windows lifted high. The car, which had been in the garage, now was parked on the circular driveway directly in front of the house.

He watched, but saw no activity. After a while, and mostly out of boredom, he ate two peanut butter and jelly sandwiches and drank a pint of water. After another little while, he treated himself to a bag of astronaut ice cream he had bought at a camping store. The ice cream looked like jagged shards of vanilla taffy, but through some miracle of 1960s chemistry, melted in his mouth and actually felt cold. Rather than use the barn bathroom, he went down the stairs and out the back door to pee in the short grass.

The Lonergans came out of the house at exactly 7 P.M. The judge wore a maroon warm-up suit, his wife a pair of canary yellow shorts and a pink blouse. They walked past the car and onto the circular drive. At first, Cannon thought they were heading to the barn, and for a time they stopped walking and gazed up at the second floor as if discussing something. He pulled even farther back from the window and listened for the latch. But when enough time passed and no sound came, he crept back to the window. The Lonergans were around the circle, heading back toward the house.

They walked the circle a second time, then climbed onto the front porch. The sun was well down now, and the tall pines cast long shadows that completely covered the distance between the barn and the house. Cannon lifted the binoculars. In the failing light, he could just make them out. The judge sat with one long leg crossed over the other, his foot bobbing. His wife hugged herself as if cold, each hand rubbing the opposite elbow.

They sat for about ten minutes before the judge's wife got up. She patted her husband's cheek, then took his hand and lifted him upright. A moment later, they went inside, and a few moments after that, two windows on the second floor lit up.

Cannon put down his binoculars and picked up his cell phone. Slowly, he tapped out a text message: CALL ME WHEN YOU CAN TALK

———————

There were no further words after the brief exchange. No more whispered questions, no more squeezed responses. Foxx got up, restarted the morphine drip, and sat back down. Ralphie was not going to make it, and neither would he. He sat there all afternoon and would sit all night. However long it took.

The nurse eventually came in. She nodded at Foxx, and he nodded back. Then she set about logging the numbers on the monitor, tapping the IV bags with her finger, and tightening the sheets under Ralphie's stick-figure body.

"Would you like something?" she said. "A sandwich?"

"I'm fine," said Foxx.

"It's good that you're here," she said, and left the cubicle.

There were events in life where the passage of time seemed to stop. Foxx had heard about, but not experienced, three-year-olds' birthday parties, elementary school Christmas pageants, and modern ballet. He had done his share of hospital visits, though. And now, not for the first time, he was holding a deathwatch.

He pulled the stool away from the bed and leaned his back against the wall. Time stretched, and when that position became uncomfortable, he moved back to the bed and laid his forehead on the edge of the mattress. He listened to the beeps of the monitor, the rush of the oxygen, the whistle of Ralphie's breaths. The sounds gathered into a rhythm, fell out for a while, then constructed a more dissonant beat.

There was nothing else to say, because anything he said would be a lie. And Foxx believed that you couldn't lie to the dying. It wasn't out of respect; it wasn't because it was cowardly. It was because the dying would soon be dead, and lies didn't work with the dead because the dead knew the truth.

The rhythm of beeps and rushes and whistles lulled Foxx to

sleep. Sometime later—he had no idea how much later because he had been completely removed from time—he awoke with a start. The cubicle was quiet except for the oxygen rush. He heard a click, and the oxygen fell silent.

He lifted his head off the mattress. The nurse stood on the other side of the bed.

"I'll get the doctor," she said. "I'm sorry."

Foxx rubbed his eyes. He had seen death too many times, and he knew there was a huge gulf between the dead and the dying. Still, he leaned down to Ralphie's ear.

"I'll get back to you on this. Promise."

CHAPTER 42

I t was a routine back then. Cannon would send her a text and then he would wait. He would imagine her rounding up the foster kids, getting them bathed and then into bed. An hour or two might pass before bedtime ended and she could find a place away from Buck where she could talk without whispering. Whispering was good, though, with its breathiness and its desire. But that was back then, before Buck found out and she needed to choose.

Night fell completely. On the far side of the circle, the lights in the second-floor windows went out. The moon rose above the tall pines, past full but still big and bright enough to cast shadows. Cannon checked his phone again, measuring the minutes since he sent the text, making sure the text had gone through.

Alone with his thoughts, he could rub off the patina of guilt over the affair with Sarah. Deep down, he wanted to rekindle it, stoke it, let it burn its course. He could do it; he should do it. As Dave said in a different context, what did his motive matter if he could prove Luke's innocence?

Across the circle, the front door of the house opened. The judge's wife stood silhouetted in the bright rectangle, then dissolved into a darker part of the porch. Cannon lifted his binoculars. He could make out her grainy image leaning forward in a chair as if about to get up. Then she settled back and rubbed her temples.

Cannon carefully opened the window a couple of inches, and

the cool night air fell in around him. A car passed on the road. He lifted the binoculars again. She lowered her hands to her cheeks and stared forward as if entranced. She sat virtually motionless for almost an hour, and then Cannon's phone buzzed.

"Are you still at Dave's?" said Sarah.

"In the Berkshires. That judge I told you about? I'm at his house."

"At his house? After all those days he ignored you?"

"He doesn't know I'm here. He has a house and a barn. I'm in the barn, watching."

"That sounds insane."

"Not really. I know what I'm doing. I know exactly what I'm doing."

"Which is what?"

"Watching and waiting," said Cannon. "I saw him. Kehoe. Yesterday, outside the courthouse in New York City. He killed Ken Palmer and Daniel Kaplan and Maxine Rosen, and now he's stalking the judge. When he shows up here, I'll nail him."

"I hope you know what you're doing."

"I do," said Cannon. "Rousma thinks I'm crazy. Buck thinks . . . Well, who knows what Buck thinks. But I'm not. I figured this out."

"I don't think you're crazy."

"Thanks."

"But still, I hope you know what you're doing. Because if anything ever happened to you . . ." Her voice trailed off.

"Nothing is going to happen to me."

"But if something ever did."

"If something ever did, then what?" he said.

"I couldn't live with myself."

"What are you saying, Sarah?"

"I think you know what I'm saying."

"Did something happen tonight?"

"No."

"Sarah, did something happen tonight? Did he—?"

"No. Nothing happened. It's just that some things came clear to me. Things about you, things about Buck. And then hearing you talk so passionately to the sheriff, and seeing Buck sitting there like a dead fish, I just . . ."

"Just what?"

"Not over the phone. Not with you in some barn."

"It's a nice barn," said Cannon. "Not a speck of dirt. Not a hint of cow manure."

"I'm down at the bottom of the road," she said. "Soon as Buck nodded out, I just started walking. And now I'm here."

"Watch yourself."

"I know. Coyotes, foxes, bear."

"Get back to the house."

"I will. Walking now. When this is done, when it's over, we need to talk."

"The things you won't tell me over the phone."

"That's right," she said.

"Promise?"

"Promise."

The call ended, and Cannon got up from the camping chair. He couldn't believe what he'd heard, what she'd said, how close she came to saying what she'd come so close to saying a long time ago. He paced between the chair and the closet, replaying her words in his head. Then he remembered the judge's wife. He picked up the binoculars. She was gone from the porch.

———

By the time Barbara got Bill to bed and herself out to the front porch, her headache was in full bloom. It felt like a tension headache, the kind that started in one temple and worked its way around her forehead to explode in the other temple. But she wasn't tense, not since New York City vanished from the Town Car's rearview mirror, and certainly not since arriving at the house, with its quiet, remote setting. She sat on one of the Adirondack chairs and made small circles with her fingers where her skin was tight as a snare drum over her temples. This was more of an anticipation headache, she realized; tomorrow worried her.

She closed her eyes as her fingertips chased away some of the pain. The air was cool. Crickets chirped softly. The moonlight was bright enough that the dull gray finish of their old sedan took on a gunmetal cast. She wondered how Bill would react at the Keystone tomorrow. She had mentioned it to him three times now, the latest being just a few minutes ago as she sat sidesaddle on the edge of the mattress and rubbed his back. He seemed to understand that he would be a resident in the Keystone for thirty days. Then again, as a five-year-old, she understood that her first day of kindergarten would be only two hours long. That didn't stop her from bellowing the moment her mother let go of her hand.

———

Cannon woke up well before the cell phone alarm. He had stayed up past midnight, though there was little else to see but the moon moving across the sky and a few deer poking out of the trees behind the house. He thought less of Kehoe than about his conversation with Sarah. He wasn't quite sure exactly where they were headed, but the morning light did not chase away the distinct impression that good things were in the offing.

He crawled out of the closet, then stretched until his joints stopped creaking and his muscles stopped aching. He should have bought the inflatable mattress the camping store salesperson had suggested. He was too old for a damn sleeping bag.

By seven, he was at his post, the antiseptic scent of the disposable wipes still in his nose, the taste of lukewarm oatmeal and powdered orange juice still in his mouth. Outside, early morning mist hung below the tree line. Straight up above, a pale blue sky promised a clear day. Nothing about the house had changed. The door was closed, the first-floor windows were shut, the second-floor windows were open. The car was parked in the circle.

He sat for half an hour, watching with his binoculars but seeing nothing inside. He got up from the stool and walked around the room, bending his knees and windmilling his arms to keep his blood moving and his mind sharp. At eight o'clock, the Lonergans came out of the house. The wife helped the judge down the porch steps, holding him firmly by the elbow and taking one step at a time. She opened the passenger door and waited for him to settle inside. Then she went around to the driver's side, tossed a small duffel bag into the backseat, and got behind the wheel.

Didn't anticipate this, thought Cannon as he watched the car turn off the circle and head down to the road. He waited awhile, wondering whether the Lonergans were taking a quick trip into town or would be gone for the day. He considered texting Sarah, but decided to leave well enough alone. He could be overbearing, and thought it best to contact her only when he had something concrete to communicate. Instead, he would take advantage of his relative freedom and go outside for some air. He would hear anyone coming from a long way off.

He went down the stairs and out the back door and then bellied his way into the brush. Funny how he could sit for enormous periods of time, but once he started moving, he had a terrible urge to pee. He was just about to lower his fly when the world went dark.

———

"Dr. Feldman knows you are here," said the woman behind the desk.

Barbara glanced back at Bill, who sat on a sofa so low that his knees bent up to his chest. He had been paging through a *Sports Illustrated,* but the magazine now lay beside him. He stared at the ceiling.

"Does she understand it's about my husband?" said Barbara.

"Yes," said the woman. "She is well aware."

Barbara sat beside Bill and took his hand in hers.

"I'm sorry, dear," she said. "I didn't think it would take this long."

Bill grunted and lifted the magazine onto his steep lap. Meanwhile, Dr. Feldman appeared and huddled with the woman behind the desk. The doctor looked harried today, not like the neat, young professional Barbara had met the week before. The woman finished whispering, and Dr. Feldman straightened up, her mood darkening as she met Barbara's eye.

Barbara forced a smile. She got up from the sofa and tried to usher Dr. Feldman away from the desk. The doctor resisted, turning just enough to create a modicum of privacy.

"It's not Sunday," she said.

"I know," said Barbara, "but I need to get him admitted early."

"I'm afraid that's not possible."

"But something happened."

"Something medical?" said Dr. Feldman.

"I'm not sure. Maybe. I don't think I mentioned that my husband is a judge."

"You didn't."

"He was attacked on Monday afternoon by a litigant who is angry because my husband ruled against him."

"Physically attacked?"

"Yes."

"How terrible," said Dr. Feldman. "Did he require medical attention?"

"No, fortunately," said Barbara. "Someone intervened, and my husband wasn't hurt. But I believe the attack affected his mental state."

"How so?"

"He goes back and forth between agitation and detachment. And . . ."

"And?"

"He wet himself on the drive up yesterday," said Barbara. "That's a first."

"I see," said Dr. Feldman. "He may need medication, but it is strictly against our policy to prescribe medication to anyone not actually admitted here. I can refer you to some doctors in Lenox or Great Barrington."

"So you're saying you can't admit him early? Even if we pay?"

"It's not a payment issue. It's a bed issue. I thought I made that clear."

"You didn't," said Barbara. She reached out her hand to Bill. "C'mon, honey, they'll be more interested in you on Sunday."

———

Kehoe didn't linger around the bodies. He released the old lawyer and let the current pull him downriver. He pushed himself up off the chaise and didn't give the forensic psychologist a second look. He sat on a chair and watched his former lawyer tumble off the deflating float and writhe until his lungs filled with water. Here, though, he could not just walk away. His target was Bill Lonergan, and right now, he didn't know where Lonergan had gone and when he would return.

He probed the back of the man's head. There was no blood, luckily, but he could feel where the pipe shattered the skull. He rolled the man onto his back and crossed his arms on his chest. The force of the blow had knocked off the man's glasses, and Kehoe, obeying some weird sense of propriety, folded them into the man's pockets. The man's eyelids were slightly open, revealing pale slivers of his eyes. Kehoe closed them with the side of his hand.

He remembered seeing the man twice before, most recently in that bar in Lower Manhattan and, a few months back, at Simcoe's Garage in Upstate New York. He passed off these brief encounters as glimpses of similar but distinctly different people, but the man's wallet proved otherwise. Robert Cannon. Resident of Roscoe, New York. Retired court officer. Licensed private investigator. Kehoe remembered him now. He could call to mind Cannon's younger version, sitting at the desk in the lobby of the Delaware County Courthouse.

Kehoe dragged Cannon by the ankles to the closet. He opened the sleeping bag, rolled Cannon onto it, then zipped it shut. Sleeping bag to body bag.

Cannon hadn't been on the list. He had been nothing but a glorified doorman, not an active participant in thwarting the paternity suit. Kehoe almost felt bad for him, but then not really. Cannon's wallet contained no clue to why he was squatting in Bill Lonergan's barn. But it couldn't have been a coincidence. Soon, he hoped, whatever brought Cannon here would be irrelevant.

From outside came the sound of a car. Kehoe went to the window to see who had driven in.

———

Barbara's unsuccessful encounter with Dr. Feldman put her in a bad mood that hardly improved during the ten-mile drive back from the Keystone. What she found when she reached home made her mood even worse. First, there was the car parked on the same segment of the circle where Jack usually parked. The car was old, had New York plates, and did not belong to anyone she knew or, given her funk, cared to know. Second, as she swung around the car and parked directly in front of the porch, she spotted someone sitting in Bill's Adirondack chair.

"You wait here," she told Bill.

She got out of the car, pressing the button to lock Bill inside. As she reached the bottom step, the man pushed himself up from the chair. Out of context and out of uniform, he looked strange until his silver hair and cock-hipped stance gave him away. Barbara's hand froze on the rail.

"You need to leave," she said.

Foxx grinned. He glided past her down the steps and cupped his hand against the passenger window. Inside, Bill stared straight ahead.

"You have no right to be here," said Barbara.

Ignoring her, Foxx tapped the window and waved at the judge.

The judge smiled crookedly, flapped his hand in an awkward wave, then turned away.

"I said you have no—"

"Right?" said Foxx. "What right I have isn't the point. What duty I have is something else."

"I don't understand," said Barbara.

"I didn't think so." Foxx jabbed the window with his finger. "He doesn't look like himself."

Inside, the judge stared straight ahead as if he were frightened and hoped that by not looking, Foxx would go away.

"He doesn't act like himself, either, right? Hasn't for a long time now, right? Shouldn't even be on the bench, right? But he made, or maybe you made, some sort of deal with Judge Patterson."

"That's not true," said Barbara. "And even if it was, it's none of your business."

"Oh, but it is, Mrs. Lonergan. See, I may look like just a court officer, but I also work for the inspector general. And the inspector general would be very interested in what's going on in your chambers."

"The inspector general has no jurisdiction over judges," said Barbara.

"True," said Foxx. "But she has jurisdiction over judges' law clerks and judges' secretaries."

Barbara mulled that for a moment. Then she came down the steps and elbowed Foxx out of the way. Behind the window, Bill wiped his wrists across his sweaty brow.

"I'm not saying I believe you," said Barbara. "But if I believed you, why are you up here now? The judge isn't on the bench. We're on vacation. We're not even in New York state."

"You're right. I could wait and we could sort things out in September," said Foxx. "But I'm here about something else."

"That boom-boom room you asked me about," said Barbara.

"Cut the innocent act, Mrs. Lonergan. You lied to me when you said you knew nothing about it."

"And why is it the inspector general's concern?"

"It's not. It's mine. Ralphie Rago didn't kill Calvin Lozier. I promised him I'd find out who did before he dies."

Barbara leaned back to the window.

"My husband is sweltering in there," she said. "I need to get him out."

Foxx stepped away so she could open the door. The judge slowly unfolded himself from the car. He seemed weaker and less balanced than Foxx ever had seen him, and as Barbara took hold of one arm, Foxx reached for the other.

"No," she said. "I'm perfectly capable of getting my husband inside without your help."

The Lonergans climbed to the porch one slow step at a time. Foxx trailed behind, hearing Barbara softly encourage the judge forward. Inside, she let go of the judge's arm long enough to point Foxx toward a large room that looked like something out of a hunting lodge, with a fieldstone fireplace, cathedral ceiling supported by rough-hewn timbers, and a wagon-wheel chandelier hanging from the center beam. Foxx waited there. He could hear Barbara talking after she and the judge disappeared into a room at the back of the house, things like "here" and "there" and "how's this" and "look at that."

Barbara returned a few minutes later as Foxx studied a print of a fox hunt that hung over the mantel. Two armchairs faced each other in front of the fireplace. Barbara settled tensely on the edge of one. Foxx sat opposite, leaning forward.

"You know," said Barbara. "It just occurred to me that I don't even know your name."

"Foxx," said Foxx.

She nodded as if his name meant something, though Foxx doubted that it did.

"Well, Officer Foxx," she said. "Let me be very clear. My husband can function as a judge. But on Monday, he was physically attacked during our lunchtime walk, and that had left him traumatized."

"Which is why you shut down for vacation a week early."

"With Judge Patterson's approval," said Barbara, "and so that my husband can seek medical treatment. In fact, we were just returning from a doctor's appointment. The doctor expects a full recovery. But you don't care about that."

"Not unless I'm asked," said Foxx. "I'm here about Calvin Lozier."

Barbara started to speak, but quickly stopped.

"I know you saw him for a number of months," said Foxx. "You were in the steno pool, he was a judge's law clerk trying to work his way onto the bench. You would use the boom-boom room at lunchtime. Tell me if I start getting cold."

Barbara said nothing.

"Sometime around June of that year, he started to believe that his long shot bid to become a judge wasn't such a long shot. In fact, he believed it was a lock. And at about the same time, he broke off with you. His reason was that he didn't think you would make a good judge's wife."

"That damn Bertha," Barbara muttered.

"What was that?"

"Nothing."

"It must have hurt to hear that," said Foxx. "You didn't know he was married. Except for the people in the personnel office, no one had a clue until the wake.

"But look at you now. Barbara Lonergan, the wife of Judge Lonergan. You're exactly what he said you never could be."

"Do you have a question?"

"I think you know what it is," said Foxx.

"The answer is complicated," said Barbara.

CHAPTER 43

Kehoe used the trees as cover. Near as he could tell, there were three people inside the house—the two Lonergans and the man who had driven in while the Lonergans were out. He knew the general lay of the property from his exploratory visit in the spring, knew also that the Lonergans employed a caretaker to look after the place during their long absences. The caretaker was a man of about his height and his physique. He was not the man who was now inside with the Lonergans. That man was smaller and had arrived in a car with New York plates.

Kehoe was mildly troubled. That hoary old lawyer had been fishing alone on a secluded river. That bitch of a forensic psychologist had been midway through a solitary drinking binge on a deck screened off by trees and shrubs. That asshole Kaplan had been entertaining a guest, but obviously not one so committed to his hospitality that a good scare couldn't send her running off. He had hoped for the same general luck at the Lonergan estate. Instead, he had three people concentrated in a house rather than spread out among the acreage. He was getting down to the end, but more than that, he wanted to get beyond the end.

He had started out with boundless energy, bottomless patience, endless creativity. He found them, observed them, laid a specific trap for each of them. But something had happened, and he wasn't quite sure what. It could have been seeing a cartoon version of himself in that twisted Andrew Norwood. Or—and he hoped this could be the case—it could have been the surprising comfort he felt with Olga. He could see himself returning to the rooming house and living out the rest of his days as her man. Yes, her resemblance to Greta attracted him, and eventually that resemblance might fade. But it could be replaced by something more enduring. Couldn't it? He wasn't exempt from falling in love. Was he?

He picked his way through the brush, drawing abreast of the house. The windows were open, and the curtains spread wide. But the windows had screens, and in the daylight, screens effectively blocked any view from the outside. He stayed in the trees until he reached the point closest to the house. Then he lumbered, crouching, to the wall. He ducked beneath a window, his shoulder scraping the concrete foundation. He could hear two voices speaking in turn, one soft and trembling, the other harsh and loud. Not Bill Lonergan's, thought Kehoe. He still recalled the sonorous, lawyerly tones that had convinced that hick judge to rule against him and his son. There was no way those tones could have aged into this barking. Either Bill Lonergan wasn't in the room or he wasn't speaking.

Kehoe crept away from the window. He peeked around the back corner of the house, mindful that the caretaker could be anywhere. A semicircular sunroom curved out from the rear of the house. It had rectangular panes of floor-to-ceiling windows and several skylights poking like bubbles through the roof. Delicate bird feeders hung from the eaves, and on the lawn behind the house, several sturdy ones stood on posts.

The sunroom windows had no screens, and the skylights lit the room enough for Kehoe to see Bill Lonergan standing inside and staring intently at a hummingbird that hovered at a feeder.

Kehoe watched for a moment, then slowly moved close enough to scare the hummingbird away. Lonergan tilted his head as if confused, then slowly turned until his eyes fell on Kehoe. He blinked and then he smiled.

Smiled? What the hell, thought Kehoe, and then he lifted a hand and waved. Lonergan waved back.

A door stood in the middle of the semicircle, indistinguishable from the windows except for the tiny wooden platform and the three steps descending to the lawn. Lonergan pushed the door open and clomped down the steps.

"Hi," he said.

"Hi," said Kehoe.

They locked eyes for a moment, and then Lonergan pointed at the hanging feeder.

"Hummingbird," he said.

"I don't see anything," said Kehoe.

"It flew away."

"I guess it did," said Kehoe. "Do you remember me?"

Lonergan grinned. "You're Jack."

Jack? Lonergan obviously took him for someone else. The caretaker, most likely. Seemed incredible, but maybe Lonergan never actually met the caretaker or glimpsed him only at a distance. And so Kehoe decided to let this mistake play out to his advantage. He'd need to correct Lonergan eventually, but there was time for that later.

"You like birds?" he said.

"My hobby," said Lonergan.

"Then you'll be interested in something I found."

Kehoe grabbed Lonergan by the arm and tugged him toward the trees. But Lonergan planted a foot and twisted free.

"What?" he said.

"It's a nest," said Kehoe. "Like nothing I've ever seen around here. And the bird, it's colorful."

"Red?" said Lonergan.

"And some gold and some green," said Kehoe.

Lonergan looked back at the sunroom.

"C'mon," said Kehoe, deciding his mistake had been to take Lonergan by the arm. "It's not far. Just a little way in the trees."

———

"I admit," Barbara said. "I met Calvin in that room that day."

"Which room?"

"The room at the bottom of the stairs."

"You mean the boom-boom room."

"If that's what you insist on calling it," said Barbara. "Yes, the boom-boom room."

"What time?" said Foxx.

"Lunch hour. Shortly after one. I couldn't get away from the steno pool any earlier."

"But you two broke up, what? Two months earlier?"

"Yes and no," said Barbara. "Sure, what he said about me not making a good wife for a judge hurt me terribly. Not so much because I didn't think it was true as because I didn't want it to be true. But two months passed, and not seeing him for so long, I re-interpreted what happened. I thought maybe I pushed too hard and scared him away. Maybe he said what he said out of fear. I also realized that I missed being with him. So I thought that if I talked to him, we could start over again."

"Then it was your idea to meet?"

"It was in my head," said Barbara, "but I didn't act on it until someone suggested I should."

"Who was that?" said Foxx.

"You know her," said Barbara.

"Did you set up the meeting, or did she?"

"I did," said Barbara.

"You called him and asked him?"

"Yes."

"And he came?"

"Yes."

"What happened?" he said.

"Not much," said Barbara. "There was no argument. No breakup sex. He didn't admit that he missed me, so I didn't admit that I missed him. We each said our piece, and that was it."

"Who left the room?" said Foxx. "You or Calvin?"

"I did."

"And he was alone?"

Rather than answer, Barbara raised her hand.

"Did you hear that?" she said.

"Hear what?" said Foxx.

"Bill?" she called.

Foxx turned toward the hallway, where brighter light spilled out of the sunroom.

"Bill?" Barbara called again, louder now. She got up. "Wait here."

She went into the hallway and called her husband's name three times before falling silent. In the silence, Foxx imagined she was tending to his needs. He didn't believe that the judge had been attacked. Word of something like that would have spread through the courthouse pretty damn quick, and even if the story had been squelched, Kearney would have alerted his troops. Which brought Foxx back to the theory that Judge Lonergan suffered from some sort of condition.

Foxx crossed his legs and pinched his eyes. Ralphie Rago. He needed to keep his focus on Ralphie Rago, not divert to thoughts of Judge Lonergan, who had no connection to Calvin Lozier or the boom-boom room, who wasn't even a judge back then.

He heard a latch click, then muffled footfalls. Close to a minute passed before he replayed these sounds and realized that Barbara Lonergan must have gone out a back door. He unfolded himself and went to the hallway. At the end, a doorway opened into the sunroom. The sunroom was bright and it was empty.

CHAPTER 44

Kehoe remembered everything he ever knew about Bill Lonergan. It wasn't a huge amount of information; he never spoke directly to the man except from the witness stand. But he heard enough of his blather with the hick judge, with Kenneth Palmer, with the Van Gelders, even with Daniel Kaplan to pick up some facts. Over the years, he would trot out these facts like precious stones and polish them to such a finish that they still shone brightly in his memory. Lonergan had been a college basketball star, had been drafted by the Knicks, had suffered a career-ending knee injury in his first preseason game. He married a woman from a higher social stratum than his own working-class roots. She applied to law school for him while he was still laid up with his knee. He landed a job with a Wall Street law firm, less due to his grades or his legal talents than his basketball career. He had no children.

Beyond the facts were the impressions, again highly polished over time. Lonergan liked to play the regular guy, the guy who just happened to be a successful lawyer but deep down was still a kid who could dribble a basketball. He told everyone they were doing a great job (even that fat-assed officer who sat behind the lobby desk and now lay cooling in his sleeping bag in the barn). The old expression "hail-fellow-well-met" had been coined for Bill Lonergan.

The sight of *Judge* Lonergan strolling around the park was much what Kehoe expected. The height, the athletic frame, the shock of white hair. But now, up close and with the rush of time slowing down, he felt a sense of disappointment he had not felt with Kenneth Palmer or with Maxine Rosen and certainly not with Daniel Kaplan.

————————

Barbara was not sure what she heard or if she heard anything at all. But she sensed an absence, maybe, or a subtle shift in the fabric that was her relationship with Bill. He did not get close to very many people. His deceased first wife, his first secretary, and now her. Twin roles bound up in a single person. At first, Barbara thought Bill's aloofness was a condition of the bench. Now she understood it was his essence: give him one person he could love and trust, and everyone else became superfluous.

Barbara was not built the same way. Though she gave herself to Bill more deeply than she ever thought possible, she kept a part of herself separate. But these last few months had worked a change in her. Thinking for him, doing for him, she felt herself becoming him.

She looked into the sunroom first, then knocked on the door to the small powder room nearby. Bill was nowhere. He could have gone up to their bedroom, but she would have seen him pass in the hallway, and if not, would have heard the loud creaking as he climbed the stairs.

She went back to the sunroom and inspected more closely now. The blanket on the chair was rumpled. The field guide lay closed on the small wooden table. She settled into the chair, trying to see what might have attracted his attention. It was still relatively early. Sunlight slanted through the skylights and streamed in through the tall windows. She noticed a smudge on one of the panes and got up for a closer look. The smudge was high on the pane, at precisely the height where Bill's nose would have pressed while looking at a hummingbird feeder hanging outside.

Then she noticed the lawn. The grass was still glazed with sunlit dew, except for two dark sets of footprints crossing toward the trees. She pushed out the door and followed the trail.

────────

They walked a footpath that dipped into small hollows and cut through the remains of ancient stone walls. Birds twittered in the branches; twigs crunched underfoot. In the distance, a chain saw fired up.

Lonergan walked haltingly, stopping often to look back as if he needed permission to keep going. Kehoe prodded him forward. They were deep enough into the trees that the sense of being near the house faded. Still, Kehoe pushed deeper.

The footpath curved around a knoll, climbed a long rise, then sloped down to a fast-running stream. There was no bridge, just boulders one could cross when the water was low enough. Today, the water poured over and through them.

Kehoe stopped Lonergan at the top of the slope and clamped a hand on each elbow.

"I'm not Jack," he said.

Lonergan tilted his head as he did when the hummingbird disappeared from the feeder.

"Jack. I'm not him."

Lonergan blinked but said nothing.

"My name is Thomas Kehoe. We know each other from long ago."

"I don't know you," said Lonergan.

"Sure you do. You must remember," said Kehoe. "Family court. Delaware County. Twenty years ago. Kehoe against Van Gelder. A paternity case about a boy who had everything that he wanted but nothing that he needed. Remember now?"

Lonergan banged the heel of his hand against his temple.

"Don't joke with me," said Kehoe.

"I don't remember. I can't remember." These last words sounded like a wail.

"The Van Gelders were your clients."

"I don't remember."

"Kenneth Palmer was the law guardian. He was supposed to protect the interests of my boy. There was Maxine Rosen. She was a psychologist who interviewed me and the Van Gelders. And then there was Daniel Kaplan, my jerk of a lawyer. You tell me you don't remember any of them?"

Lonergan shook his head, and Kehoe's heart sank. This wasn't the man he expected to find. He'd lost his memory, maybe even lost his mind. That's why he looked so feeble, clinging to his wife for support as if he might forget how to walk.

He should have known. He should have read the signs and not wasted his time pursuing a man who'd already given him the slip. Palmer, Rosen, Kaplan, they all knew. He saw the recognition in their eyes, the realization that their sins from long ago had come back to roost.

Lonergan was the worst of them. The case had been going well, even with Kaplan at the helm, until Lonergan rode into town with his athletic pedigree and his regular-guy façade. He was the one who implied, in the most subtle way, that there was something funny about a stranger seeking paternity of a five-year-old boy. He was the one who sold the hick judge on ordering psychological evaluations. Rosen's report, he knew, had swung the case against him.

There were so many things he planned to tell Lonergan. *That boy was my son, and I was the only good thing in his life until your lies cut me off from him forever. You got your fee. He got a life where he was pampered but not protected, provided for but not loved or cared about or taught anything of value. Like how to find a calling, earn a living, become a productive member of society. Now he's dead, and it all goes back to something that was just another case to you.*

But all that he wanted to say was meaningless now. Lonergan couldn't remember, which meant he couldn't understand. And he needed to understand for this to have meaning.

The hell with it, thought Kehoe. He dropped his grip from Lonergan's elbows, turned away, walked back the way they had come.

"Hey," called Lonergan.

Kehoe walked fast. He wanted to get to his car, drive back to the rooming house. He never would return to the cemetery, never would glue the fourth and final pebble to the gravestone. He was done.

"Hey," Lonergan called again. He was right on Kehoe's heels, hobbling quickly to keep up.

"Get away!" barked Kehoe.

He shoved Lonergan in the chest. Lonergan staggered backwards, but caught himself before falling. A moment later, he was at Kehoe's heels again.

Kehoe grabbed the old man by his shirt and lifted him off his feet. Lonergan's eyes were red, his white hair was mussed. Saliva leaked from a corner of his mouth. Kehoe threw him down onto the hard dirt of the footpath. Lonergan sat up, sucked air, then slowly got to his feet. Kehoe threw him down a second time. Again, Lonergan got up.

Kehoe grabbed Lonergan by the belt and the shirt collar and ran him down the slope. He stopped at the edge of the stream, changed his hold into a bear hug, then waded into the water, half dragging, half swinging the struggling Lonergan on his hip. At the other side, he threw Lonergan onto the bank, then got out of the water and dragged him up the slope. Lonergan lay panting and groaning. His eyes were closed. Kehoe waited until he was sure Lonergan would not get up again, then he waded back across the stream and trudged up the slope.

"Ken Palmer."

Kehoe stopped and turned around. Across the stream, Lonergan sat and hugged his knees to his chest.

"Ken Palmer," Lonergan repeated. "He took me fishing one day. Most boring day of my life."

Kehoe walked back down the slope and crouched at the edge of the stream.

"We were on a case together. Family court in Delaware County."

Lonergan gazed past Kehoe as he spoke. "The judge ordered DNA testing to see whether the boy and the man who claimed to be his father were related. That's when I got involved. The boy's grand-parents fired their first lawyer and hired me. They knew how that DNA test would come out and they wanted me to stop it at all costs. So I did. I argued the DNA test wasn't recognized by the law yet. The judge didn't buy that. I argued that a stranger suing for paternity of a young boy had funny stuff in mind. The judge didn't buy that either. But then I argued that even in a paternity case, the court needed to consider the best interests of the child. It wasn't exactly relevant, because if the test proved paternity, the case was over. But the judge bought that and ordered psychological tests, and the psychologist looked a little deeper into the situation than she needed to."

Kehoe stood up and plodded into the water. He had no idea whether Lonergan had been putting on an act or whether he was truly addled and something just clicked in his memory. The ex-planation didn't matter. Lonergan remembered. He remembered every little detail.

Kehoe scrambled onto the other bank and hauled Lonergan to his feet.

"You know who I am," he said.

Lonergan cringed. Kehoe clamped a hand on his jaw and twisted his head to face him.

"Look at me. You remember. Tell me you remember."

"I remember," said Lonergan.

"You remember me."

"I remember what happened."

"Tell me again what happened," said Kehoe.

"What happened when?"

"With the case."

"What case?" said Lonergan.

"Jesus," said Kehoe. He shook Lonergan by the jaw. "The paternity case. Delaware County. Ken Palmer."

It wasn't an act. It was too authentic to be an act. Lonergan was genuinely addled. Maybe demented. Something tripped a wire in his head, and he was able to remember for a moment. But then that connection broke, and now Kehoe needed to trip that wire again. He spat words, names, anything he could think of in no particular order. He held Lonergan by the jaw, and Lonergan stared at him, eyes wide and lips trembling as if he wanted Kehoe to trip that wire just as much as Kehoe wanted to trip it himself.

". . . forensic . . . report . . ."

Lonergan's eyes narrowed; his lips stopped trembling. He stared past Kehoe into a distance of time rather than space.

"The report," he said. "The forensic report to the judge said that the boy was scared of the man."

"What was that again?" said Kehoe.

"The psychologist reported that the boy was scared of the man."

Kehoe loosened his grip on Lonergan's jaw because now it was his turn to gaze into the distance of time. He remembered Kaplan explaining that a forensic report was confidential. The judge read it, the lawyers read it, but the parties to the case were not allowed to read it. Their lawyers could discuss it generally with them, but no more. Kaplan had been very vague about the report. In fact, he'd told Kehoe only that it was something they needed to work around. But he didn't need to see what he could feel, and he definitely felt a change in the hick judge's attitude after the report dropped. Even Kaplan seemed standoffish.

Kehoe let his hand drop. The proof he never had needed overwhelmed him in a rush. The boy being his son was not a disputed fact. Everyone knew it to be true: the Van Gelders, Kenneth Palmer, Maxine Rosen, Bill Lonergan, even his own damn lawyer. But they all had conspired against him. Of that, he now had the testimony of a crazy old man as proof.

"You all knew," said Kehoe. He reared back and slapped Lonergan across the face.

"No," said Lonergan.

"No what?" said Kehoe. He wound up and slapped Lonergan again from the other direction. " 'No' as in you didn't know? Or 'no' as in stop hitting you?"

Lonergan covered up with his arms.

"I don't know," he whimpered. "I don't know."

Kehoe shoved him in the chest, and Lonergan lost his balance on the sloping dirt. He landed flat on his back. Kehoe jumped onto his chest. He pried down one arm, then the other, then used his knees to pin them to Lonergan's sides.

"But you know why I'm going to kill you," he said.

CHAPTER 45

At first, Barbara seized on a logical explanation for Bill's disappearance. Bill not only liked Jack but also admired his abilities. Jack could build things and could fix things, while Bill, for all his athletic prowess, could do neither. Bill watched Jack work like a spectator sport. So it was logical to assume that Bill might be tagging along with Jack right now. But as Barbara crossed the lawn, careful to walk alongside the two sets of footprints left behind in the dew, a certain fact gave a lie to that logic. Jack had the morning off today. So unless Jack arrived early and did not report to Barbara to discuss the day's chores—two departures from usual practice—someone else walked Bill into the woods.

Barbara stopped where the footprints ended and a path that she and Bill often walked cut through the trees. A hush descended the moment she picked her way onto the path. She could hear birdsong, but that quickly faded as she tried to listen through it, hoping to hear voices. Bill's voice. Another voice. Any voice. A chain saw started up. Probably the owner of the next property.

She kept going. The chain saw cut out, and again there was silence broken only by the occasional birdcall. The path unfolded before her, passing through breaches in old stone walls and curving around sudden rises. There was a stream up ahead, she remembered, but she was still too far away to hear the rushing water.

She rounded a bend and then climbed a long rise, her steps

hurried along by worry and fear. None of this was her fault. If Foxx hadn't turned up here, if she hadn't agreed to talk to him, if there had been a bed at the Keystone.

She reached the top of the rise. The stream was below, wider and deeper and faster-running than usual for August. On the far side, two men seemed to be wrestling. She ran down the slope, and as she ran, the men spun into perspective. One was Bill. He lay on his back, his legs splayed out, his warm-up pants wet and muddy. The other man straddled his chest.

"Hey!" Barbara yelled.

The man turned, and Barbara's perspective shifted again as she recognized the Good Samaritan from the park. Rather than wonder what he would be doing here, hundreds of miles away, straddling Bill's chest on the bank of a stream, her mind constructed an instantaneous scenario. Bill had fallen into the stream and nearly drowned, and the Good Samaritan was performing CPR to save him.

Barbara plunged into the stream. It was ankle deep, then knee deep, and then suddenly waist deep. The current was strong, the water cold. The Good Samaritan glanced her way and then focused his concentration on Bill. From her new angle, Barbara could see that he was not performing chest compressions. He was strangling Bill.

Barbara lurched forward, losing her balance, tumbling downstream, and then righting herself. Finally, she pulled herself out and crawled up the slope.

"Tell me you knew the truth!" the Good Samaritan screamed at Bill. "Tell me!"

But Bill could not speak. His eyes bulged, his face was flushed, his tongue stuck out of his mouth.

Barbara jumped onto the Good Samaritan's back. She pummeled his shoulders with her fists, but he kept throttling Bill's throat. She wrapped an arm around his neck, and he let go of Bill long enough to throw her off.

She hit the ground hard, got back up, and dived at him again. This time, she raked his neck with her fingernails. This time, she bit into his ear.

He let go of Bill and slapped at her, but his slaps did nothing. She kept raking, kept biting. Scrapes of skin curled under her nails; blood salted her tongue.

He stood up and tried to shake her off, but she clung to him. He spun around, and still she held on. Then he stumbled down to the stream and dived in.

The water loosened her. She couldn't bite and breathe at the same time. She couldn't rake his neck and cling to his shoulders. He broke her grip and shoved her facedown into the water.

She thrashed her arms and kicked her legs, but he kept pushing her down. His hand pulled away, and she started to rise. Then his foot slammed into her back and pinned her to the bottom.

She clenched her teeth and sealed her lips, trying to hold her breath as panic seized her. His foot pressed harder, twisting as if crushing the life out of a bug. Finally, the pressure on her back and the burning in her lungs overcame her. She blew out her air, and her next breath drew mud and water.

And so this was it, she thought. Fear became detachment. Confusion became idle curiosity. She knew not why this man wanted to hurt Bill, wanted to kill her. The reasons were beside the point. Her last conscious thoughts turned back to the frogs. Frogs buried themselves in mud to survive the winter. She would be here among them, next winter. Because she understood that her life always had been about the frogs. They were the first secret she had buried.

―――――――

There were three distinct tracks in the dew of the grass and three distinct impressions in the soft dirt of the footpath. But as Foxx reached the top of the rise, he saw only two people down below. Judge Lonergan stood on the opposite side of a stream. His warm-up suit was soaked and muddy; his big round face was bright red. He stared at another man who was waist deep in the stream and using his arms to pull himself to the bank. The judge seemed to stiffen as the man clawed his way out of the water. He turned sideways and raised his fists John L. Sullivan style. The man walked toward the judge. When he got within range, the judge took a wild, roundhouse swing. The man feinted and, using the judge's momentum, sent him sprawling. He was on the judge instantly. He rolled the judge onto his back and locked his hands on his neck.

Foxx jumped into the stream. The current knocked him down, but with a few strong strokes, he reached the other side and pulled himself out. The man was still strangling the judge. He looked up just in time for Foxx's fist to meet his chin.

The man let go of the judge. He leaned back and rubbed his chin, and Foxx could see that his punch stunned him but not much else. The man stood up. He was bigger than Foxx. Older, too. But he looked like he could handle himself. Foxx did not give him a chance. He dismantled him with a kick behind one knee, a punch to the gut, and, as the man sank, a two-handed slam to the back of the head. The man landed facedown in the dirt.

The judge sat up, coughing and fighting for air. Foxx raised his knees and lowered his head. His breathing seemed to strengthen.

"Where's your wife?" said Foxx.

The judge coughed.

"Your wife," said Foxx. "Where?"

The judge pointed at the stream.

Foxx got up and ran along the bank. Fifteen yards away, a torrent of water sluiced between two boulders. Something was caught in the sluice. Barbara.

Foxx jumped in and let the current take him. He unwedged her from the boulders and carried her to the bank. She felt cold and heavy. From the water, he hoped.

Drowning wasn't a risk at 60 Centre Street, so Foxx wasn't officially trained in the art of resuscitation. But he had lived all his life along the water and knew what to do. He lay her on her back, opened her mouth, and scooped out a handful of water and twigs.

"Come on," he said. "Come on."

Nothing happened. He turned her onto her side. A tiny stream of water leaked out of her mouth, then stopped.

He rolled her onto her back, opened her mouth, and pulled her jaw forward. Nothing happened, so he locked his lips over hers and blew hard. He blew two more times before he saw her chest rise. He leaned back, waiting and hoping, and then her eyes popped open and she coughed up a mess of muddy water.

CHAPTER 46

The state police needed the rest of the day to sort things out. After the judge, Barbara Lonergan, and Kehoe were taken away in separate ambulances, only Foxx remained. Flashing his tin meant nothing.

"So you don't know the man you say was attacking the judge," said the investigator.

Foxx bristled at the "you say," but kept his bristling under wraps.

"Never saw him before," he said.

"And you think the man put the judge's wife in the water, but you didn't actually see that."

"It's the only logical conclusion," said Foxx.

The investigator, who wore reading glasses to make notes on his pad, stared at Foxx over the rims of those glasses.

"I'll decide what's logical," he said. "Now, tell me why you drove up here."

"It's a personal matter," said Foxx.

And so an adversarial wariness hung between Foxx and the investigator as the other officers worked the scene. The wariness only worsened after Jack arrived for his day's chores and discovered Cannon's body zipped up in his sleeping bag. Foxx recognized Cannon, and though he explained that Cannon had inquired about Judge Lonergan's whereabouts at the courthouse not two days ago, could advance no conclusion, logical or otherwise, as to how Cannon got dead in the barn.

The police moved their operations into the house. Foxx was not technically in custody, but was not free to go. He sat in the same armchair where he had talked to Barbara Lonergan while the investigator phoned Cannon's next of kin and then immediately made a second call. He paced during this second call, and he paced a long time. He ended the call and sat in the armchair where Barbara earlier sat.

"That was a Sheriff Rousma," he said. "Cannon's family told me I should tell the sheriff what I told them. So I told him, and when I mentioned the name Kehoe, all I got was a very long silence."

The investigator pushed his reading glasses back up his nose and paged through his notepad.

"Looks like you walked in on the tail end of an old story."

––––––––––

After sorting out everything they had learned, the state police formally arrested Kehoe and transferred him out of the hospital to a lockup. Foxx strolled into the hospital at dusk. Judge Lonergan showed some bruises on his face and some red strangulation marks on his neck, but otherwise looked fairly decent, considering that he probably had been a minute from death when Foxx clocked Kehoe. The judge smiled when he saw Foxx and told him that the doctors and nurses were doing a great job. As Foxx backed out of the room, the judge told him he was doing a great job, too.

Barbara, across the corridor and three rooms down, did not look so well. She lay waiflike on the bed, her slim-enough body barely a bump under the covers. Her hair looked scraggly, her lips thin, her skin ashen.

Foxx sat on a chair, thinking he'd been at two too many bedsides lately. Barbara mumbled in her sleep, and when Foxx jumped the chair closer, she woke up.

"You again," she said, barely above a whisper.

"Sorry," he said. He wanted to claim credit for saving her, but thought it bad form right now.

"Bill?"

"Down the hall," said Foxx. "He seems okay. At least he's telling everyone they're doing a great job. Me included."

A laugh bubbled up from Barbara's chest. Her hand groped toward Foxx. He took it in his. Too much bedside hand-holding, he thought.

"You're a good friend," she whispered.

"To who?"

Barbara cleared her throat. Her voice came out stronger. "Ralphie Rago."

"The exact opposite. There were years I ignored him when I could have been a better friend."

"A fast finish makes up for a lot."

"Do you really believe that?"

"I'd like to," said Barbara. "How is he, by the way? You told me he was dying."

Foxx said nothing.

"I see," said Barbara. "Well, we left off somewhere. Funny, I can't remember. But there is something else I need to tell. It may as well be you."

She tried to sit up, but did not have the strength, so she asked Foxx to adjust the bed. He pressed a button, and the motor hummed and the mattress contracted until Barbara was sitting up. Her head drooped as if she fell asleep, but she shook herself back.

"Thank you," she said.

She told Foxx the story of the birthday gifts that first year on the farm—the bicycle for her and the BB gun for her brother—and the strict rules they needed to obey.

"We had a pond on the farm, not far from the house. I thought it was neat to have my own pond where I could ice-skate in the winter and skip rocks in the summer. Then came the day when I stood on the edge of the water and heard the plip of a frog jumping in. Suddenly, the pond looked like it was filled with blinking dark eyes and darting white tongues.

"I'd always been afraid of frogs. Don't ask me why, but it was like a primal, run-for-your-life fear hardwired into my brain. And so I ran back to the house and swore I'd never go back to the pond again.

"Except I did.

"Near the end of the summer, I stayed home with a fever while my parents and brother drove to the new mall in Big Flats to buy clothes for the school year. There was a daybed in the small room off the living room, and I lay there drinking juice and reading a book. In the quiet, I thought I heard a croak. I listened, heard nothing else, and passed it off to my imagination. But a few moments later, I heard it again. I sat up and when I heard it a third time, I zeroed in on a pile of books in the corner. I crawled out of bed, unpiled the books one by one, and found a small, pulsing frog. I freaked out.

"After I cleaned up the mess, I went into my brother's bedroom and took his BB gun to the pond. The water was low, and the frogs crouched in shallow puddles. Their constant croaks sounded deafening in my ears. I pulled the trigger; the BB gun hissed. I kept shooting till the croaking stopped.

"I didn't think my father would notice the frogs were dead, and if he did, I didn't think he could see they were shot. But the BBs left these perfect little round holes in them, so it was easy to see. Of course, he blamed my brother and whipped him good. And I just let it happen without saying a word.

"Years passed. I always planned on owning up to killing those frogs. But I never did, even as my brother and father grew apart, even after they stopped talking completely. My brother died at thirty-four. By then, he hadn't spoken to my father for half his life. With him gone, I thought I could get past what I did and what I didn't do. But there are some things you can't get past, no matter how hard you try to cover them over. You think the years will bury them deep enough that they can't work their way to the surface. But they do."

"Okay," said Foxx. He wondered where this was going.

"So now I remember where we left off," said Barbara. "And I remember what I wouldn't have told you. But what happened out there made me realize there was something else I needed to un-bury."

"I understand," said Foxx, and hoped that he did.

"It's true that I met Calvin in the boom-boom room that day," she said. "It's true that I left him there alive. But I didn't leave him there alone. The room had a closet. Someone was in the closet with the door cracked, waiting for me to leave. But they were only going to talk. That was the deal. They were only going to talk."

"About the old photo," said Foxx.

"How do you know?"

"Sidney Dweck."

"He told you, huh? Did he tell you what the photo showed?"

"He only said it was something pretty bad."

"Unimaginably bad," said Barbara. "And if it had gotten out, Calvin would have become a judge."

"But you never would have been his wife," said Foxx.

She turned her head, her eyes moistening but not quite squeezing out a tear. Despite the years, despite her reinventing herself as Mrs. Lonergan, those words still worked their way to the surface.

Foxx leaned back in the chair and waited for her to finish.

CHAPTER 47

Foxx arrived at the courthouse midway through the lunch hour. Foley Square was in its August languor. The air was thick and humid. A hazy sun baked the pavement from a white-hot sky. Pedestrians drifted, very few choosing to climb the thirty steps from the sidewalk to the courthouse portico.

Foxx stood at the top, dressed in jeans and a short-sleeve button-down shirt. His shield hung over his waistband. He raised one foot onto the square plinth of a column, leaned his elbow on his knee, and let his cigarette dangle. Even his fingers were sweating.

He had called Bev on the drive down. Failure stuck in Bev's craw, so she was delighted to hear that Foxx had reopened and then closed one of her failed investigations. Foxx felt certain he'd recognize the two senior investigators Bev promised to send to clean things up. They would wear dark suits and white shirts and dark ties. They would wear sunglasses, too, and despite the heat, not a bead of sweat would glisten on their skin.

Foxx's cell phone vibrated. He killed his cigarette and read the text message. DELAYED. HANG TIGHT.

He pocketed the phone. Everything was falling into place.

He went into the cool of the courthouse and took the elevator to the fourth floor. He walked the circular corridor until he found the internal stairway that would take him to a door that opened into the chambers corridor on the fifth floor. The door was permanently locked so that no one who intended to harm a judge could bypass the security desk. But Foxx had a key, and the door had a small window, and it was through this small window that Foxx saw Larry Seagle return to Judge Lonergan's chambers shortly after 2 P.M.

Foxx silently unlocked the door. As Seagle pushed into chambers, Foxx crossed the corridor and slipped in behind him. The sound of Foxx locking the dead bolt caught Seagle's attention.

"Good boxball game?" said Foxx.

Sweat beaded on Seagle's reddened face. His gray T-shirt hung dark and heavy. Salt streaked the lenses of his athletic glasses.

"Yeah," said Seagle. "What's it to you?"

"Nothing."

"Then you can leave."

"I saw the judge and Mrs. Lonergan," said Foxx. "Spent the night with them."

"You had that talk with her?"

"Yeah."

"Then you must be happy," said Seagle.

"Not completely," said Foxx. "I'm looking for something."

"If it's something of theirs, you'll need to wait till they get back." Seagle took off his glasses and rubbed them with the end of his T-shirt. "Or they could call and tell me what you're looking for."

"They won't," said Foxx.

Seagle put his glasses back on and blinked.

"Why not?"

"Because what I'm looking for belongs to you."

Seagle leaned back against his desk and folded his arms.

"What can I have that interests you?"

"Your Get Out of Jail Free card," said Foxx.

"My what?"

"The thing that insulates you from the consequences of all the shit you pulled in your illustrious career."

"Hey, I work hard," said Seagle.

"Maybe now because you need to keep Judge Lonergan afloat."

"I don't know what you're talking about."

"It's a photograph," said Foxx. "Dates back to your days as a photographer for your college newspaper."

He glanced toward the wall where Seagle's college diploma hung among several framed certificates. He noticed that Seagle didn't follow his glance. Studiously so.

"I still don't know what you're talking about."

"Yes, you do," said Foxx. He slowly unhooked his shield from his waistband and placed it on a bookshelf. Then he unbuckled his belt and pulled it off like a sword from a scabbard. He folded the belt in half and snapped it. The crack of leather on leather echoed in chambers.

"I heard about you," said Seagle.

"Heard what?" said Foxx. "From who? Heard from your friend Orlando Cortez that I hung him out a window? Is that what you heard?"

He snapped the belt again. Then he raised it over his head and whipped it down. It didn't actually hit Seagle. At most, it grazed his arm before smacking the top of the desk with a loud crack. But Seagle went down on the carpet and hugged himself into a ball.

Foxx hit the desk one more time. Seagle hugged himself harder and began to snivel. Foxx stepped around him and lifted the diploma off the wall. The frame was cheap, the backing the same grade of cardboard used for legal pads. Foxx pried up the tin grommets with his thumb.

A photograph and a folded page from an old newspaper were pressed between the backing and the diploma. The photograph looked like something snapped surreptitiously, perhaps from under a coat. The angle was skewed, the composition off-center, and the colors were muted by lack of lighting. But the faces of the young men were clear and identifiable. Sidney Dweck was right. This photograph would mean political death in New York.

Foxx buckled his belt and hooked his shield over his waistband. Seagle stood in front of his desk, leaning heavily on one hand and rubbing his gut with the other. He wasn't sniveling anymore, but his eyes were red. Foxx peeled him away from the desk like a damp sheet of paper. They went down the corridor to a back stairway, Foxx gripping Seagle's arm and quartering behind his left shoulder. He held the diploma in his other hand.

At the stairway, Seagle veered toward the down, but Foxx pushed him up.

"Where are we going?" said Seagle.

"You'll see."

"Not the roof."

"The roof?" Foxx shook his head. "Jesus."

The stairway ended at the sixth floor. They walked one length of the hexagonal corridor, hit the angle, and started down the next. Seagle must have thought there was a defenestration in his immediate future because Foxx could hear whimpers in his breathing and feel rubber in his legs.

They turned the next angle. Seagle balked at the sight of Judge Patterson's chambers.

"No, you're not," he said.

"Sure am."

Seagle tried to wrench himself away, but Foxx yanked his arm across his back and up between his shoulder blades. Seagle yelped in pain. Foxx ran him to the open door, then planted his feet and flung him inside. Seagle crashed into the front of Bertha's desk and melted to the carpet.

"Is he in?" said Foxx.

Bertha, aghast, managed to nod her head.

"Then you won't want to be," said Foxx.

Bertha sidestepped around her desk, stared at Seagle for a moment, then hurried out the door. The zipping of her stockings faded in the corridor.

"Get up," said Foxx.

Seagle rolled onto his side and hugged his knees to his chest.

"Ah shit," said Foxx. He set the diploma on Bertha's desk, then clamped one hand on Seagle's waistband, the other on his collar, and hauled him up.

Seagle wobbled, unable or unwilling to keep his feet under him. Foxx spun him around, pinned him to the desk, and smacked him across the face. That stiffened him.

The door to Judge Patterson's office opened inward, and Foxx pushed Seagle so hard that he barreled right through. The judge sat at his desk, his reading glasses low on his nose, his pewter hair studiously mussed. He stared over his glasses as Seagle wobbled toward him.

"What the hell, Larry," he said. Then he saw Foxx. "Can I help you?"

"You can," said Foxx. He stepped past Seagle, lay the diploma facedown on the desk, and pried up the grommets.

"I didn't give it to him," said Seagle.

"Didn't give him what?" said the judge.

"He came in," said Seagle. "Smacked me around. Went right to the wall like he knew it was there."

"I remembered seeing the same diploma somewhere else," said Foxx.

"What are you talking about?" said the judge.

Foxx lifted off the cardboard backing.

"These," he said.

He lay the photo down first. The colors suffered from the original lack of light and the passage of many years, but still showed clearly enough in the red armbands, the brown shirts, and the red, white, and black flag hanging limply from a flagpole in the background. Five young men stood in a row, their arms raised in a familiar salute.

Foxx stabbed his finger at the face of a young man standing in the center.

"Nice clean-cut look you had back then," he said, "though a bit reactionary for my taste."

"That's not me," said the judge.

"Sure it is."

"You have no proof."

Foxx unfolded the sheet of newsprint. The black-and-white photo that appeared in the student newspaper was smaller and grainier than the color original, but obviously was the same picture. The headline above the photo read: NATIONAL SOCIALIST "CLUB" DISCOVERED ON CAMPUS. The caption below the photo listed the names of the five young men. Third from the left—the name corresponded perfectly with the younger version of the judge.

"I didn't give it to him," said Seagle.

"Shut up," said Judge Patterson. He leaned back in his chair, stroking his beard with one hand while fiddling under his desk with the other.

Foxx recognized what was happening. He expected it, too. Every judge's desk had a panic button that sent a distress signal to the captain's office. The smug grin on Patterson's face meant he'd just pressed the button.

Foxx knew the drill. He'd been part of the team that responded to these panic button calls. The response was fast and overwhelming. Get into chambers. Safeguard the judge. Take down anyone present. Ask questions later. Tolerate no bullshit.

Foxx felt, or thought he felt, the pounding of footsteps on distant stairs. He looked around the office. The judge sat with his hands folded on the desk. His eyes gazed thoughtfully up at the ceiling, as if he listened for the same footsteps that Foxx now definitely felt in his chest. Seagle looked a wreck, red-faced, wearing ratty gym shorts and a sweaty T-shirt, his glasses askew. Foxx himself was in civvies, his sole mantle of authority the shield wedged in his waistband. This would be an easy one for the response team. Take him down, take Seagle down. Form a protective ring around Judge Patterson. Even if things got to the talking stage, it would be his word against the judge's.

The pounding Foxx felt became pounding he heard. The team was up on the sixth floor now, running down the corridor. The judge heard it, too. He lifted the photo, the newspaper article, and the diploma and dropped them into the top drawer of his desk.

The pounding stopped.

Foxx looked at Seagle, who stared at the floor as if completely unaware of his surroundings. He looked at the judge, who gazed at the ceiling again as if expecting the sound of footsteps to resume. Instead, there were whispers. An exchange of whispers. Incoherent but harsh, sharp, at swords' points. Then came silence.

A moment later, two men stood at the door. They wore dark suits, white shirts, dark ties. One folded his sunglasses into his pocket. The other kept his sunglasses on.

"Who are you?" said Judge Patterson.

"IG's office," said the man without the sunglasses. "We need to speak to you."

CHAPTER 48

One month later, Foxx borrowed Ellen's car and drove to the Berkshires. It was a sunny but cool day, the air breezy and fresh. Barbara insisted that they talk on the front porch. Each of the Adirondack chairs had a tartan blanket draped over the back. Barbara spread hers on her lap. She looked much different from the nifty fiftysomething Foxx would have taken for a tumble back in August. She had lost weight and her hair had lost its body, the combined effect being that she literally looked longer in the tooth.

Foxx listened to her talk about Judge Lonergan because it was only polite. The judge was not returning to the courthouse and was not opposing Andrew Norwood's grievance. That chip would fall as it may. He was still a resident at the Keystone. The bounce back Barbara believed would occur never occurred, and she doubted he ever would live anywhere else again.

Jack came around from the back of the house on the riding mower. Foxx and Barbara sat in silence as Jack cut the small swath of grass in front of the porch, then crossed the driveway to cut the circle. Orange and yellow mums filled the flower bed around the flagpole.

"An investigator from the district attorney's office was here last week," said Barbara. "I told him what I knew, which was more than I allowed myself to know all these years."

Jack finished in the circle and headed toward the barn.

"What did you think when you heard Calvin was dead?" said Foxx.

"I immediately thought it was Neville. How could I not, when I knew that Neville was hiding in the closet while Calvin and I spoke? But then when I heard Ralphie Rago was arrested, that made sense, too."

"Why?"

"He was odd. When Calvin and I were together, I would get strange looks from him."

"Strange how?"

"Like he was accusing me of something."

"I heard Patterson is considering a plea," said Foxx.

"Let's hope," said Barbara. "I don't want to testify at a trial. I'll do it, don't get me wrong. I'd just rather not."

She got up and walked across the porch to grip the rail. Doddering, thought Foxx. He wondered how much was real and how much might be an act.

"I never will leave here again, not even for a minute," she said. She gazed across the circle as Jack bumped the riding mower into the barn. "I need to be a good wife to my judge."

———

Another month passed. Judge Neville Patterson pled guilty to murdering Calvin Lozier and was sentenced to fifteen to twenty-five years. No one else was prosecuted, because the statute of limitations had run on all of the related crimes except for murder. But Orlando Cortez lost his job and Larry Seagle, suddenly without the power to manipulate, finally was banished from the court system. Meanwhile, after the murder charges were dropped against Luke Godfrey, the district attorneys in Sullivan, Delaware, and Columbia Counties sparred over the right to prosecute Thomas Kehoe.

———

After the plea, the *Daily News* ran a feature story about the murder of Calvin Lozier and the rise and fall of Neville Patterson. A photo credited to a college freshman named Lawrence Seagle appeared prominently. As the race for the nomination began that year, Seagle first offered the photo to a politically desperate Calvin Lozier. But Lozier could not put together enough money to meet Seagle's price, so Seagle played a different angle by telling Patterson that Lozier had offered him money for the photo. Patterson tried to talk Lozier out of releasing the photo before the nominating convention, but the conversation turned violent. In the end, Seagle put the photo to his own use.

Foxx bought two copies of the newspaper and razored out the stories. He pressed one into an encyclopedia atlas and burned the other to ash.

As happened every year, Foxx waited in vain for the goblins and witches, princesses and pirates who wandered the neighborhoods of City Island on Halloween night. There was no bang for the buck of traipsing up from the avenue to visit a single house on a broken backstreet. Still, he set a salad bowl of candy on the front steps. Some years, he counted what was left and could convince himself that someone or something had spirited a few pieces away.

At seven o'clock, he took the urn and envelope and crossed the empty lot where the Rago house once stood. Out on the sound, a fog-horn moaned, but after he climbed the stone fence and dropped onto the other side, all he could hear was the blood pulsing in his ears.

There was no special spot, no particular grave they dared visit at midnight, no tree where they would drink beer or smoke ciga-rettes. Foxx simply walked into the darkness until he felt the hairs stand up on the back of his neck.

He lifted the lid of the urn and walked a small circle while shaking Ralphie out over the grass. Then he did the same with the news article.

"Now everyone knows," he said. "Godspeed, Ralphie."

At the house, he found the salad bowl upended. He stepped over the few remaining pieces of candy and went inside.